SUSPECTED

Rori Shay

Contents

The fissures from your absence are only stitched together by the sweetness of the memories. Grandma Lea, Grandma Marie, Grandpa Bill, Grandpa Al, Adam Rayman, Sarah Firebaugh, Uncle Jesse, Aunt Pearl, and Uncle Al

1

EVEN THE TERRAIN IN Mid Country senses we are intruders. Jagged rocks and thorny brown weeds jut out of the earth, scraping our ankles and slowing our progress. I didn't have as much trouble hiking up East Country's side of the border, but now that the three of us, me, Griffin, and Margareath, descend the steep slope into Mid, we're constantly catching ourselves mid-stumble.

"You okay?" Griffin asks, reaching out a hand to steady me.

"Uh-huh." The lie sounds hollow, even to my own ears. But I say it anyway and pick up my pace. I don't want Griffin to convince me to turn back again like he tried to do as we waited for Margareath at the hill's crest. Going back to East Country is the one thing I can't do, and Griffin doesn't even know the whole reason why. All he thinks is, I left East Country to spy on our neighbor and to help him escape our country's death penalty.

Yet there is another reason, and thus far, there has been no good time to tell Griffin he's going to father not one, but two children in the Elected family. My pregnancy is something I want to divulge in a special way, not as we run like fugitives, breaking almost every law of our forefathers.

When the lights from Mid catch my attention again and almost set me into a forward tumble, I try to focus on doing one thing at a time: get down the hill, cross into Mid Country, *then* tell Griffin the news.

Everything about Mid so far is offensive: their flagrant display of electricity, the strange way Margareath didn't remember her family when asked about her children moments ago, even the air on Mid's side of the

Nirogene mines smells different than ours. There is a faint scent of wet metal and something sweetly acidic, which I can't quite place, but that's causing me to gag. I stop for a second, burying my face into the fabric of my shirt sleeve to take a deep, clean breath. Vienne warned me that newly pregnant I'd have a heightened sense of smell. That, on top of my perpetual nausea, is overwhelming to say the least.

I blink my eyes once hard before proceeding forward again. The massive amount of illegal light emanating from Mid's epicenter miles to our west is tremendous. It's so dark on the mountain and so bright in the distance; our direct path seems even bleaker.

"Just a little more to the bottom of the hill," says Margareath. She pants in between every other word, the exhaustion of our trek down this treacherous mountain evident on her features. "Once we reach the bottom, it's about a day and a half walk to Mid's city."

I try to estimate the number of miles from the border to Mid's center. Maybe fifty, given Margareath's statement and the fact that our pace is relatively slow. How long, I wonder, would it take a group of fighters from East to traverse the plains if an invasion was required? Every nugget of data on Mid gets me one step closer to understanding why they're trying to invade my country, steal our resources, and kill my people. And closer to figuring out how to stop them.

I turn my head to peek at Griffin. Even in the inky darkness, I can see his brow furrowed in concentration. He's been trying to act calm as we make our unlawful descent into enemy territory, but I can see the uneasiness in his eyes. He's an escaped convict, and I've just broken at least two of the world's Eco Accords. He's as determined to thwart Mid as I am, but sneaking into the country is dangerous for both of us.

And Margareath is only barely helping. She's been strange ever since we met her at the hill's peak, giving hints about Mid Country, but not really telling us anything tangible. Her apparent glorification of our enemy and its "amazing" capabilities is unnerving.

What if it's a trap? Could Margareath, the first and only spy I sent into Mid, have defected? Would she dare lead us straight into the hands of Mid's Elected? Breaking the Eco Accords and country isolationism would be a good enough excuse for their leader to execute me and Griffin right on the spot.

I squeeze my eyes shut, trying to block the blackest thoughts from my mind, but they keep welling up like sewage from an overflowing chamber pot, rank and unwanted.

"Eyes open at all times," says Margareath, pursing her lips. "Wouldn't want you to hurt yourself."

Something about the way she picks her words makes me shiver, but I do as she instructs, refraining from anything but blinking. Griffin locks eyes with me behind Margareath's back, raising his brows, and I just shrug in reply. If she is indeed now our enemy, there's little we can do until the time is right.

When we reach the bottom of the border hill, I can't help but glance behind me. All views of my country have vanished. I can't see anything of East behind the looming mountain we just traversed. I put my head down and keep plodding forward. Maybe it's better this way. If I can't see East any longer, I won't be as easily reminded about what I'm giving up.

"I didn't bring a lot of food. Didn't think I'd be travelling back with companions," says Margareath, rifling through her knapsack as we walk. "But I have a little to share, if you're hungry." Griffin and I both look at the round object she's holding out to us.

"Thank you," I say. "We didn't realize Mid's city would be farther away from the border than our own, so we didn't bring many provisions."

When the United States was divided into three countries, it was the Nirogene mines that created borders. One long mine in Maryland between East and Mid Countries and another mine at the Rocky Mountains to divide Mid and West Countries. Why, I wonder, wouldn't Mid Country have situated its epicenter right next to the mines like we did in East? Nirogene is the only substance I know that stops the rusting process, and we need to conserve as much of the old metal as possible. Mid must still dip into their side of the mine; I just don't know why they're not stationed closer to the mineral.

Margareath's voice jolts me before I can ask her the question out-right. "Here, take the orange." She thrusts the fruit into my hands almost forcefully. "You look ill, and this is infused with vitamins." I ignore her bluntness. If she only knew why this hike was stressing my unaccustomed, exhausted body, she'd be stunned. In her eyes, I'm East's Elected and by all rights, a man. I'm not about to tell her exactly why my pallid face and dark-circled eyes aren't indicative of an actual malady. They are telltale signs of a particular blessing I never envisioned my future held.

Instead, I focus on the food. I don't understand the word "vitamins" that Margareath uses. It's not a term East's people use, and I don't remember it from my history lessons. However, the orange she's just handed me isn't an orange color at all. It's neon pink, an absurd color for a piece of fruit.

Griffin eyes it suspiciously, too. "This doesn't look natural," he says, taking the orange from my upturned palm.

Margareath shifts on her feet. "I grew it. Mid tries to recreate foods from long ago, but they don't always turn out the same."

"Is it safe?" asks Griffin. I know what he's thinking as he fingers the fruit's bumpy rind. Not only does this fruit look slightly radioactive, almost glowing, but it could be part of a trap.

"Of course it's safe!" Margareath says, one hand on her hip. She rolls her eyes at us and then looks toward the sky. "We don't have a lot of time. Eat it or don't. It's your choice."

Griffin nods his head, resolute, and then takes a large bite, not bothering to peel back the fruit's outer layer. "I'll test it before you eat any," he says toward me. At once, the sweet acidic smell I sensed earlier wafts out of the orange and hits me hard in the nostrils. I feel my gut cramp from the sickening pungency.

Griffin wipes his mouth with the back of his hand, still holding the fruit. "It's fizzy."

Margareath smiles. "That's the injected vitamins. It contains every nutrient needed to sustain a person for a whole day, so you don't have to waste time eating when you're busy working. See? Mid is making things better." She turns on her heel, ready to keep walking. With her back to us, Griffin and I exchange another grave look. Making things *better*? Like how? By growing strange new fruit concoctions and threatening to wipe our country off the map?

"Now that we're officially on Mid's side of the border, we have to walk under this," Margareath says, completely oblivious to the signals Griffin and I convey between ourselves. Margareath reaches behind a nearby boulder and produces a thin, black rectangle, about the size of a door. "It's risky to walk through the border land. Mid flies around the vacant outskirts of the country on constant alert for invaders."

"Do they have a lot of invaders?" I ask.

Margareath shrugs. "They're prepared for it, in any case."

Margareath tries to explain the mechanics of how the black rectangle shields us from Mid's view. Griffin listens carefully, absorbing every word, but I take the opportunity to rest my legs against the boulder, sinking into a crouch. The adrenaline rush I've had to maintain, breaking Griffin out of prison and then leaving everything I've ever known behind, is finally starting to ebb. I'm so tired; I could fall asleep sitting up with my head in one hand. My shoulders start to slouch forward and my eyes drift closed, but that only causes my other senses to heighten. I can feel the hard rock against my spine and the crumbling dirt shifting underneath the soles of my sandals. In another instant my eyes bolt open. Griffin and Margareath are so engrossed in their conversation they don't hear the whirring noise I do.

"What's that sound?" I ask, cutting off Margareath mid-sentence.

She cocks her head to the side, listening, and then yells, "Duck!"

Griffin and I both scramble next to her under the screen, squeezing close against the boulder. In seconds we see a dark object cast an ominous shadow across the ground. I'd know the outline anywhere, even if I hadn't seen one of Mid's airrides in the Mind Multiplier months ago. The futuristic helmet I'd worn twice, once under Tomlin's supervision and once on my own, showed me Mid's airride hovering over our side of the border, killing a man who'd deposited bullets at the entrance to East's Nirogene mines.

We huddle closer together, trying to ensure not an arm or leg is visible outside the screen's perimeter. I keep my eyes fixed on the sky, hoping Mid's airride will redirect elsewhere. It purrs overhead, so quiet in fact, that I'm surprised I heard its engine. The airride sounds like a mere wind. I wonder if right at this very minute the machine is transmitting evidence that there are interlopers in Mid who need to be eradicated. I brace myself for additional airrides to congeal into an angry swarm out of nowhere.

My brow perspires, sending tiny droplets of sweat running down the bridge of my nose. My hand instinctively clutches around Griffin's. His skin, in contrast to mine, is cool to the touch, and it's the one thing that keeps me from visibly shaking. When I think the jet is listening and can hear our very intakes of breath, it's in that moment the airride swooshes away, leaving a trail of silvery exhaust in its wake.

"Close call," says Margareath, dropping the screen at our feet.

"Should we expect more of them?" asks Griffin. He stares into the sky, searching for more. "Did they see us?"

"I think we're safe," she says. "The screen blocks all ultraviolet light, and it's impossible to see through. If Mid noticed us, they wouldn't have left."

I'm looking up into the night sky too, and my next words come out quickly before I can stop myself. "This is an anti-solar panel, isn't it?"

Margareath spins around to stare at me. "Yes. How did you . . . ?"

"Books. That's all." I've said too much. Margareath gawks at me with a different expression than the annoyed one she's displayed so far.

"You know technology," she says. The look I didn't discern at first is now written all over her face. Her cheeks are red, and the whites of her eyes are bright. Awe.

I've seen the same look twice before. On Griffin, when he showed me the illegal light he'd manufactured. And on members of East Country's Technology Faction years ago when Griffin's father brought forth the power tool for their inspection. It's one of the most dangerous expressions I think I've ever witnessed. It conveys wonder and excitement over technology, and it's the biggest transgression one can make when our world views technology as the sole contributor to environmental destruction. We aren't supposed to want to use the technology that ruined our planet almost two generations ago. We can't manufacture it. We can't proliferate it. We can't make the same mistakes our forefathers made. I break eye contact with Margareath, looking instead toward Mid's city.

Griffin squeezes me around the shoulders, almost imperceptibly, but enough that I would do almost anything for a moment of privacy to lean back against his hard frame and let his body wrap against mine as I sleep.

He coughs out loud, gravitating Margareath's stare from my face to his. "So what's the anti-solar panel used for?"

"Planting. I'm a Grower in Mid Country. These screens shield all of Mid's vegetation so the sun's radiation doesn't affect the food. Everyone knows no one can be seen underneath the panels. The panels are the main reason why Mid's government uses real guards instead of video surveillance to monitor the Growers at work."

"How'd you sneak this panel out?" I ask.

Margareath smiles, the curved yellow of her teeth looking like a too-ripe banana. "Pretty stealthy, ha?" She leans on one leg and runs a hand through her auburn hair. "I cracked the corner and reported it broken. While it was with the engineers for fixing, I told them the panel was decommissioned for use as scrap material. When I took it, the engineers thought the guards had possession and the guards thought the panel was still with the engineers." Margareath nods her head up and down in self-congratulation.

"Is Mid really that trusting?" asks Griffin.

"In certain ways, yes. They're paranoid at times and blind to human nature at others." Margareath points to a jagged flaw in one corner of the screen. "But it never did get fixed. Be careful of this part when you're holding the panel. Last thing we need is for one of you to cut yourself and have to visit the doctors in Mid right when we get there."

I stifle a grumble under my breath. If Margareath thinks I'm setting one foot in front of a Mid doctor, she has another . . .

"There's only one screen," Griffin interjects, breaking my thoughts. "Are you saying we have to huddle under this the rest of the way to Mid?"

"Well, I didn't very well expect to have company on the walk back. We only have to huddle under it if we hear or think we see an airride coming. Elected seems to hear them well enough." Margareath whistles out air through her front two teeth. Motioning toward me she says, "Why don't you take the first shift holding it? If you hear another airride coming, raise it over our heads. Whoever's holding it will get the most coverage. We'll take turns."

I nod and reluctantly lean down to pick up the panel she's left in the dirt by our feet. My wearied body wants to defy her suggestion, but I don't want to look weak and tired. I hold the flexible panel against my side, feeling the awkward bulk poking into my ribs. But I take care to hold the screen so it doesn't drag against the ground.

We start moving away from the semi-protection of the border hills, walking along the open ground for miles ahead of us. There's nothing out here. No trees. No vegetation of any kind, except for a few tufts of grass peeking out of the packed soil. I remember the Mind Multiplier's view of my parents walking through a lush paradise, trees and forest all around them. They couldn't have been anywhere near this wasteland. I sigh, thinking about where my parents are right now and what they'd say if they could see me. Would they be proud or profoundly disappointed?

We walk straight for the next hour. I can tell by looking at the stars it's roughly two a.m. I'm trying to be strong, but after a while of moving the screen from arm to arm all the blood is pooling in my hands, which have started to throb. Finally Griffin wrenches the edges of the panel out of my clamped fingers. I can hardly release my hands; they're so rigid.

"I'll take over now." His lips are tight and a line of concern is etched across his forehead.

I start to protest, thinking I haven't held the screen for my fair share yet, but Griffin easily grips the panel with one hand and rubs one of my arms with his other. "Don't worry, I'll make sure you're completely covered if something flies near."

"That's not what I was . . . " I start to say, but I see the devilish grin erupt on Griffin's face and stop protesting. I know he's trying to lighten the mood by teasing me.

"So, Margareath," Griffin says. "Looks like there aren't any other airrides out tonight."

We've been quiet for the last hour, worried that someone or something in the dark will hear us. But when it's apparent we're the only ones out here, we start to talk.

"They'll be more at some point. Believe me. Mid has scores of them flying around. Especially at night."

"What in the world is Mid doing?" I ask. "Why do they have so many of the old world flying machines?"

"Defense," Margareath says. Her word is simple, and I can tell she unequivocally believes it.

"Defense from West Country?" Griffin asks.

"West doesn't exist anymore." Margareath looks at her hands, flicking dirt out from underneath a fingernail as we walk.

"What?" I ask. "How can a whole country that existed at the start of the Accords in 2100 be gone just eighty five years later?"

"Earthquakes. West's fall is actually a good thing for you," Margareath says. "It'll be your alibi. Lots of people from West keep migrating to Mid. Lots of refugees for you to blend in with. Mid's graciously opened its doors to all of West's immigrants."

"You talk like Mid's the best thing since sliced bread. Do you even *want* to come home to East Country?" Griffin asks, his voice tight. For the first time, his words are tinged with anger, and I'm sure he's about to ask Margareath, point blank, what her intentions are with us. Has she defected or not?

"Of course I do."

"Because of your family," I say quietly, letting my words roll off my tongue like eating the frosting off a cupcake in smooth, long licks. My voice is gentle and coaxing.

Margareath is quiet for a few beats, and I think I've broken through her facade. But after a moment, she turns to stare at me. "What family?"

This time, when she pretends not to know what I'm referring to, I don't let it go like I did when we first met her on top of the border. "Your family," I say again. "You have three kids and a husband. More children than most."

Margareath makes a small bubbling sound in her mouth, and she almost stops short, causing me and Griffin to bump into her.

"Do you remember them?" asks Griffin. His voice is low, devoid of its earlier accusatory tone.

Margareath lets out a sharp, loud laugh that I swear can be heard through the nothingness for miles.

"Shhh!" I say, putting one hand on the back of her shoulder.

"I don't have a family in East Country." Margareath laughs again. "Good one, Elected!"

I glance at Griffin who's already watching me with big eyes. We don't fully understand Margareath's mental state, but I decide not to push the issue of her family anymore. I don't want her to snap, when we're in the middle of nowhere, possibly being pursued by Mid's mechanical beasts. I shake my head at Griffin, willing him to drop the topic too. Instead, I start quizzing Margareath on other things about East to see what she does remember.

"You said you're a Grower in Mid, right?"

"Yes, got the job right away."

"Okay, well, you were a Planter in East. Do you remember that?"

"Of course!" exclaims Margareath. "Why do you think they like me so much in Mid? I remember a lot about what we planted at home. I'm very helpful. Of course, I tell Mid's officials I grew vegetables in West

Country. If they knew I was from East, they'd have disposed of me long ago."

My face crumples on her last sentence, but I go on. We keep asking her more questions about East, and it's clear that she remembers everything except her family. When Margareath is facing forward once again, I whisper in Griffin's ear, "Maybe it's a defense mechanism."

He bites the side of his lip and nods his head, whispering back, "I wish Vienne were here. She'd understand what was going on inside Margareath's brain."

He refers to Vienne's mastery of psychology, a skill my wife was taught specifically to deal with me and my gender issues. For a split second, I feel the color rising to my cheeks, burning with leftover jealousy for Griffin's longtime friendship with Vienne. Griffin wishes she were here. I wonder if he'd rather have her skills in this endeavor than mine. Vienne would be a more advantageous partner right now. I swallow thickly but tamp the feeling down. I wish Vienne were here too. I picture her nurturing demeanor. She'd be able to elicit a lot more information from Margareath than Griffin and I can.

My mind starts to wander, and I imagine how Vienne will inform everyone in East that I've left. Perhaps at the next town hall. Will my people equate my departure with my brother, Evan's, years ago? Will they think I ran away? Or will they understand I'm trying to find answers? It's only been a few hours since I left Vienne, but I already miss my wife. She had an easy way of allaying fears. Just a few words from her could have soothed even a wild boar from the wilds of East.

We continue walking through the night, into the next day. We sit and rest a few times, but we don't dare sleep. My legs feel as if they'll shatter like glass if we don't rest soon, but I've been quiet about the pain so far. It's no use whining about the discomfort, and I agree it's best we get out of the plains as soon as possible. Mid should be made to think we've come from West Country, so the sooner we move into the city and aren't seen arriving from this eastern angle, the better.

When it finally gets dark the second night, we collectively decide to take our first extended break. Margareath leads us to a small group of scraggly bushes she's obviously scouted out previously. She lays the panel down nearby. It's the first time none of us are holding it for protection, and we can all three rest at once.

"We're close enough now," says Margareath, yawning. "Even if they found us out here, we could make something up." Her words are tinged with the beginnings of sleep already setting over her body. I wonder what story she'd concoct exactly. I start trying to think of one as a backup, but I'm so tired I have trouble lacing together anything realistic.

Griffin pulls out remnants of the orange from his backpack. "I think it's pretty safe," he says to me. "I'm still alive. You should eat something." He's only taken one bite of the fruit, so there's a lot left for me. It still smells atrocious, but I dive into the orange like a half-starved wolf and am amazed at the fruit's juiciness and flavor. I almost believe Margareath about the vitamins Mid's injected into the orange because after just a few moments I feel satiated, like my body's received a much needed boost.

I'm still sucking on fragments of the orange, thinking about eating the rind too, when Margareath falls asleep on her side, snoring for all the world to hear. I consider nudging her with my foot, because last thing we need is Mid's guards descending on us due to some loud breathing. But Griffin and I finally have privacy, or at least as much as possible given the circumstances. Who knows when we'll have a real chance to talk again soon. I snuggle in close to him, letting our bodies touch conspicuously for the first time since we met with Margareath.

I feel the heat from his skin against mine, and the color rises to my cheeks before I can even decide how exactly I want to kiss Griffin. Full on the lips or soft and gentle running in a line up his neck? I let myself loosen up, my muscles aching from our long walk. Griffin wraps an arm around me. He shifts even closer so I can almost make out the pattern of his hard stomach behind the linen shirt. Despite my exhaustion, a buzz shoots through my chest.

"You still think it's a good idea to sneak into Mid Country?" asks Griffin, a whisper in my ear.

"Yes. I couldn't just let you walk into the lion's den alone."

"It would've been the smarter decision."

I smile into the dark. "And never see you again? I don't think so." I should tell him soon the other reason behind my insistence on travelling into Mid. How I wanted to hide my pregnancy from our countrymen and that it's his baby I'm carrying. But with Margareath just inches away and Mid's airrides lurking, it still doesn't seem like the right time to tell him that news.

"I'd have found a way back to you eventually," Griffin says. He leans down and our faces are so close, I can feel the hint of stubble, rough across his cheek. Griffin kisses me under my right ear, down my neck toward the collarbone. I stretch, angling my head to savor the sensation of his lips against my skin. One of his hands falls lightly down my back. Where his palm lies, I feel heat emanating in all directions, warming my entire body.

I want to kiss him back, grasp him around the shoulders with both my arms, and indulge in the feelings I've been carrying for so long. But one glance at Margareath's sleeping body reminds me she might not slumber that soundly for long. We can't let her know I'm female. If she wakes up and thinks it's two men kissing, that wouldn't be so bad, except I'm supposed to be East's Elected, married to Vienne. I can't let her in on everything yet, especially with Margareath's confused mental state still looming as a big question mark.

So with all the force I can muster in my body, I grip Griffin's biceps and push back. It's not very hard, as I'm not that resolute. But he feels the change.

"I know, I know. We shouldn't," he sighs.

Griffin extracts his arm from behind my back, and I'm instantly sorry for ending our intimacy so soon. An inch of moonlight is now visible between our two chests, and I'd give almost anything to take that short distance away again.

I breathe out, letting the passion from his kisses evaporate off me like steam. I can't look at Griffin. If I do, I'll just go right back to rubbing my hands up his arms. And then who knows where our touching will end. So instead, I stare into the darkness toward the west.

"I wish we could see something of Mid's city center ahead." If I can't voice my frustration at Griffin's and my unrequited desire, I can at least ruminate on another irritation. As soon as we had walked close enough to make out patterns of the city, Mid cut off all lights. We were plunged back into inky darkness without being able to see much of anything.

"We'll get a good view when the sun's up."

"Do you think they cut the lights because of us? Like they knew we were coming?"

Griffin doesn't answer, just stares into the dark along with me.

"You see those shadows, though, right?" I continue.

"Yes." Griffin is short with his words, like he's also worried about the shadows we see, but doesn't want to convey his anxiety to me. It's like him to keep his feelings bottled up in an attempt to protect me. I wonder when he'll stop treating me like something fragile about to break. And when he does, will I like how it feels?

In place of the thousands of lights we'd seen in the distance before, there are now just immense, monstrous shadows, making the world seem even darker. I swear, I think the shadows are blocking light from the moon, although I don't know how. Pictures of childish nightmares run across the inside of my shut eyelids, as I allow my imagination to run wild. But before I know it, I'm falling asleep, my head resting heavy on Griffin's lap.

And then, as if my eyes were only closed for a minute, I feel a hand rousing me awake again. "Elected." Griffin's murmur reaches into my dreams. I'd like to keep sleeping, letting our mission and the rest of the world wait a bit longer, but his touch opens my eyes. Only Griffin could have lured me awake right now.

"Alright, I'll take the next shift." I groan as I lift myself on one arm, readying myself to take the next watch. "You can sleep now."

"No, we're ready to leave. Come on, I'll help you up." Griffin eases himself out from under me and extends a hand.

I open my eyes wider as I see dawn light on the horizon. "Wait, it's morning? You let me sleep straight through?" I start turning around. There's a thick fog covering the ground, making me feel like we're floating in something damp. I clutch at my exposed arms for a second, thinking the fog's brought droplets of acid rain with it, but I feel no tell-tale pinpricks.

"You needed it," he says. "You both did." He gestures to Margareath who's just starting to stir too.

"You didn't sleep at all?" I ask, standing up taller. My voice is high. He couldn't have stayed up straight for two nights in a row. I look at his eyes. There's a deep, purple circle starting to form under each of them.

"It's alright," he says. "My father forced me to stay up longer than this, running errands for the Technology Faction. I'm used to it."

I look at him hard once more. We're about to enter Mid's city. He's going to need all of his strength, and it's not fair he's let me sleep, making the decision to sacrifice his own welfare without consulting me. But

Griffin's always making sacrifices for me: putting himself in harm's way as arrows point at my head, keeping my gender a secret when he knows it implicates him in a messy web of lies. I suppose lack of sleep isn't the worst thing he's had to bear for my benefit.

I turn, facing him. "Thank you. But you don't have . . . "

"Wait, Elected," he says, using my formal name, cutting me off with a low voice. The hairs on the back of my neck stand up at his sudden change of tone. He slowly raises a hand, pointing, his eyes travelling higher as the fog around us curls away with the rising sun.

My back faces what he's seeing, and I start to think he's pointing toward a group of Mid's guards, here to capture us—silent stalkers who've encircled us in the night. Or maybe it's an airride that's landed nearby without us knowing until the fog lifted. I silently pray to the heavens we haven't been found while I slept so foolishly. I turn, preparing for whatever is there.

But it's not a group of guards. Or an airride. And no matter how I've braced myself, I couldn't have prepared for the sight of what looms over our heads.

2

Out of the receding mist, two gigantic, glistening swords appear over us, bending the sun's rays in a blinding glare. My breath catches in my throat, the monsters from my dreams having come alive to skewer us. These unearthly creatures reach all the way from the ground into the heavens. I can almost see them swaying, bending closer and closer to fall forward, slashing us to pieces. Each of the two monstrosities has sharp metal edges and is covered with thousands of rectangular eyes.

I grasp Griffin's arm, my fingers tightening on his biceps. "We've got to run!" I say in one gulp.

Griffin crouches next to me, already grabbing up our few belongings. I search for the best escape route. The two of us are in sync, ready to dash away from our supposed hiding place before these monsters blink and focus on us. "Margareath, come on!" I plead.

I'm about to take my first stride forward, the kinetic energy building in my calves, when a gurgling noise erupts to my right. I swivel to see Margareath bent over, hands on her knees, her face a muddle of features. Something's wrong with her. She's delirious with fear.

"Margareath!" I yell again. "Let's get out of here!"

"You're . . . you're . . . scared of those . . . " She points toward the metal swords cutting the sky in half.

"I don't think they've seen us yet," I say. My voice is urgent, trying to break through her obvious hysteria. "Hurry!"

Margareath hits her knee and doubles over even farther. She gives another choked noise, but this time it doesn't sound like a sob. It sounds like she's laughing. Griffin's shaking his head, implying he thinks she's gone crazy and I should stay away. But we can't just leave her here like this. I move inches closer until I can put a hand on her shoulder. She looks up, and she's got tears streaming down both of her cheeks.

"I guess I should've warned you," she says.

This is it—where Margareath finally admits she's turning us in—that she led us straight into the clutches of these awful monsters.

"If you've betrayed us . . . " Griffin's voice is a growl. "Come on, Aloy. Let's get out of here." He doesn't bother using my formal name around Margareath anymore, so I know he means to leave her behind. Griffin grips my upper arm, and he doesn't even have to pull me. I don't need persuading. I'm right there in step with him.

Margareath laughs even louder, her cackles now high-pitched. When she finally realizes we're actually leaving without her, she calls out, "Wait! Wait!"

"Get away from us! We don't need your help anymore!" I yell backward.

"You do!" Margareath shouts. She runs to catch up with us. I almost put out a hand to push her away, but before I do, she says, "They're skyscrapers. Elected, you've seen these in your history books before, haven't you? Or at least something like them?" She's panting, trying to match our pace.

As I continue to run alongside Griffin, I sort through her words. Skyscrapers. Massive structures that Tomlin said were so tall they could almost touch the sky and scrape the blue clear of all clouds. But these creatures look different than the ones in my books. They look alive, swaying in the morning breeze, the tips invisible within the limits of our vision. They aren't *almost* touching the clouds; they're up *in* the clouds.

"What are all those eyes then?" I ask Margareath who's still struggling to keep up with us.

"Windows!"

I twirl around, my boots kicking up one final spray of chalky dirt. "Buildings? But they're so sharp and thin. They look like they're falling forward."

"I swear, it's just an optical illusion, based on their reduced surface area toward the tip. They're truly buildings. We all live in them."

I grasp onto Griffin's shirt, preventing him from continuing forward. I remember one large, flat book Tomlin showed me once. It was full of glossy pictures of a place called New York City. The skyscrapers there couldn't have been much more than a hundred stories high. The ones we run from here look slightly similar, if massively taller.

"I think she's telling the truth," I say to Griffin. He stops, but his legs stay locked, ready to bolt.

Margareath takes our temporary stop as a signal to explain the structures in more detail. "We all have apartments in them. Mid's Elected wants everyone to live close together, not like in East where people own separate houses. Mid think it's the best way to accomplish the country's goals."

Griffin winces as she says the word 'goals'. "And those would be?"

Margareath ignores his question, still looking toward me for confirmation that we're staying.

"All the families live together up there?" I ask pointing at the two structures, my eyes thin lines against the bright sunlight.

It's Margareath's turn to look at us confused. "Families? No, just one person per apartment."

It's like she doesn't even understand the concept of families anymore. She must be mistaken. Where do all the children stay?

"Mid's Elected built those towers a few years ago when everyone from West started migrating to Mid," she continues. "He needed a place to house all the new citizens. He was very accommodating."

"I bet," Griffin grunts. "More people to make babies and grow his population."

"Make babies? Oh no," says Margareath. "We just focus on our work in Mid."

Griffin and I exchange a look, but stay quiet. Every word Margareath says now is more of an explanation of Mid's ways then we've gotten out of her before. And if I truly intend to stop Mid's advance against our country, I need this exact type of intelligence. I turn toward Griffin. "We should keep moving into the city."

He nods but doesn't take his eyes off Margareath, like she'll morph into a gargoyle, claws ready to attack if he turns his back for an instant.

"Good!" says Margareath, gathering her own pack more closely over one shoulder. "You won't be disappointed. Mid has a lot to offer."

It's like she's quoting from some kind of brochure. Griffin shakes his head but follows her lead once again.

"You'll need to register and choose a job when we get there. We should start thinking about possibilities," she continues.

"How did you get out of work for three days?" asks Griffin, ready once more to poke holes in her story. "How'd you get away unnoticed if you say Mid monitors everyone so closely?" I know he's still thinking she's somehow deceiving us, working with Mid's government to root us out.

But she doesn't show any signs she thinks we distrust her. Her face is now open, smiling broadly. "I broke!" she says. "Just like the anti-solar panel."

"Broke?" I ask, mild distaste for her word obvious across my creased brow.

"You know. Got sick. Mid calls it breaking."

I look down at the ground. Kind of like they think everyone is a machine. Like the human body is one big mechanism that just needs some oil and a bit of tightening to get repaired.

"So they just let you off work for pretending to be sick?" Griffin asks.

"Not exactly. I had to really be sick. There's no faking in Mid." She gets quiet, leaning toward the two of us as we keep walking. "They'd know."

My eyes squint involuntarily. "Sick, how?"

"I ate rotten cabbage for three days in a row. That way, the cameras got a good image of me vomiting. I was released from work, no problem."

I cough slightly, thinking about the lengths Margareath went through to help us after all. "Well . . . " I hesitate, thinking of the right words. "Thank you. Now that we're here, there's no more need to make yourself ill."

Margareath just shrugs, like she doesn't care about throwing up violently. She really has changed. I remember the well-spoken, delicate lady who gifted the Aloe plant to Vienne, trying to heal her wound. That woman is nothing like the flippant guide in front of us now. I wonder again what happened to Margareath in Mid throughout the past two months. Or if maybe my shunning her from East is the reason she's so off kilter. I meant to save her by eliminating the threat of her execution, but maybe I've enacted harm against Margareath in another form.

The three of us proceed in silence, growing steadily closer to Mid's epicenter. As we walk, I stare ahead, watching the looming skyscrapers creep closer and closer. They still look imposing, but now that I know they're just buildings, I'm not afraid to look in their direction, even peer into their gaping windows. Other buildings pop up along Mid's skyline now, too. Shorter ones, but they're still so different from the houses we have in East. These are all constructed with precise angles, shiny metal, and glass. At home our dwellings have rounded corners fashioned out of mud or pieces of scrap material scavenged over the years. Mid's structures all look new, gleaming in the sun.

In the silence I take Margareath's advice, trying to think what kind of job I'll apply for in Mid. It's not like I can put down 'Elected' as my choice. What else would I be suited for, though? Margareath has a skill working with plants, and Griffin can obviously care for animals again. But what trade do I know? I can fence. I can whittle. I can speak publicly about the dangers of abandoning the Accords. At this last thought, I laugh inwardly. That's the exact thing Mid doesn't want to hear. They obviously abandoned the Technology and Ship Accord.

I'm about to ask Margareath for other ideas, when something smacks against my cheek. I instinctively protect my face and duck. There's a trilling noise hovering near my ear, but it's gone again in a flash.

"Something grazed me! A bullet!"

Margareath and Griffin immediately dive onto the flat dirt next to me.

"Your face is bleeding!" Griffin says, crawling to me on his stomach.

I check to see what he means, and my hand swipes a line of red off my cheek. "We must have been spotted!" My voice is panicked and my eyes dart around for airrides circling overhead. But there's nothing above us. Could Mid have found a way to become invisible now too?

We hear the trilling noise again, and Griffin thrusts his own backpack over my head, leaving himself open to the attack. We form a triangle with our bodies, our backs leaned up close to each other as we all stare at the sky, expecting yet another onslaught. When I hear the trilling noise again, something sharp lashes through my hair. This time Griffin and Margareath turn in time to swat the thing hovering near our heads. We each bat the air, determined to take down the intruder with our hands before it reaches a vital organ.

"I've got it!" shouts Margareath, stomping something small on the ground. Out of the corner of my eye it indeed looks like a golden bullet, small and round. Margareath disables it with two hard jolts of her boot heel. The object crunches and finally lies still, the trilling noise extinguished.

We all stand over it, leaning down to see the tiny object.

"It's a bee," Margareath says, her words rushed. Suddenly, she laughs again. It's the high-pitched crazy hoot she made earlier. "A bee!" she says again. "A bee!" She's almost hopping.

Griffin bends down and pinches the smashed orb in between two fingers, careful not to let its stinger brush his hand. "This doesn't look right."

"Well, of course not," Margareath laughs again. "This one's mechanical, and you thought it was a bullet!" She doubles over again, clutching her sides as she chuckles.

I don't find the situation or her degrading tone amusing at all. "Let me see," I say, squinting my eyes at Griffin's fingers. The "bee" is yellow with black plastic hairs in stripes across its body. The stinger is elongated, sharper than anything I ever saw in Tomlin's picture books, and there are two plastic, black beads for its eyes. It looks like something out of a horror story children tell around fires in East Country. A piece of metal coming alive. A robot with a brain, attacking us.

As if Margareath reads my thoughts, she says, "It can't think for itself. It's not artificial intelligence, although Mid is trying to recreate that technology too. It's just made to look like a bee."

"Why would they make this?" asks Griffin, still holding the bee away from us like the thing will come to life once again and sting uncontrollably. "Why produce a fake animal? It's not like this bee will make honey or any other useful substance."

"Simulation, of course," says Margareath. "They're trying to recreate all the animals that inhabited the earth before the climate change. Sometimes they don't always work right. Not sure why this one smacked you in the face, Elected, but it's probably an early version. Wait until you see what else Mid's created, though. The technology is fascinating!"

She's finally admitted it. She finds the technology intoxicating, like it's some kind of drug that's seeped throughout her veins. It's strange how excited Margareath is to talk about Mid's technology, but I'm starting to get used to her enthusiasm. I suppose I shouldn't be too surprised. She *was* part of the Technology Faction in East Country.

We initially leave the bee on the ground, its battered mechanical body almost too small to see within the thick dirt. But I scoop it up at the last second. Maybe the sharp point of its stinger will come in handy. I ease it into my backpack, swathed in a scarf.

We keep walking, but not in silence this time. Griffin pelts Margareath with a litany of questions. "So there are veterinarian jobs in Mid?"

"Sure thing!"

"And do the cameras watch people all the time?"

"Yes, Mid utilizes cameras almost everywhere. Not in your apartment, but everywhere else."

They continue asking questions and answering them like a volley of balls across a net. As long as Griffin's asking about technology, Margareath is more than happy to share her thoughts. I am interested too. We've finally found the key that unlocks Margareath's information. I'm about to ask a question myself, specifically how Mid seemed able to block out the moon's light last night, when something else grabs my attention.

I see a patch of green within what's been a steady terrain of brown dirt. "What's that?" I ask, pointing into the distance. It's so green in that direction, it's almost too vividly colorful.

"It's Mid's forest," says Margareath, like the word itself is commonplace.

A forest? Mid's managed to maintain a full expanse of trees? There's been no lush growth like the dense trees we're heading toward in over fifty years. However, I immediately picture the pine needles and tall foliage I saw surrounding my parents in images from the Mind Multiplier months ago. Could this be where they travelled? I pick up my pace, as does Griffin, both of us curious to see vegetation this thick. If my parents were here once, maybe this is where they've stayed! Their names are welling in the recesses of my throat, almost bubbling up to the surface in a shout. If I can find my parents this fast, then maybe the rest of our plans for Mid will come together just as easily. Closer to the edge of the forest, I start to run.

The dirt at our feet turns into thick green grass, the likes of which we've never seen in East. "It's incredible!" says Griffin, falling to his hands and knees. I continue to run through the forest, reaching the other side faster than I would have imagined. I turn left quickly, hoping to see some kind of campsite where my parents could have sheltered. But I find the edge of the foliage too rapidly again.

I race back to where Margareath stands. "It's just a patch of green."

"Small, I know."

I can practically see the ends of the forest on both sides. There are no signs of my parents. No makeshift tent. No supplies. It's just plants and grass and trees. I sigh, inwardly knowing that finding my parents couldn't possibly have been that easy, but disappointed all the same. I take a moment to look around me at the foliage, no longer searching for people behind the tree trunks. I hear a din of insects surrounding us, and I like the sound of their vibrations.

Griffin is sitting cross-legged in the grass, a piece of greenery between his thumb and forefinger. I fall down by his side, and for a moment, I pretend the forest is endless, that we can't be seen within its green walls. Griffin and I crawl on our knees, letting the tiny blades of grass brush through our outstretched fingers. Around us trees of every size and shape, ones only imagined in my dreams, climb tall. It even smells green.

For the first time I can understand Margareath's appreciation of Mid's technology. They've been able to bring plant life back to its original health, and it's fantastically amazing. After a few minutes, I turn to look at Margareath. Surprisingly, she's not as entranced as we are. Has it all become commonplace to her?

"How did they grow this?" I ask.

"They didn't *grow* any of it." Her voice is short. It's the first time she actually doesn't sound enamored with Mid.

I turn to peer at her with more focus, leaving the grass at my hands alone. "What do you mean?"

Margareath throws both of her hands up in the air. "It isn't real. It's plastic."

"Plastic?" Griffin picks one thin blade of grass. His eyes become thin lines as he leans closer to inspect it.

"Deceiving, right?" asks Margareath.

"But . . . but . . . it looks so . . . ," I stammer, the air drained from my balloon of joyfulness.

"As a Planter, I find it all a bit offensive. You can't just simulate grass and trees and expect that to satisfy people. We need technology to grow real live trees!"

She mumbles on about the simulated greenery for a few minutes, but I can't help turning back to the fake trees around us. I tune her out easily, pretending that the grass in my hands is indeed real. It looks like the fairy tale forests from my forbidden childhood books. I half expect a leprechaun to peek from behind a tree trunk.

Griffin keeps eyeing the forest too. He rubs his hands across the molded bark of a nearby limb. Without turning around he says, "It almost looks like the oak between East's White House and the prison, doesn't it?" I smile, thinking of the old tree with its great big branches hanging down like an ancient, wrinkly man. The one under which Griffin and I became friends. The one where he first touched me, and I knew his feelings weren't just camaraderie. "My father would have loved this," Griffin continues. "All the fake insects. The fake grass. He would've thought it was enough." Griffin rubs both hands across his arms. "But it's not."

I look up into his dark eyes. They're almost black in contrast to the bright green around us. "You're hoping to find a paradise somewhere deep in the wilds?" I ask. People have been trying for over a century to renew our planet to the glory of long ago. But it's futile. We destroyed Earth with our carbon monoxide, our pollution, our wars, and our greed. Our smog suffocated not only ourselves but the world around us.

"No. Grow a new one, blade of grass by blade of grass, if we have to."

I breathe in deeply, pretending the smell of pine wafting out of small manmade holes in the tops of the tree trunks is actually a real fragrance.

"Can we get on with it?" asks Margareath, waving at us from the side of the woods. "I have to get back to work soon." We stand, no longer lingering over the plastic woods.

On our way out, I have the urge to take a few blades of grass—to preserve them in my pocket. I suppose I just want to show them to Vienne when I see her in another two weeks, but I leave without any specimens. For all I know, each blade is wired and picking them would set off an alarm. Plus, Vienne and I will have more important things to talk about when we meet again.

After just a few more minutes, we finally enter the city through tall metal arches. "Just decoration," Margareath says. "They're not meant to keep anyone in or out. We'll pass my workplace first, so I'll leave you there. But then immediately go register." She points to a squat, square shaped building.

Like the two skyscrapers we saw before entering the city, all of Mid's structures are sleek silver, made of metal. I see myself distorted in the mirror-like reflections. I look tired and dirty, but no one here seems to notice. Even with our dissimilar clothing, Griffin and I don't attract attention. People scurry past us, as if they have more important things to do. Shoulders knock hard into my arms as people make their way through the city center in a hurry. What kind of place is this where no one even meets my eye to mumble an 'excuse me'?

"They'll assign you rooms and a job when you register too," Margareath says. "Just go along with everything, and I'll meet up with you later."

I nod at her, but don't bother meeting her eyes. Instead, I can't help looking around me in amazement, taking in the foreign sites. We're like the tourists from the past. Tomlin once told me about them. How they would travel to other places just to feel small and insignificant, knowing the world was larger than they'd ever imagined. He questioned why they'd leave home when loved ones and everything that matters was back where they started? Now I understand the pull, though. It's overwhelming to see Mid, but part of me can't believe this was all here without me knowing. It's like a light's been turned on and now I can see.

We've entered another world. Not a future one, but one from the past. Griffin squeezes my hand. His neck cranes back multiple times, trying to take in the enormity of the building up close. The depth of Mid Country's reliance on technology is both mesmerizing and chilling. Griffin keeps discreetly pointing things out to me. Like the strange looking robots gliding around us that no one seems to mind. Even when we think one of these automatons is about to smack right into us, at the last second the robot deftly circumvents our path. We keep pace with the rest of the crowd, steady drum beats of feet briskly scooting along the paved, interlacing walkways.

Bordering the walkways are scores of metal sculptures, their thin limbs reaching in haphazard directions toward the sky. I start to think it's nice that Mid included art throughout their otherwise monotone cityscape until I realize these metal sculptures aren't art at all. They're supposed to be trees. Each sculpture originates from the ground, silver and sleek. Limbs twist in all directions to form branches, almost looking like liquid metal oozing snakelike from multiple points on the trunk. Is this really enough for them? These fake trees? Or was this just the first model, and the forest beyond the city walls is Mid's second phase? Either way, what I've seen of Mid's vegetation so far leaves much to be desired. Except for the surprisingly zesty pink orange, Mid's attempts to recreate nature don't seem very far along. It's a sharp contrast to the other technology showcasing itself around us in the moving walkways and red-eyed robots. Apparently nature isn't high on Mid's list.

We keep walking between dozens of silver buildings with the two gargantuan skyscrapers flanking our right. There's also a tall dome, covered in something billowy and white. The cover flaps in the wind but doesn't fly off the dome.

"What's in there?" I ask, glancing toward Margareath for an answer.

She shrugs, barely looking at the structure. "Never went inside."

I purse my lips, looking up at the white cover sometimes flapping so high it covers the sun.

"But don't worry," Margareath continues, "my workplace is much more amazing, and I can tell you all about that." We grow steadily closer to the crops she refers to. Vegetation lines a square directly to the north like straight sewn lines on a quilt. Above the patch of green are hundreds of the anti-solar panels held overhead by workers. "If you can't think of a job," Margareath whispers into my ear, "you could be a Holder." She points to the people with the panels raised in the air, held up with a fold-out handle almost like umbrellas of old. Each Grower has a Holder and one panel dedicated to him as he works. "Holder's a mindless job." Margareath's voice grows even quieter as she breathes close to my cheek. "For the people who aren't quite all there. Yes, Mid could keep the screens up with poles, but everyone needs a job to do. Even these people. They'll force you to choose *something* when you register, and if you can't think of anything else . . . " Her voice trails off.

I decide right then and there, I don't want to be one of these Holders. I stare at the other people surrounding the gardens. About twenty men and women walk along the edges of the precise rows, just watching, pacing back and forth.

"Who're they?" asks Griffin.

"Guards," says Margareath. "The ones who watch us since cameras can't see through the panels. They're the only ones who carry weapons, so don't antagonize them."

"Wasn't planning on it," says Griffin, shooting one of the guards a hard look. Again, I expect the guards to stop us for questioning, but they're focused on watching the Growers. Their eyes never leave their work.

"What're you growing here?" I ask.

"All sorts of food." Margareath's eyes are alight with her passion. "I'm working on green beans lately." Margareath shows me a row of low plants. She bends down and snatches a slender cylinder off one of the stalks. "Here, try it."

I delicately place the vegetable in my mouth for a taste. Surprisingly, it's incredible, just like the orange from Mid. This green bean exudes earthiness, like sun and dirt mixed together. It's fresh and crisp, and I find my mouth waters for more. "It's good," I say. Then I pass a tip of the unfinished bean to Griffin who also takes a bite.

"You can have more in your apartment, if you want. There will be directions on how to get them. It's not hard." I nod at Margareath and think longingly of a chance to rest and eat. "I've got to start working. I'll look for you later," she says.

We leave her, walking out through the rows of different brightly colored vegetables. Again, the growers and guards don't bother with us as we stride by them as quickly as possible. But without Margareath near us now, I worry once more that we'll be called out as intruders.

"Registration is in that building over there, right?" asks Griffin, confirming what Margareath told us earlier. We step over the ankle-high fence surrounding the gardens. I grab hold of his hand firmly now that we're finally on our own.

"It doesn't look too assuming, does it?" It's the most subtle, discreet building of all so far. The registration complex is just a short, square box, made of something other than metal. "Are those bricks?"

"I think so," Griffin says as we get close. He runs his hand over the rough exterior. It's such a contrast to the sleek buildings behind us. "Maybe it's from before the wars."

We stand in front of the double glass doors for a moment, looking at each other to bolster our resolve. "No going back after this," Griffin says.

"Nope."

"One more chance to turn back, Aloy. I'd walk back with you to East tonight, if you wanted."

"Nope," I say again and press firmly on the entrance door. Inside, cool filtered air hits our faces as we pass through into the sterile hallway. It's eerily quiet here, and for a moment I wonder if we misunderstood and stepped inside the wrong building. "Maybe we should turn back," I start to say before a voice in front of us interrupts me.

"Right this way." A man stands up from behind a high counter to our side. "Come to register?"

"Yes," says Griffin. He drops my hand and goes to shake the official's, but no hand is offered back to Griffin. Finally, Griffin looks away, confused, and pulls his hand back. Maybe they don't have the same customs here. I watch to see if the official will bow to us or make some other kind of sign, but he just looks down on his desk, adjusting thick glasses.

"Where do you originate from?" asks the man. He still doesn't look up.

"West Country," I say without hesitation.

"You're late." He glances at us, pushing the rims of his black frames low on his nose.

I cough a little, thinking the jig is up. "Doesn't matter, though," says the man before I can even think what to say next. "We'll take you either way. Always good to increase our numbers. Don't know how you survived out there longer than most, though. Your brethren all mostly came a year ago. Just dribs and drabs of people now." The man seems to be talking to himself now, staring down at a book in front of him.

"What do we have to do to register?" asks Griffin. He's leaning forward just a bit, trying to see the big book behind the desk.

But the official doesn't try to hide it. At once, he grasps hold of both thick ends and grunts, pulling it up on top of the counter.

"You need to sign in. Do you know how to write?"

"Yes," I answer, surprised at his question. Were the people in West illiterate?

"Sorry, just have to ask. You're all pretty uncivilized over there."

I try not to seem offended. It's not even my country he's talking about, but the superior tone he uses when referring to West is unnerving.

"Alright, sign your name here." He points to a blank line on one of the large, yellowed pages in front of us. Griffin grabs the offered writing implement first, scrawling something non-committal for his name. All I can make out is a large G. The rest is purposefully indistinguishable.

The man twitches his nose at Griffin's scrawl but doesn't ask him to redo the signature. "Okay, your turn," he says, handing me another writing implement. It's not like the charcoal sticks we used in East Country. This stick is white and long with a blue tip on the end. I set it against a spot on the page and start to write an A-L-O, before thinking better of it and finishing my A-L with an I-C-E-N. Alicen. That'll be my name here. It could be either a boy's or girl's name, ambiguous. I like how the thin stick glides across the page, and I take an extra second letting the letter N slide off my hand into text.

"What do you call this?" I ask the man, holding the writing implement out in the middle of us.

"What? The pen?" he asks.

I nod.

"You've never seen one of these before? The rest of your people did."

I stop holding the pen in front of my face with interest, instead dropping it with a tiny clack onto the white desk in front of us. I need to be more careful. We don't know anything about West, and even this tiny question could show us for who we really are.

"We were poor," I respond, my voice low and quiet as if I'm ashamed. I don't have to fake the tone of my answer. I'm so scared, my voice cracks easily on its own.

This seems to pacify the official. "Many of you people from West were." He shakes his head in condemnation and turns the book back toward himself. "Alright, I'm going to assign you places to stay. It'll just take a few moments. In the meantime, look through this listing of jobs. Everyone works here, so you'll need to pick something."

He thrusts a thinner book in front of us and turns it to the first page. After each job, there's a short description and two numbers in parentheses. Griffin immediately sees the listing for "Animal Caretaker" with the number "10" in back of it and another number "2".

"What do the numbers mean?" he asks.

"Oh," says the official looking up at us from behind another stack of papers. "The first number is the amount of openings we have in that area. The second is how many weeks the earliest one's been available."

Griffin puts his finger on the page and silently traces the description next to the listing while glancing back up at me. I lean in, reading what he's pointing to.

"Animal Caretaker: Consists of generating clones of existing mammals, reptiles, insects, and birds. With more experience, creation of new species."

This is not what either of us was expecting, and we both scan down the page to see if there's anything else involving care of animals. But this is the only listing dealing with animals at all. Griffin sighs and shakes his head in disgust. It's almost enough to catch the attention of the official, though, so I don't answer it back with any recognition. I just keep looking down the list for any job that I could do.

"I'll take this one," Griffin says, motioning to the official. The two of them start to talk about Griffin's experience, and the man is obviously satisfied. This time he's clicking keys on some type of machine to input Griffin's information.

"Alright, this will just take a moment to go through the system and get accepted," the official explains, pointing to the small, square machine in front of him. "I'm sure you'll get the job, though. Don't worry."

I keep peering down the list. The jobs are listed in alphabetical order. I page through to the middle and see "Engineer (20-1), Guard (80-4), Holder (90-3)." I grimace at "Holder", redoubling my efforts to find something I'll be qualified for. On the same page as Holder I see one interesting listing. It catches my eye because of the numbers in back of it. "Historian (1-110)". I squint at it closer. There's only one position? And it's been open for a hundred and ten weeks? That's a long time. I read the description, not quite understanding it even after the third review.

"Historian (1-110): Knows things forgotten."

"What's this one?" I ask the official. He's almost finished typing Griffin's experience into his machine, but he stops to quickly look at the job I'm pointing to. Once he sees it, he stands up, leaving the machine altogether.

"I'm sure you don't want that one," he says, squinting at me. He looks at me harder than he's done before, this time removing his glasses completely. Maybe I've made some blunder. Requested something I shouldn't.

"I don't know. I might," I say. "What does this job entail?"

He doesn't answer me. Just states the obvious. "It's been open for a very long time. No one is qualified."

This makes me mad in a way I remember feeling years ago when I asked my parents if I could leave the White House and constantly got 'no' for an answer. It makes me feel young and stubborn again. My fingers start twitching in my clasped hands.

"Well, maybe I am. How do you know?"

"Historian? You think you know things others don't?"

At this, I stare at the man without looking away or down at the floor in defeat. His thick brown hair leaves sweat marks on his forehead. He's not good-looking, and his face, contorted as he looks at me, makes him look even more like a troll from my old fairy tales.

"I might," I say. "Try me."

The man humphs. "Fine. What is a turbine?"

"Any of various machines in which the kinetic energy of a moving fluid is converted to mechanical power by the impulse or reaction of the fluid with a series of buckets, paddles, or blades arrayed about the circumference of a wheel or cylinder," I blurt out without even giving it a second thought.

Both Griffin and the official stare back at me with wide eyes. I shut my mouth hard. What have I just done?

The official starts to stammer, still looking at me in amazement. "Umm . . . I suppose that answer is correct. I'm . . . I'm not too sure, actually. Let me just type it in here."

He bends down to thumb my answer into his machine, asking me to repeat parts of it a few times. We all wait in silence as the machine registers my response and pings back after just a few seconds. It gives a small, upbeat "ding".

The official looks back at me, eyes still wide. "Okay, answer this then. What kind of weapon did governments use back in 2030 for assassination?"

I look at the official like he's joking with me. But when he just stares back, completely serious, I answer, "Long arrows."

He types my answer in again, and it only takes a second for the machine to ding.

This time the official fumbles nervously with the keys in front of him, typing in something fast. He peers at the screen, pushing his glasses back on his face to see clearly. Finally, he looks back at me and says, "Ummm . . . alright. What year was the last Accord dictated and which one was it?"

I think back to my lesson with Tomlin the day I saw my first execution in East. I got the answer wrong back then, but this time I'll be right. "The Ship Accord. 2115."

The official chokes loudly and immediately turns back to his machine to log my answer. The computer doesn't just beep once this time. It comes back with a fast "bing, bing, bing." The official turns to me, his mouth open wide.

"You got the job," he says. He thumbs through the book again, looking once more at how long the position has been open. More than two years.

Griffin mouths "Way to go" at me while the troll-like man paws through the book. Griffin smiles big, proud that I've been able to knock the official down a peg or two.

"How . . . how . . . did you know those things?" the official stammers, looking up once again.

I shuffle my feet in front of me. I can't very well tell him I'm the Elected in my country and was raised on all this information. So I just look over his shoulder, letting my facial expression go flat and closed. "Books," I say. "My father collected books." It isn't a lie, so it comes off my lips easily.

"Well . . . " The official shakes his head in confusion, trying to comprehend how I've been able to answer questions that others haven't. "Report to building thirteen tomorrow morning at eight a.m. sharp. You got the job. But," and at this he smiles slightly, feeling his own power leveling the playing field once again. "You'll be on probation for a few months. You'll probably have to come back here in a few weeks and pick a new job."

I nod noncommittally, not wanting to fully acknowledge the official's warning. He starts talking to Griffin again, inputting the last bits of Griffin's answers into the machine. The two converse back and forth, and it affords me a few seconds to flip through the big book of names on the official's desk again. I pretend that I'm just checking my signature, but it doesn't matter. The official is so caught up typing in Griffin's information that he doesn't pay me any attention.

I'm looking for just one thing in the book, and it's not my signature. I flip back ten pages to a date months in the past. My fingers fly across the names. I'm frustrated that I can't find what I need until my eyes finally rest on the hard scrawl I've seen many times in my life. This signature's written on official documents, birth certificates, execution warrants, speeches. I can't help smiling slightly, and I pull my finger along the small indentation the two signatures made into the pulpy paper.

"Claraleese and Soyer." My parents' names. They're here.

3

PART OF ME CAN'T believe my parents made it to Mid after all. It's almost too good to be true. I wish I knew what jobs they took, but that information is only on the official's machine, and I don't think I can get to it. I could ask him outright, but it would seem too suspicious. I'll just have to look for my parents in the city's epicenter and hope I stumble upon their faces in a crowd.

"Here we go," says the official. "You're both in Tower One. Griffin in room 10233. Alicen in room 11399. Pretty good views. Your jobs grant you the higher rooms." He pronounces my name Alyken. I don't correct him because I haven't yet thought how my name should be said. "Griffin, you need to report to the animal warehouse now, but Alicen, you are free until tomorrow morning."

"I'll just go to my apartment," I say toward Griffin, grabbing my pack from the tile floor. I'm tired, but I wish it were reversed—me going to work and Griffin getting a chance to lie down in a bed. I'm the one who's had sleep; he hasn't had a moment of rest in almost two full days.

The official puts up his hand. "No, you can't. No one's allowed into their apartments during work hours unless they're broken." I think of how Margareath called herself broken when faking sickness.

I look up at the ceiling and square my shoulders. All I want right now is to lie down in some semblance of a cot and fall into a hard sleep. "Well, when can we go in?"

"Any time after six p.m. There are digital clocks all over the city. You can't miss them, so you'll know the time."

I wince. They don't even tell time by the stars like we do in East. Mid's completely succumbed to reliance on technology. I shake my head at the official. "Well, what am I supposed to do in the meantime? Should I just start working now too?"

The official laughs slightly, indicating he knows something I don't. "No, you were already given instruction on when to report. Best not be late tomorrow." As an afterthought, he says, "The doors to everyone's apartments are locked at 8:01 sharp. Anyone left inside is given demerits."

"Demerits?" asks Griffin.

The official shuffles some papers on his desk, impatient that he has to explain all this to us. "Yes. Points against you."

"What happens when we get points?" I ask, looking back and forth from the awful official to Griffin.

"Less food doled out in your kitchen when you reach ten demerits. Less water in your sink and shower when you reach twenty. Inability to visit the Satisfaction Room after thirty." He smiles at me wider. "But you'd best not be late to your new job either way." He points a stringy finger at me when he says 'you'.

I try not to think of the harshness of taking away our food and water. Instead, I ask, "What's the Satisfaction Room?"

At this, the official looks up at me with a cocked smile. "You have some time now. You could go look into it yourself."

"Fine," I say. "Griffin, let's go. I'll walk you to the warehouse."

We leave together, and I'm happy to leave the sterile registration building behind. I don't intend to fail at my job, so I won't be giving the official the pleasure of seeing me again.

The animal warehouse is a three-story building, long and rectangular, made out of silver material, same as most of the other structures. Outside of the main doors, we stop and look at each other.

"You going to be okay on your own?" asks Griffin. "I don't mind ditching work and just wandering around with you."

"No. That's okay. I have a feeling they'd come find you, don't you think? Or at the very least you'd get demerits. We don't know how much food they give us in the first place. I don't want to be responsible for you getting less right from the start."

"Alright, but I'll see you tonight. I'll meet you right outside of your apartment at six, okay?"

I nod and squeeze Griffin's elbow tight. Part of me doesn't want to let him out of my sight. Who knows exactly what's behind those doors? The thought of us separating in this strange city sends chills down my neck. So I breathe in deeply, trying to collect myself. At least we'll see each other tonight and be able to talk alone. I can think of a few other things I'd like to do with Griffin in private. This last thought makes me smile, and it's with this grin that I let go of Griffin's arm and push him lightly toward the double doors in front of us.

"Go. I'll be alright. I promise."

"Okay." He leans in and kisses me on the forehead, so fast and light I don't think anyone would notice even if they were looking.

I watch for a second as Griffin's long legs walk around the silver folds of the entrance doors, into the semi-blackness inside. The doors clank shut in back of him, and then I'm truly alone. I turn around slowly, wondering what I should do first. I look up at the towers to my left, counting up to floor one hundred thirteen. It's right below the lowest cloud but far enough away I have to squint into the sun. I wonder which one is my window.

I gather myself and start walking straight ahead. I don't know where I'm going, but I have three hours to look around. I figure I'll be working every day after this, so these few hours may be my last to explore and find out more about Mid. I'm intrigued by the Satisfaction Room, but I decide to get a lay of the entire city in my head first before entering any specific building. I walk in a large circle around the outskirts of Mid. The entire epicenter is about two and a half miles around; it only takes me thirty minutes to make the entire loop before I end up at the great stone and metal arches where we first entered. As I walk in a circle, I count the numbers on the buildings. They're all in order from one to twenty. I'm supposed to go to number thirteen tomorrow morning, and I pause outside that building for a moment longer than the others. It's about twenty floors high and made of metal just like all the others. But this one has a gold rim on the top, as if it's more special than the other structures. There are gold diamonds etched on the top four sides of the structure. Maybe the diamond is Mid's country symbol. I wonder what it could signify.

When I've gotten my bearings and feel like I wouldn't get lost even if I were walking here in the dark, I make my way to the white, billowy-topped building I first saw with Margareath. It, like the registration building, is the only one that looks completely different from the others. Maybe that's where I'll get the best clues about Mid's intentions.

As I get to the bottom of the white dome, I see there's barbed wire surrounding the structure in a circle. A few men mill around the entrance. None of them stop walking or look at me as I walk closer, so finally I reach out and tap one of them lightly on the shoulder.

"Excuse me."

The man jumps at my touch and finally looks at me. He has pin-straight, white hair, but he's not old. And when his eyes shift to mine, I see that his are a very pale pink. He's an albino. But that doesn't explain the dull expression emanating from his heavily lidded eyes. The man doesn't say anything, just stares at me like I've burned him with my fingers.

"Hi," I say again. "I . . . um . . . I'm new. I was wondering if you could tell me what's inside here."

"Inside this building?" The man finally finds his voice. He seems a little slow, and for a second I wonder if he's actually a Holder.

"Yes." I smile at him encouragingly. "It doesn't look like the other buildings."

"Mid's . . . finest accomplishment . . . ," he stutters, looking furtively left and right over the top of my shoulders.

"Accomplishment?"

"Mac!" The albino seems to come out of his stupor all of a sudden and yells to another worker who's about to enter the building. I take a step back, not wanting to cause a scene.

"I don't want any trouble. I'll just g—," I start to say.

The man the albino called turns on his heels, walking over to us. "What's up, Aaron?"

The albino points a finger at me and stutters, "He . . . he wants to know what's inside here."

"Well, tell him then," says Mac, patting Aaron on the back with a thump. "Everyone should know. It's not a secret anymore."

Aaron jumps at Mac's touch, just as swiftly as he did with mine. "But . . . but I thought . . . " he says, looking down.

"Hi there," says Mac, interrupting Aaron and looking directly at me for the first time. "Don't worry about Aaron. He's been a little broken lately. He might not remember, but the Elected's said it's not a secret any-more. You of all people should remember that, Aaron."

Aaron keeps looking down at his feet, rubbing the top of his head with one hand.

My voice catches in my throat as I stare up at Mac. He's an extremely tall man and the first one here in Mid who seems comfortable. "Sorry. I didn't mean to disturb you."

"No problem. I'm the foreman here at building one." Mac points a finger into Aaron's chest. "You can go ahead into work. Share a shift with Brice today. You're not yourself."

Aaron's white face turns beet red, but Mac hardly notices. Aaron looks at me for one more second before dropping his gaze again. Even after he's gone behind the double doors of the dome, I continue to stare after him.

"Don't worry about him," says Mac, laughing again. "Just a bit of confusion after visiting the doctors. So what were you asking again? Oh! What's under the dome?"

I stop staring after Aaron, focused again on my original task. "Yes. You said it's not a secret anymore? Then why's it covered up?"

"Have to make sure no outsiders can see it. We're so close now. Don't want it destroyed before it's of use, you know?"

"Before what's of use?" I ask, impatient for the answer now.

"Our nuclear warhead, of course!" Mac's voice is full of pride as he looks up toward the top of the billowing white material flapping gently in the wind. "And our rocket launcher. Pretty neat, ain't it?"

I'm stunned. A rocket launcher and nuclear warhead? These are the villains of the earth's destruction years ago, and they're back? Now I completely understand what Mid is going to do. They'll try to take over the world again, just like countries did over a century ago. I stand there dumbfounded as Mac rattles on.

"Love talking about it, as you can probably see. Been a long time coming, this technology. We've been working around the clock. Special permission from the . . . " He pauses a moment and then guffaws, smacking one hand to his forehead. "I guess you could say from the Elected!" He's positively jolly referring to the equipment, but I can't return his enthusiasm. "Would love to build a laser ray gun. Like the ones they used to have way back. I'd show you what I have so far, but can't do that, unfortunately. You'll just have to wait like everyone else 'till we use it one day."

Use it? My head is swimming. I'm sure Mac must notice my discomfort, but he just keeps looking up toward the top of the dome.

"I'd better get going," I choke out.

"Hey, come back, ya' hear?" calls Mac after me as I start to turn. "Always love fans of my work! And what's your name?"

I turn back for just a moment. "Alicen," I say, pronouncing it with a hard "c" like the official from registration.

"Well, see ya around Alicen!"

I raise a hand, but keep walking away at a brisk pace. I want to get as far away as possible from the weaponry. The situation is more dire than I thought. If Mid is going to take over the world with this awful technology, East is the first country that will feel its wrath. I almost contemplate heading back to East right now to launch a full scale defense. But what would we do in such little time? Maybe Griffin's father was right. Maybe we should have been breaking the Technology Accord ourselves years ago, if only to build up a cache of fortifications. There's no way we'd catch up in time now, even if East used technology full-throttle, starting tomorrow. It's best if I stay here and find some way to upend Mid's plans from within. How, I have no idea, but I've got to try.

It's ten past six before I even notice how much time's passed. I make my way to Tower One and see a heavy stream of people all doing the same. When the throngs reach the front of the building, people proceed in an orderly manner, one at a time, through the main doors. They place their index finger up to a silver sensor pad, wait for the 'bing' and then walk through the turnstiles. I look wildly around me for my parents. If there's a crowd here, maybe I'll be lucky enough to see their faces. I wonder if they know about Mid's weapons and what they've been doing to stop it.

I get to the front of the line before I have the opportunity to see any familiar faces. I stick my finger out and feel the cool piece of metal scanning my skin. It tickles, and I'm impelled to pull my finger away, but I wait out the sensation. The screen sprouts a picture of my fingerprint. It's like an unending circular labyrinth. I've never seen my print outlined all in black like that. I stop a moment, staring at the picture until someone bumps into my lower back. I turn, but the woman directly behind me doesn't say anything, just stares ahead like she didn't push me. I shake my head but keep walking forward to a square box that everyone else enters.

At first I don't know what it is, and I'm afraid to step in with the others. But I remember Tomlin's skyscrapers and how I asked him if people climbed all those stairs. He'd explained about elevators, and I think this contraption must be what he meant. I jump slightly over a small gap in the floor, unsure if the elevator will start moving with me half in and half out. Once the little room is packed with people, it starts a rapid ascent. I don't know how it can tell at which floors to stop, but the elevator makes no mistakes, slowing down and opening its doors only at the right ones. There are only four people left as the elevator climbs past the hundredth floor, a small enough number to start a pleasant conversation, but no one speaks. The other three people just stare straight ahead.

I feel my throat closing in on itself. We're so high up. We could fall at any second. I remember Tomlin telling me how elevators were another flawed piece of technology: cables holding up the tiny box snapping at any second, elevator doors shutting on people's hands, and women birthing babies while stuck inside the miniscule room. How are all my fellow passengers so calm? If Tomlin were here, would he even trust the equipment enough to have gotten onboard? What will Griffin think of it? Will he ride one or stubbornly take the stairs? Do they even have stairs in these towers?

My questions and fears are endless, but in just a few more moments we reach floor one thirteen, and the doors open for me. I step out of the lift into the tower's hallway.

At once I see Griffin standing a few meters down the carpeted hallway. "Hey!" I call out.

He turns on the balls of his feet, his forehead furrowed in neat, straight creases. "I was starting to get worried, Aloy! This is your apartment number, right?"

I nod and catch his hands within mine before he can throw his arms around my waist. "It's Alicen now, remember?" My voice is a whisper in the hallway where Mid's cameras are surely in use. "Come on, let's get inside."

"Just put your fingertip on the slab of metal like downstairs in the lobby."

I do as he instructs, and the steel door automatically slides open. The two of us halt in the entrance to my new apartment, taking in the sights before venturing further. We're standing in the living room and ahead of us is a kitchen. The first room contains one chair and a small table. It's minimalistic but luxurious at the same time. I can't help flopping down onto the seat once we've agreed there's no apparent danger inside.

I groan. "It feels so good to sit."

Griffin walks past me, touching the sides of the living room walls. "I think these are compartments." He pushes on one, and another door slides open. When he turns back around he's holding a piece of clothing toward me. "Sexy. Looks like you got what everyone else wears." A thin brown robe hangs from a piece of metal wire. It isn't a pretty thing, but I realize it'll suit my purposes perfectly. Under its wide, triangular shape, my pregnancy will remain hidden for a long time.

"It'll be hard to tell the difference between men and women underneath those things," I say.

"Yeah, about that," says Griffin. He's still scoping out my rooms, wandering into the kitchen. "Have you noticed anything strange about how people act around each other? Like the opposite sexes?"

"Absolutely. They don't like to be touched. I made the mistake of touching someone today, and he almost jumped out of his skin."

"True. But more than that. Men and women don't interact. And when they do, they don't even make eye contact."

"It's definitely not normal," I agree.

"Hey, look at this."

I stop massaging my calf and stand up to see what Griffin's inspecting.

"Doesn't look like much of a kitchen," I say. "There's nowhere for a fire to be built. How're we supposed to cook?"

"I don't think you need to worry about cooking." Griffin laughs, poking his finger inside a box built into the wall. "How do you think this works?"

"I have no idea." Suddenly, I'm so tired I could sleep right here on the floor. But I'm hungry too. I don't like that eating here will be yet another riddle to solve.

"What did Margareath say about getting green beans?"

"That it would be easy to get whatever we wanted."

Griffin pauses for a moment, running his hand slowly over the sides of the cut-out. "Anything we wanted. Hmm . . . like cornbread?" He emphasizes the word, directing his voice into the metal box. He watches the cut-out intently but nothing happens.

"You think if you just ask for something, it'll appear?"

"Maybe." He's still fiddling inside the cut-out, and I take the opportunity to glance around the room now that I'm in it. There's a small metal box on a counter to my left. I pull on its doors, which open with a 'thwump' of controlled air. At once my face is hit with the coolness. "Food! Look!"

Griffin peeks into the ice chest with me, and we hungrily pull out the few contents. A single cup of purple liquid and a wrapped plate. I pull back a thin sheet of metal from the plate and see a slab of brown meat, a mash of white vegetable and more of the delicious green beans.

"Let's eat!" I say, and we both tear into the portion. It's not enough for two, but we don't care. It's more than we've had in the last two days.

"Mmm," moans Griffin with appreciation.

"What is the white stuff? It's sweet."

Griffin shrugs but loads his finger with another dollop of the concoction. When we're finished, I look around for somewhere to put the dirty dishes. There's only a small counter, not big enough for our little plate and cup, so I set both down inside the cutout in the wall. Instantly, a voice erupts through the wall.

"Thank you. Would you like some more?"

I instinctively duck down onto the ground, looking wildly around for a person in my apartment.

Griffin chuckles out loud. "So this is how it works!" He points to the cutout. "It only starts once we've finished our original food. That way there's no waste." He cocks his head. "Ingenious, really."

I stand up quickly and join him in front of the kitchen wall. "Yes, tell it we want more."

"Maybe you should," Griffin says. "In case it only recognizes your voice."

It's a good thought. I lean forward with my head almost inside the cutout. "Yes, more food please."

Immediately there's a whooshing sound from within the wall and a moment later a flap in the cutout slides open to reveal another plate of food. It's more of the same, and we tuck into this meal too. We keep eating, replacing dishes and asking for more food until we've had four platefuls.

"I can't eat anymore," I say, holding my stomach in the living room. I can't stop smiling. I haven't felt this satiated in a long time.

"I could, but I don't want to make myself sick," says Griffin.

I walk over to the cutout, replacing our last dishes and say "no" when the voice asks us if we'd like more.

"Do you think it's keeping track of how much we're eating?" I ask.

"Yeah, sure. But what does it matter? Mid seems to have quite enough of everything. It's not like we're taking food away from others. Tracking our food isn't my worry. It's whatever else Mid is tracking." He looks around my apartment pointedly raising his eyebrows. I get his drift. Somehow Mid could be listening to every word we say. Even though Margareath doesn't think they employ cameras in the apartments, she didn't say anything about listening devices.

"I need to tell you what I saw today," I say quickly, whispering right next to Griffin and shielding the view of my mouth against my arm. I know news of the rocket launcher will squelch this good mood we're in after eating. But there's no better time. As my father used to say, 'bad news doesn't get better with age.'

"And you have to hear about the cloning they're doing," says Griffin. "Mid's experimenting with genetics. They can tell what kind of diseases we'll have before we even contract them."

"Yes, but can they then cure them?" I ask. "And if they can't, what are people supposed to do with that information?"

We exchange stories for what feels like hours, moving from the kitchen to the living room and then eventually into the sparse bedroom, whispering at all times and even turning on the water when discussing the most sensitive of information. Griffin is aghast at my explanation of Mid's nuclear weapon, as I knew he would be. We discuss ideas for foiling Mid's offense. Sabotage the rocket launcher. Turn people, one-by-one, against the Elected. Even assassinate him. Finally, my head feels heavy, and I have trouble devising any more attack plans.

The bedroom holds a twin-sized bed, small but comfortable with a plush mattress. I lie down while Griffin sits upright on the bed against the wall.

"There only seems to be room on here for one person to sleep," Griffin says, patting the bed with one hand and twirling one of my short curls with his other.

"I don't mind sharing," I say in the middle of a drawn out yawn. I grasp onto his biceps, pulling him toward me so that Griffin's head rests next to mine on the pillow. I burrow my head into his neck. "Maybe I don't want to sleep right now after all."

Griffin kisses me, softly at first, but then with more intensity. He shifts to encircle me, and I wholeheartedly fall into his embrace. Our bodies are like two planets that have revolved around the sun for decades without ever feeling the warmth. Now we melt into each other. I run my hands through his jagged hair, holding on tight as he continues to kiss my neck. I bite down softly on his shoulder as he starts pulling up my linen shirt.

I should tell him. I *need* to tell him that I'm pregnant. But I don't want to interrupt this moment that's finally ours. I moan as he makes his way lower, kissing my chest and then my hip bone. I arch my back, begging him silently for more, knowing where this is going and wanting it.

"GET OUT NOW!" A shrill voice echoes around every room in my apartment, reverberating against the metal bedframe.

Griffin instantly stops kissing me and tumbles off onto the floor. I sit up, again looking left and right for someone inside the room.

"What . . . what's . . . going on?" I stutter, not able to completely catch my breath.

"Did they see us?" asks Griffin, grabbing frantically at his shirt that lies next to the bed.

"EVACUATION SEQUENCE ONE!" says the voice again, and I realize it's coming from the walls. There's no one here. But the word 'evacuation' piques my senses, drawing the blood from my flushed face back down into my body.

"Griffin, I think something's wrong!"

I grab his hand and the two of us run to the front door. When I open it, I see people milling into the hallways from all rooms around ours. This time the people aren't as calm as when they were coming home from work at six p.m. Citizens walk briskly, some run. But some also turn to look at me and Griffin coming out of the same apartment. Their eyes are wide, not just from the evacuation, but also from the sight of us. I go to drop Griffin's hand, but he won't let me. He keeps a hard hold on it.

The metallic voice is here in the hallway too, booming over hidden loudspeakers. "MID IS UNDER ATTACK! WALK SINGLE FILE TO THE STAIRCASES! GET TO THE TOWER'S BOMB SHELTER!"

No one is walking single file, but my earlier question about stairs is answered. Mid has stairs, it's just that no one uses them if it's not completely necessary. Just like everything in Mid so far, if there's a way to use technology, the people here will do so.

Griffin and I jog in back of the crowd toward a lit door at the end of the hallway. The stairs are wide. Everyone steps onto the top and then seems to hold onto a rope at the side.

"Don't let go of this!" Griffin yells at me over the loudspeaker voice, thrusting one of the ropes into my arms. He still holds my other arm hard, and I'm glad because I refuse to lose him in this confusion. I wonder how we're going to possibly run down one hundred thirteen stairs in time before these supposed bombs rain down. But my worry is answered instantly as the ground underneath our feet slips away. The stairs become a slide, each step clicking backward into itself. We all hold tight as the rope propels us down the slide at an amazing speed. A minute later, we're coming closer to the ground floor. I wince, thinking that we'll all crash into a pile at the bottom, body upon body, struggling against each other. But again, Mid's technology surprises me. At floor two, the slide slows, gently depositing each person, one at a time, onto their feet. The rope flies up into the air and begins its ascent back up to higher floors. We've been deposited onto a moving platform, so we're out of the way of people in back of us. I stumble on the moving walkway, but Griffin rights me. He's steadier on his feet than I am. People step off the walkway, and we follow, letting them lead us into the bomb shelter located beneath the lowest level of the tower.

Everyone crowds into the dark rooms. There are a few light bulbs hanging from the ceiling, but they only serve to make the room spooky, and everyone's faces look like apparitions. We're coated in shadows, making our features seem hollowed out. But it doesn't stop me from looking around. I hope to see my parents in this crowd. After searching the faces for a moment, I realize they're not here. But I realize something else too.

I pull Griffin close so that I'm talking directly into his ear. "There aren't any kids here."

He looks around, taking in my words. His eyebrows go up and he shakes his head. "No, no kids."

"Where are they all?"

But before Griffin can answer, I hear a man to our left talking to another citizen of Mid. "Again? Won't they ever stop bombing us?"

"What do you think they need this time? What'll be missing when we get out of here?" the other man asks. "Our food this time? Or maybe the rocket launcher?"

"It won't go on like this for long. Elected says we're already striking back. This is what we've been planning for."

I turn to the men. "Someone's stealing from Mid?"

The first man looks surprised that I've spoken to him, but he answers quickly enough. "Damn East Country!"

I almost fall to my knees. If it weren't for Griffin still holding my elbow like an anchor, I'm sure I would have buckled.

They think it's *East Country* stealing from them? Bombing them? Why?

Most importantly, if it's not my country, then who is it?

4

GRIFFIN AND I WHISPER to each other as far away from the others as possible.

"It's not us, obviously," he says.

"Obviously!" I shudder. "Why would they pin it on us? What they said back there about already striking back—are they talking about how Mid stole our Nirogene and bombed the hills?"

"Seems like it. And they're talking about starting a bigger offensive soon."

"We've got to destroy that rocket launcher as soon as possible!" My eyes dart around to ensure no one can hear us.

The doors to the bomb shelter are pulled back suddenly, and the room is bathed in harsh light.

"Everyone out!" a guard yells. "Evacuation ended. You can go back to your apartments."

People start filing out of the room, but not everyone goes directly to the elevators. People crowd inside the lobby.

"Saw it all . . . they've handicapped us!" yells one man toward the group starting to form around him.

A throng of citizens follow the observer out of Tower One's front doors into the black night. Everyone's looking at something in the sky, but I don't follow their eyes. I can only focus on the hundreds of guards surrounding the towers. Each one carries a huge weapon, nothing like the tiny guns the guards carried by the crop. I shrink back against Griffin, horrified at these different sorts of killing machines surrounding us.

Griffin, however, stares along with the crowd. "Look," he says to me, pointing into the sky.

I follow his finger up to the dome in the distance. The white canvas is thrown off the tip, and we can all see the top of the rocket launcher. But it doesn't look like it should. The metal has been blown apart. It hangs there like a limp arm, ready to fall at any moment. Something small moves on a section of the bending metal, waving precariously in the wind.

"Looks like we won't have to do a thing," Griffin says. "Whoever led the bombing did our job for us. The rocket launcher is ruined."

I know I should be happier at this sudden good fortune, but I can't help squinting upward to see the thing balancing on a wayward piece of the building's skeleton. "What's moving up there?"

"Broken pieces of the rocket's rail structure?"

"No. Look right there." I point specifically to a tiny figure balanced on the broken rail.

Griffin follows the angle of my finger and finally sees what I'm referring to. "That's a person!"

"Come on! It doesn't look like anyone else notices. We've got to get over there!" I start running in the direction of the cylinder-shaped building, and Griffin has no choice but to follow me. We arrive at the dome, and I immediately see Mac, the foreman, standing outside the barbed wire fence, looking up to the top of the broken weaponry.

"Mac! There's a man up there!"

He swivels to look at me. "Oh, hey there." His demeanor isn't rushed, but he looks pained. Mac puts his hand to his brow and then points upward. "Look what they did to my rocket launcher." He shakes his head and drags a sweaty hand across his eyes.

"I know, but there's someone up there!" Now that we're closer, I stare upward, shielding the bright lights from my eyes, trying to see better. "Wait a second . . . " The person's white hair flies wildly in the wind. "That's Aaron, isn't it?"

Mac leans forward. "Reckon it is. Shame, really."

He isn't moving fast enough. I almost reach out to push Mac through the gates. He's got to do something.

"You know that guy up there?" Griffin asks me.

I don't have time to answer Griffin, but I nod. "Mac, come on. You've got to get Aaron down!"

Mac shakes his head. "Not possible. Up way too high. Too dangerous."

I move to face Mac so he has to look me in the eyes. "Wait, you're going to just let him stay up there? He's going to fall. Look at him holding onto the bar!" I stare up at the tiny figure above us. Aaron's gone from walking along the beam to holding onto it on his knees. "No one's going to help him?"

"Impossible with the bombing. Elevators aren't working."

"What about the stairs?" asks Griffin, getting the drift. The people of Mid are just going to wait for Aaron to fall to his death rather than devise a way to save him. "Don't you people have some sort of ladder or something?"

Mac stares at Griffin for a longer beat when he says the words 'you people' but then cocks his head to the side and just shrugs. "No one uses stairs for going up. Just elevators."

"This is ridiculous! I'm going in!" I say, throwing my hands in the air.

Mac finally looks at me seriously. "You can't." He reaches out to grab me, and Griffin automatically wraps his hand around Mac's collar before the big man can touch me.

"Well, someone's got to do something!" I yell back at Mac. Without thinking, I run through the open, barbed wire gate and straight into the dome's gaping entrance. I ignore the shouts coming from behind me. This might be my only chance to not only save Aaron but to see the rocket launcher. With all the chaos tonight, the doors for the dome are wide open and the guards are otherwise occupied. No one stops me as I search the bottom floor of the building for a stairwell.

"Wait!" I glance back at Griffin who's running in after me, yelling. "There's no way you're going up there alone!"

"You have to stay down here and divert anyone from stopping me."

"No, you don't understand. They're not coming in after us."

I stop for a second. "What do you mean?"

"I mean, Mac isn't going to stop you. No guards are coming. When Mac realized you weren't kidding, he just grunted and turned away. He doesn't really care. None of them do. It's strange. It's like that guy's life doesn't matter to them. Since you're hell-bent on fetching him, it seems Mac's resigned to losing you too." He stops for a second, catching his breath.

"Alright. Then, come on. I have no idea how long Aaron's already been up there in the wind. He could fall at any moment."

We scramble together through the door into the tall stairwell.

"How many flights, do you think?" asks Griffin, huffing by my side as we ascend to the twentieth floor a few minutes later.

"Maybe thirty more?" I look up to the open sky peeking through the ripped white canvas. I honestly don't know how I'll make it up that many floors without passing out. We've fueled up on Mid's superfood, but the lack of sleep is slowing me down.

"Can't understand why we're the only ones trying to save him," I say in between heavy gulps of air.

"The loss of one person is better than endangering a bunch of others, I guess."

I think about Griffin's words for a couple more flights. If we were in East Country, would I sacrifice one person to potentially keep others safe? I remember the day the mines were bombed. I sent people in looking for survivors even though the hills could have caved in at any second. I couldn't leave any of the trapped miners without hope of escape. If this was my country, I'd have multiple people up here trying to save Aaron, even though he's just one person.

By the time we've reached the fortieth floor, my lungs feel like they'll burst. I'm panting, bent over with hands on both knees.

"You alright?" asks Griffin. "We can stop. He might not even be up there anymore, anyway."

Griffin's words push me back upright. We might only have minutes before that big piece of metal Aaron's holding onto splits and falls. I clutch the stairway handrail to scale a few more steps in one bound, trying to make it look effortless, but Griffin can tell how much this climb is costing me.

"I'll go get him, okay? You just stay here," he says.

"No way. I'm not letting you sacrifice yourself for my half-brained scheme."

"Well," laughs Griffin, hurtling himself up to the next landing, "at least you're admitting it's half-brained. How're you planning to reach him once we get up there anyway?"

"You're going to have to hold the metal at its joint while I give Aaron a hand."

"No way I'm letting you climb out on that overhang while I just watch!"

"You'll have to," I say, trying to keep my voice calm, even though the idea of shimmying across a rail fifty floors in the sky isn't my idea of fun. "I'm the lighter of the two of us. The metal might crack under your weight, and anyway, I'm not strong enough to hold up the joint if it starts to break like you are."

"This is idiotic," says Griffin, scaling a few more stairs next to me. "Why don't we let Mid save its own people?"

"Because they won't. They'll all just watch from below as this guy falls to his death."

Griffin doesn't say anything, but I know he agrees. Something's weird about this country. People are too excited about technology and too disengaged from their own neighbors. And where are the children? Besides finding my parents and learning about Mid's nuclear capabilities, now we have a new mystery to unravel. It's only been a day in Mid, yet we already have more questions about the country than when we arrived.

It takes us ten more minutes to reach the top of the stairway, where we feel wind licking at us through the gaping hole in the canvas above.

"Everything from this point on has been structurally compromised," says Griffin. "So be careful where you step."

We climb out of the stairwell and navigate our way through pieces of broken building until we feel stronger gushes of air from our left. "There," I say, pointing to a section of the damaged outer wall. "We're next to the highest platform."

Griffin peeks through the hole in the wall. It's big enough for us both to climb through.

"He's straight out that rail!" I yell, seeing the albino man swaying like a rabbit in a tree snare. He's still alive, holding onto one rail with both arms and a slender twine of rope. He's slipped from last we saw him. From this vantage point, I can tell that Aaron could hoist himself up if he didn't have to use both hands to hold the rail. I can also see straight down to the growing crowd below us. There are maybe two hundred people watching, but not a soul is tromping up the stairs behind us to help. I feel like yelling something caustic down at them all, but in this wind, they wouldn't hear me anyway. Instead, I try to get Aaron's attention. "Hey!"

At first I don't think he's heard me, but then his head whips around, and we lock eyes. Aaron seems to recognize me, but his look isn't one of relief. If anything, he looks angry.

"We're coming for you!" I scream.

He shakes his head wildly in our direction.

"Aloy," says Griffin, now that we're both looking out the precipice. "You still think this is smart? Even this guy doesn't think we should go out there."

"He's just scared." I start scooting myself forward, sitting with the bar in between my legs, testing my weight on the rail.

"What if you fall?" Griffin pleads. "Is this stranger's life really worth yours? If you die, you realize East Country is left abandoned, right? You're willing to sacrifice both your life and your people for one man?"

I already have my answer ready. "I never believed 'the greater good' was a valid excuse not to do the right thing."

Griffin shakes his head, hearing the resolve in my voice. "This is crazy." There's a length of rope lying near the busted outer wall, probably the same kind Aaron has with him. Griffin grabs the bulk of it, tying three lengths around my hips and securing an intricate knot. Finally, he nods and then lies on his stomach with his legs and feet locked under the lip of the building's floor. He puts all his weight into holding the beam steady. It helps a little bit. The metal bar doesn't sway as much in the wind with Griffin using his body as a dowel. I look back and try to smile reassuringly at him even though my stomach starts to lurch. I can feel my heartbeat straight from my toes to the tips of my fingers. When I look down again I don't just see Aaron and the crowd but the head of an intact missile peeking through the damaged frame of the building. It protrudes about thirty floors down, suspended between a dozen different rails.

I try to breathe deeply, pushing myself forward again. Everything will be fine, I say over and over to myself with each pull of my body. Just a little more and I'll be close enough.

When I've gone about twenty yards, almost on top of Aaron, I yell down. "Give me your hand!"

"Don't push me off!" he shouts upward, the wind catching pieces of his hair and lashing them against his cheeks and mouth.

"Of course not! I'm here to help you!" I keep my eyes trained ahead instead of straight down.

His voice gets softer, but I think I can make out his words. "I don't deserve it."

"Yes, you do! You were just in the wrong place at the wrong time!" Pieces of ripped canvas fly past my face, making it difficult to see Aaron hanging underneath me.

"You don't understand," he says. "You should just go back."

He squints through the wind, his hair flying in and out of his eyes. I wait for a full twenty seconds, counting each one in my head. My arm stretches precariously far off the rail, still gesturing for Aaron to take the assistance.

Finally he gives in. "Okay, how should we do this?"

I let out a big gulp of air I didn't even know I was holding. "Like this," I say, showing him how he can propel one leg over the rail while I hold onto the rope that's under Aaron's armpits.

After a few frightening sways of his body, one of Aaron's legs extends up to encircle the metal. I hold onto the rope with a tight grip, keeping my legs wrapped around the rail. Aaron grasps onto the beam, pulling his body up so his stomach lies flat against the metal. Finally we're right next to each other, and the albino copies the hold I keep on the rail with my legs.

"Why are you saving me?" he asks from behind.

"No time for talking," I gasp, glancing back at him. "Just get back to solid ground."

Aaron nods, inching himself forward as he watches me do the same. I look down once more at the crowd. Everyone's still staring up at us, but no one's cheering or clapping like I expect. At the end of the beam, Griffin holds out his hand. We each grasp onto it, me first and then Aaron, holding Griffin's arm by the elbow to ensure maximum stability. Griffin ensures we make the leap back into the building without falling. I see him take a deep breath when we're all back within the inner walls of the dome.

Griffin whispers into the hair behind my left ear. "How many times do I have to watch you put yourself in danger?"

I just shake my head, a sort of apology.

We start walking down the forty-nine flights of stairs, going faster now on the descent and inhaling deeply like all three of us were holding our breath throughout the ordeal above.

"What were you doing up there in the middle of the night?" Griffin asks Aaron, always suspicious in this odd place.

"I don't want to be a Holder!" Aaron's frustration is palpable. His pale eyes look turbulent in the dim light of the stairwell.

"It doesn't seem like it's anyone's favorite job, but that doesn't answer the question," I say. "I thought Mac said you were supposed to share a shift with someone else. Where's your partner?"

Aaron turns toward the wall, not meeting my eyes. "I wasn't authorized to be up there." He swallows hard. "But . . . I had to show them I'm still useful!"

"Why wouldn't they think you're useful?" Griffin asks, his eyebrows raised as he looks in my direction.

"I got some basic engineering answers wrong. I keep forgetting things. So they think I'm permanently broken."

"I didn't know anyone could be permanently 'broken'," says Griffin with a frown. "That seems a . . . severe diagnosis."

"And you don't seem sick," I say.

We're at the bottom of the staircase now. Aaron pauses, like he's unsure if he wants to pass through the lobby out into the crowd around the dome.

"It'll be okay," Griffin says, picking up on his hesitancy. "We'll vouch for you. I'm sure they can't make you take a job you don't want." He tries to sound confident, but we look at each other behind Aaron's back. I'm pretty sure the government in Mid can and will make their people do just that.

Aaron walks in front of us, but I'm the first one Mac runs to when we get outside.

"What do you think you were doing?" he asks, hands in fists at his sides.

"The right thing."

Mac shakes his head. "You think so, but it would have been better if he'd fallen."

I can't believe Mac just said that, and in front of Aaron, no less. "What are you talking . . . " I start to say, but I'm interrupted by two men in white coats stepping out of the crowd and each grabbing one of Aaron's arms.

"No!" screams Aaron, suddenly aware that they're there for him. "No, you can't! I don't want to be a Holder." Aaron screeches the last part over and over again as the two men lift him off his feet and haul him away.

"Where are they taking him?" My voice is high and frenzied. "They shouldn't make him do a job he doesn't want!"

"Do a job?" says Mac, laughing. "That ain't what they're about."

"Then what exactly?" interrupts Griffin, his eyes wide.

"They'll try to fix him again."

"He was just desperate to work on his project. To prove his worth. You said the Elected lets people work on the weapons here round the clock," I say.

Mac gives me a strange look, one eyebrow cocked. "Yeah, but not him," he finally says. "Not in his condition."

"What kind of sickness is it exactly?" asks Griffin, his arm instinctively tightening around my shoulder.

Mac gazes for a second at Griffin's arm and purses his lips. "I don't have time to be answering all your questions. I've got to fill out a report on this here incident."

He starts to walk away, but as Mac almost gets enveloped into the crowd, he turns back once more in our direction. "Have you two newcomers had your monthly check up at the doctor's yet?"

I swallow.

"Yeah, didn't think so. It's mandatory, you know," he says.

I glance at Griffin, my brow furrowed. I'd rather stay away from things that Mid qualifies as 'mandatory'.

"Don't worry," whispers Griffin into my ear. "We'll pretend we already did. And anyway, you'll be in and out of Mid so fast, they won't have time to see you."

That's what he thinks, but Griffin still doesn't know I'm planning to stay in Mid for a full nine months, enough time for our baby to be born.

I glance back into the crowd and watch Mac disappear. The guards usher everyone toward the towers now that the "show" is over. I keep a lookout for my parents in the mass of people streaming along the moving paths, but again I don't see them. I watch, disheartened, as the guards pay special attention to me and Griffin making our way through the tower's turnstiles. There's no way he can sneak back into my apartment with me tonight. Griffin realizes this too.

Inside the elevator he squeezes my hand. "Good luck tomorrow. I'll be waiting at your door right at six p.m." He steps off the elevator at his floor, watching me until the doors fully shut again.

Alone in the elevator, I lean against the too-cold walls. His words remind me that I only have a few hours left to sleep before starting my next deception in Mid. I sigh, and stare up at myself in the silver mirror on the ceiling. I look tired. Exhausted, really.

Outside the door to my apartment, I reach my finger up to the metal slab. For a second I glance to my left and right, but no one even looks at me. The few people still milling around move like robots into their own rooms, keeping their heads straight forward.

I climb into my rumpled bed feeling bedraggled and ill. But Griffin's earthy scent, like pinecones, reaches up to me from the rumpled sheets. It's the thought of him being near me tomorrow night that allows me to finally drift off.

I'm awakened by a blinking light. A digital projection on the ceiling reads seven a.m., but it feels like I just put my head on my pillow. I try to ignore the ceiling clock getting brighter and brighter by burying my head under my sheets, but soon a voice, soft at first and gradually more piercing, orders me out of bed.

"Reminder: all citizens must be out of their apartments by eight a.m. You only have forty minutes left."

I sink more fully into the mattress, clamping both hands up to my ears. "I hear you. I hear you," I mutter.

But the voice is relentless. "Only thirty five minutes left."

"Fine!" I yell up to the ceiling, knowing my protests directed at a lifeless machine are fruitless. But it makes me feel better to get angry anyway. I find a labeled "hygiene station" toward the back of my apartment and wash off with the streaming cold water and sponge provided. I pull on the one canvas robe hanging in my closet and sink my feet into brown, not altogether uncomfortable, loafers. When the robe falls off the hanger, a panel in the closet wall opens and another robe slides in. "Efficient," I muse, running a hand through my still-wet hair. I look around for a mirror, remembering that I'll have to figure out a way to keep my hair short if I'm going to maintain my image as a man. But there are no scissors in this sparse place. And no mirror for that matter either. I peer at my faint image in the silver metal of my closet door. "This is stupid!" I say to no one when I can't even make out my eye color in the reflection. "And where's the underwear?" I call out, opening the closet door again to peer around inside. There's nothing inside except for the extra robe. "Just perfect. So everyone walks around practically naked?" Then I smile and keep talking to myself as I shuffle into the kitchen. "You'd think that would inspire some sort of sexuality among the people of Mid, but I didn't see anyone even looking twice at each other!"

I open the square ice box and find another small glass of purple liquid and a bowl full of cut up oranges. I tuck into the segments, and when their delicious pulp is gone, I place the empty plate into the hole in the wall. I ask for another dish and am rewarded with more of the same hot pink fruit. When I'm about to place this second dish back into the wall a light begins blinking from the kitchen's ceiling. The projected clock in this room pulses the time 7:58, and the less-than-friendly mechanical voice starts is nagging anew.

"Two minutes until demerits. Everyone must be out of the apartment by eight."

"I'm going!" I call out. I let my empty dish clatter onto the metal counter inside the wall and hurry toward the front door.

"One minute!" the voice says.

I click the apartment door closed behind me, watching with wonder as people on all sides of the corridor step out of their front doors in military precision. I'm about to head out, following the others single file to the elevator when I realize I don't know what this day will bring. I should carry my knife with me. I'm contemplating where exactly I'll store the knife under these robes while trying to get back into my apartment, when I realize nothing is happening. My apartment door won't open.

I jam my big toe into the bottom of the door, hoping to wedge it open without making a scene. A few passersby stare but keep walking straight. For a split-second I contemplate banging on the door with all my might and screaming at the computer to "Open up!" But bringing extra attention to myself isn't a smart idea, especially after I made a scene by saving Aaron last night. I can't afford to attract attention just for a knife I don't even know how I'd conceal.

Along with everyone else I shuffle head-down onto the moving walkways outside the tower. I get to building thirteen and enter the steel doors that belch out a cool gust of air. A man at the front door looks up as I click my loafers loudly on the tile floor.

"Index finger, please," he says.

I thrust my fingertip onto his scanner. He reviews my biometric information in a machine on his lap, opening his eyes wide. I'm curious to see what his machine revealed, but the official regains composure fast and merely says, "This way."

He escorts me to another elevator, but this one's different from the Tower's. The outer wall is glass and shows us the entire expanse of Mid as we climb. I get a bird's eye view of the damaged dome from last night. They've repaired the white canvas so it no longer flaps like an injured bird in the wind. I'm about to ask the official what was stolen during last night's raid, but before I can do so he announces that we've reached our destination. "Top floor."

I step into the immaculate hallway and see two decadent doors, like frosting on top of a white cake, at the end of the empty expanse. There's nothing along the walls to distract me from the long, silent walk down the corridor. As we reach the gold doors that look so out of place in this austere building, my situation hits me again. I don't know what I'll say if they ask me too many specific questions about West. I don't know what job I'll be doing. And I'm still not positive I'm qualified for whatever they have in mind. If I make a mistake, will they cart me away like they did Aaron?

The official pushes on one of the gold doors to reveal an almost piercingly bright room inside. "Wait here," he says.

I look around the room in wonder. Unlike the blank hallway, this room is full to the brim. Crystal glasses and other relics gleam under the glare from the sun shining through the windows. Instead of a digital projection telling the time on this ceiling, there's an old grandfather clock with a swinging pendulum sitting in one corner. A rack of decorated handguns in all shades of metal line a shelf. It's like a museum. And the view here is amazing. I step closer to the windows that take up an entire wall. Sunlight streams inside, hitting a chandelier and sending small rainbows everywhere. I'm tracing a fingertip across one of the rainbows reflected on the wall when a voice interrupts my thoughts.

"Like it?"

I jump, turning toward the man who's just entered the room. He's awkwardly close to me, just inches from my back, so that when I move I almost knock into him.

"Didn't mean to startle you," he says, backing up with long, steady steps. Then he leans forward, almost in a bow, with one hand out-stretched toward mine. But I remember the registration official and know that shaking hands and touching isn't something people do here in Mid. If this is a trick or some kind of test, I'm determined to pass. So I keep my hands at my sides, palms inward, the sweat leaving imprints on my robe.

The man nods slightly, a small smile starting to form at the point where his two lips meet. Something about this official is mesmerizing, and I can't help staring at him. I feel like I've almost seen him before, but that's impossible. His blue eyes are piercing, like he can reach into my heart and know all the lies I've told to get here. The man's tall, but not as lanky as Griffin. He wears the same robes as me, but I can see the muscles in his arms and neck edging up against the course fabric. His hair is so blonde it's yellow like the early corn we harvested in East Country. The sun glints blindingly off the whites of his eyes, and I almost turn away. But I refuse to give up any ground, even if it's not the physical kind, so I continue matching his gaze.

"Your name is Alicen?" His voice purrs.

"Yes, Sir."

"And you answered all of our questions correctly in the registration building." It's not a question. More a statement. I nod in agreement. His eyebrows rise and the smile on his lips widens. "You say you learned all that from your father's books?"

I think how odd it is that this information must be catalogued in my file somewhere.

"Must have been quite a man," the official continues. "Most of West's paper was damaged in the intense floods and earthquakes. It's amazing he was able to save any." His left eyebrow is slanted, daring me to give any other explanation, but I keep my face blank.

I don't have to lie when I speak about the greatness of my father, so I let my words ring true. "He was. I miss him terribly."

There's an awkward silence for a few moments, and I feel impelled to say something else, but the man begins talking again.

"And you went out on a limb to save . . . " He coughs a little and continues, "one of our engineers." He pauses and puts a hand up to his face. "Literally, out on a limb."

"Yes. About that . . . " I start to say. I'm ready to ask what will happen to Aaron and why they think he's 'broken', but the official cuts me off.

"What do you know of nuclear warfare?"

I stutter for a second, catching my words about Aaron in the recesses of my throat to instead answer this question. "I know they were used in the final country-to-country battles."

"Go on."

"Along with cyber warfare that shut off people's access to clean water and electricity, it was nuclear warfare that killed off so much of the population."

"Do you not think nuclear bombs were preferable, and by that I mean quicker, than starving people slowly?"

I consider this a moment. I don't want to show him my true feelings about what I know he's building here in Mid. If I rebuke the official for breaking the Technology Accord, will he kick me out of the country even before I can learn anything useful? But I can't willingly applaud nuclear weapons. So I swallow and answer, "Either way the end result is the same."

The official turns away from me, but when he looks in my direction again, his eyes are clear and any hint of a smile is gone.

"Back at the registration building, you displayed a breadth of knowledge, but do you know how any of the past technology worked?"

"I'm not an engineer, but I know what technology used to exist and how it was employed."

"Yes, you did know about the long arrow. A fine piece of weaponry most people have forgotten. I was quite impressed you could name it."

At this I cut in, eager to gain another piece of solid intelligence about Mid. "I heard that East Country is attacking us. Why doesn't Mid's Elected use a long arrow on them instead of building nuclear weapons?

A long arrow would just take out their Elected and leave the rest of the population alone. Mass casualties could be avoided."

The official gazes at me silently from head to toe. I think I've gone too far. Said too much. Given all of my cards away. He'll guess that I'm from East, and my whole quest here will be over.

Finally his eyes rest on my face. "Unfortunately, we do not yet have satellites that could construct a signal for the long arrow." He clears his throat and looks at me with narrowed eyes. "In those history books of your father's, did you learn nothing about warfare? When an enemy attacks again and again, it isn't about just taking out their leader. To sufficiently stop a foe, one must instill fear and widespread devastation."

I look down so that the official won't see the horror settling over my face. I understand now that Mid's government is completely corrupt, devoid of reason and sanity. If I'm going to complete my deception here long enough to gather any vital information, I'll have to be as cold and cruel as this country's Elected has turned his entire people. I'll have to fool this official into thinking I'm one of them, happy to construct weapons of mass destruction.

"I see your point."

He doesn't answer immediately, but I continue to feel his gaze sizing me up. Finally the official says, "Since you seem to have a mastery of history, your job here will be to tell us what kind of machines and weapons can feasibly be constructed with Mid's resources. You'll be our technological historian."

I should have known based on the registrar's questions, but the idea still astounds me. Me? The person who's upheld the Technology Accord along with her ancestors for seventy years will now be helping Mid Country abandon the law? It's so utterly beyond comprehension that I have to stop myself from laughing out loud at the absurdity.

"Who will I be advising?" I ask.

"The Elected, of course."

My eyes grow wide and I have to stop myself from outwardly showing any nervous energy. If they give me access to their Elected I might have a chance to make a difference. Convince him to abandon this awful campaign. "Alright. When will I meet him?"

The official lets the smile sneaking across his face grow big enough that he looks like a snake ready to bite. "You already have."

THE WAY HE PRONOUNCES the three words so precisely, I feel like I'm in trouble. "You met the Elected last night."

I think of the demanding demeanor of Mac at the rocket launcher, and my confidence wanes. "Mac? He didn't announce himself as Mid's Elected. If I'd known, obviously, I wouldn't have disobeyed . . . "

The official breaks me off. "Not him."

I reflect on all the guards I saw last night, trying to deduce which one was Mid's Elected.

"The Elected isn't right in the head as of late," the official says, giving me a final clue. "He's a burden rather than a leader now."

Awareness slides over me with a chill. Their Elected was carried away by men in white and saved by someone who obviously didn't know who she was dealing with. I finally understand why Mac said 'easier this way'. It would have been cleaner for Mid if their mentally unstable Elected died on the damaged dome than if they now must concoct a way to oust him. In this country, where weapons are more prized than people, I can imagine a hundred gruesome scenes depicting Aaron's demise. Now I've stepped in and left the job in Mid's callous hands again.

I expect this official to rant against my untimely heroism, but instead he says, "I'm obliged to you. No one else was going to save my brother."

I stare at the official, open mouthed, understanding a further piece of the puzzle. At once I see why he looks so familiar. Aaron's same eyes, albeit a different color, shine through this man's face. I let my next realization sit in the air for a moment before voicing it. "So if he's incapacitated, you'll be . . . "

"Ah, so you know details of the Elected Accord too. Yes, now that everyone realizes just how damaged Aaron is, I'll be installed as Elected sooner than later. But currently my name's Calix." He extends his hand again to shake mine, but like before, I ignore it. I've already made too many mistakes in this country. I won't fall into another trap. Calix laughs out loud and pulls back his hand.

"What exactly is wrong with him?" I ask.

Calix turns toward the window, looking out of the great glass expanse instead of at me. "Everyone in Mid gets mandatory radiation treatments once a month. Except for the Elected family, of course. We have other means of diffusing illness." He stops a moment, resting a palm against the glass. "But Aaron insisted on trying the doctors' homeopathic techniques anyway. He believed strongly in their particular work. He commissioned it. Unfortunately, their medical practices didn't work correctly on him. Aaron's been forgetful since the procedure."

I realize what exactly Aaron's forgotten. "If people just treated him with the respect he deserves, maybe he'd remember he's the Elected," I say quickly.

Calix hoots again. It's an awkward response to such a serious topic, but I'm starting to expect the disaffected cynicism Calix radiates. "It makes the dementia worse if we don't go along with his delusions. He thinks he's an engineer, so Mac lets him play it out. It's easier than holding Aaron down while he kicks and thrashes."

"Will you continue in his footsteps?" I ask boldly, stepping forward. "When you're Elected, will you continue to disregard the Technology Accord?"

Calix laughs out loud. "Ah, my favorite Accord of them all! The one that nobody seems to follow anymore. Of course I'll continue in his footsteps. It's my family's legacy. Come. I'll show you exactly how we don't uphold the precious Technology Accord." There's a sarcastic lilt in his voice as he snorts on his last words. I follow him willingly, hoping whatever he shows me will shed new light on Mid's intentions.

Calix leads me out of the penthouse, back into the hallway and down the elevator. Next to him in the city, we receive a lot of attention. People don't ignore him like they've done with me for the past few days. Calix hurries us along the moving sidewalks, as people bow and skirt out of our way. Now that they know he's to be the next Elected, they seem scared of him, or at least respectful.

We stop first in front of building five. Inside, people are head-down, concentrating on mixing a wide array of illegal fuels. Inky black oil sloshes in a drum to my left. I smell the strong, greasy scent all the way into my head, making me slightly dizzy. A great fire roasts a spinning piece of rock. Black smoke crawls out of the coal-like stone, infusing the long room with a gray haze.

"Here we have the missiles," Calix says, gesturing me away from the huge oven. He runs a hand along a sleek, black bomb. "And the semi-automatic Uzis." He points to a container filled to the brim with larger guns than I've ever seen in person. I turn in a circle, taking it all in.

"What's that?" I ask, pointing to an enormous metal disk being welded at the end of the warehouse. It's mounted against the wall and takes up the entire expanse.

Calix turns toward where I gesture. "Oh, that. We're going to eradicate cancer."

"With a disc?"

"Sure. It'll be mounted along a rail over the entire city, following the sun as it makes its daily cycle. We'll blot out the damned rays entirely."

"You're not just testing the limits of the Technology Accord," I say in a mix of awe and shock. "Mid has abandoned it completely." I breathe out slowly, letting my words sit like lead on my tongue. I can feel the tingle and taste of iron when I accidentally bite down hard on my lip and draw blood.

Calix's eyebrows rise, as he waves a hand to encompass all the technology in the armory. "It's not like we set out to create all this. We were forced to break the Accords when East started attacking twenty years ago."

Twenty years?

I contemplate how I'll tell Calix that I'm East's Elected and how we haven't stolen or raided anything from Mid. I itch to start a negotiation now, but first I need proof to show Mid that East isn't involved in the attacks.

"How did the attacks start?" I ask.

"We noticed resources vanishing. Initially, we thought it was thieves within Mid, but then we started seeing airrides. When food and minerals kept disappearing, we began building defenses. Then when the technology we created got bombed, we escalated our rate of manufacturing. We threw ourselves into developing offenses."

Mid's law-breaking sounds eerily similar to what we've begun in East. I wonder for a moment if we've begun the same cycle Mid is on, just twenty years behind. Resources vanishing, airrides appearing, creation of defenses, and on and on. If left on our own, will East eventually decide to manufacture weapons too? How different will we be from Mid?

Calix continues, "We wanted to learn more about East, so we sent in a spy."

I almost falter right there. They've done the precise thing I'm attempting now. Calix keeps talking, and I listen so hard I feel like my ears will bleed along with my now-throbbing lip.

"They have something called a 'Technology Faction' over there. Been around forever, apparently. Ever since the pacts. Can you believe it?"

I blink a few times, but I don't say anything. I'm afraid if I open my mouth, all will be lost.

He thinks I'm speechless in disbelief. "I know!" Calix exclaims. "Outrageous! They never even attempted to follow the Accords. At least we started to."

I can't believe how wrong he is about East and how ingrained his impression is. It would take a lot more than just my word to derail Mid Country's fear of us now.

"What exactly is East stealing?"

"First it was food. But lately it's almost always Nirogene. We countered their attack, though. Bombed their mines. I don't think East will be able to get their hands on any more Nirogene for a while. That should teach them."

I think of the workers we lost in the hills the day Mid bombed our harvesting area and bow my head discreetly as Calix keeps touring me around the facility, oblivious to my sadness. I have to check myself each time Calix shows me a new, astonishing weapon. He introduces me to workers inside the warehouse, who all nod their heads and bow at him as he passes. It's like he's a king instead of an elected official.

"Alicen will be helping out the engineers. Make sure to hand over everything he asks to see," Calix explains over and over again. It's funny how much latitude Calix is extending me. If he only knew.

We continue our journey through a few more buildings, and I'm starting to grow wearier by the second as I see the vast array of weapons Mid has collected. They've been building bombs and airrides for twenty years. Even if East started now, we'd never catch up. We will never be able to fight back. It will be up to my negotiation skills to stop an onslaught or my imagination to conjure a method of destroying Mid's weapons.

All of this, every bad thing they think of my country, every counter attack they're planning, is due to the spy they sent into my country. When I concentrate on this fact, I'm no longer tired. I'm fuming. Their spy did a terrible job and has endangered us all. I want to speak to that person. Find out more details. And then wring his neck with my bare hands.

As we're nearing the end of the day, I turn to Calix in front of building thirteen. The light of the setting sun reflects on half his face, making his pale features look orange, like a ghost back from the dead.

"I'd like to talk to the spy. Hear firsthand what he saw."

Calix is flippant when he answers me. He's looking at one of his hands, picking at a fingernail. "Can't."

"Why not?" I ask.

"Still over there," he says, flicking a piece of dead nail onto the ground. He finally looks up at me with a wry smile on his face. "Been in place since she was four years old."

SHE?

Four years old?

I'm throwing up before I can choke back the sensation of nausea. I remember the night Tomlin and I walked back to the White House after melting down the bullets. How I asked him about Vienne's family and he told me he found her on the border hills as a little girl by herself. How he suspected she was from Mid. Everything I've ever said to Vienne runs through my mind. Is she responsible for the downfall of our entire country?

All of the side effects of my pregnancy, which were subdued over the last few days, come back in full force. I clutch my stomach and keep vomiting until only bile spews forth.

Calix's hand is on my back. He keeps hold of me while I lean against the building's cold metal exterior.

"Don't touch me!" I sputter. The bitterness rings off my voice. I'm convinced that Vienne has warned them I'm here. This whole day has been an elongated stunt to show me how Mid will cripple my country. Then I'll be executed with this knowledge still brewing in my fore-thoughts. What will they do to Griffin? Or my parents, wherever they are? I want to sprint away before Calix can hold me here. But I'm weak from the vomiting, and I don't think I'd get too far anyway. A robot passes us, its orange eyes flashing like a warning. At Calix's command, the thing could rip out my throat in one swift movement. I'm just a pawn in his sick game. I'd rather he take me fast than draw this out anyway.

Calix pulls back at the ferocity resonating off my words. "Wow, you really do belong in Mid," he mutters, the words clotting in his throat as he looks away.

"What did you say?" I ask.

"Nothing. It doesn't matter."

I look up from the ground where my mess is stinking in a puddle. Calix's face doesn't look threatening, like he's about to apprehend me. Instead, he looks uncharacteristically concerned. Over the day, I've grown used to his sardonic, slightly entitled demeanor. Not this sympathetic one, and it confuses me.

Maybe Vienne has enough loyalty for me personally that she didn't tell them I was coming. Maybe Calix still doesn't know I'm a spy.

"You're broken," he continues. "We need to get you to a doctor."

"No!" The word reaches out of my throat like a wolf striking at prey. I can feel my own teeth bared, ready to snap.

"Why not?"

I struggle for some explanation, but nothing comes to mind. I just mask my non-answer with more coughing, pretending that I might retch again.

"Oh," says Calix, looking up at the heavens. "You don't have to be concerned about what happened to Aaron. That's a one-time thing. Everyone else has been fine after the doctors' procedures."

He thinks I'm afraid to go to the doctors because of Aaron's adverse reaction, and I let the assumption stand.

"You should really go. It's mandatory, you know. And you're broken. But . . . " He looks off into the horizon again, as if trying to convince himself of something. "I guess it's alright if you skip the procedure for now. You feel better now, right? You've stopped vomiting. No one has to know you were feeling ill."

It's like he's suddenly done a one eighty, convincing me not to go to the doctor's. I look up at him, my brow furrowed.

"You seem okay now," he continues. His eyes search mine, as if pleading me to agree.

"I'm fine," I say and stand up straight to drive the point home.

I take advantage of Calix's brief moment of consternation to ask my burning question. "How do you get information from the spy in East?"

Calix eyes me, annoyance clouding his features again, but at the moment I don't care. I'm too infuriated with Vienne and need to know the extent of her betrayal. "The spy thing again?" Calix tosses his blonde hair. "My parents set it all up. I don't know anything else about her."

I look him in the eyes to see if he's telling the truth.

He frowns. "What? You think anyone got me ready to take the Elected role? I have no background knowledge. They devoted all their attention to Aaron."

I continue to look at Calix, a light bulb growing brighter in my head. He was like me. Never intended for the leadership position. The second child, the one that was good to have around as backup but not the one his parents ever envisioned in the role. He'll struggle in this Elected role, which is probably part of the reason he needs me for guidance on history. This is how I'll turn him. These methods of Mid's, their vicious ideas on wiping out East, they aren't his. They were Aaron's. Maybe, just maybe, Calix is bitter enough about being his parents' runner up to swallow the pretty, candy-coated pill I plan on feeding him. Maybe he just needs a little push to rebel against the plans established by his family.

"They should have devoted some of that time to you. You were part of the Elected family. Just as important as your brother." I massage his ego carefully, rolling it around in my hands like raw clay.

"Ha!" Calix scoffs. "You obviously don't know how an Elected family operates!" He looks up at the digital clock projected on a building yards in the distance. "It's past six. You're free to go. But I'll see you tomorrow. Eight o'clock sharp. Meet me in building five."

He barks out commands like a seasoned Elected. Like someone who's had people say yes to him his whole life. I bite my bottom lip again, renewing the drops of blood peeking through the disturbed skin. Maybe Calix will be a little harder to break than I thought. He's like an angry cat, purring one moment and ready to scratch in another. I nod like a faithful subject, and we part ways.

Griffin's waiting for me in front of my apartment door, same as yesterday. Suddenly, the harsh facade I constructed in front of Calix cracks. My lower lip trembles, and Griffin immediately reaches for my hand. But I shake my head, turning away from him even though I'd like nothing more than to throw myself into his arms. Instead, I press my finger to the door scanner and open my apartment. Only when Griffin is fully within the four walls of my semi-sanctuary do I allow him to wrap me in a tight embrace. I held in the stress all day, allowing it to gather in the bones under my skin. But now my defenses shatter like a million icicles all falling from a rooftop ledge at the same time.

"What happened?" asks Griffin, pulling my head against his shoulder.

I tell him everything, starting with Aaron and working my way up to Vienne, whispering the whole time.

"She wouldn't do that to her country," says Griffin. I look up into his face, finally stepping out of his arms. Griffin's words are assured, but there's a deep line etched between his eyebrows.

I just shake my head and look down at my stomach that has been grumbling for the last fifteen minutes. I've ignored it as I told Griffin about my day, but now the gnawing sensation is almost overwhelming. When I investigate the kitchen for food, as before, there's a full plate waiting for me. We share it at the small living room table and ask for more as we continue talking.

"Yes, but which one does Vienne consider *her country*?" My voice is a hiss, hard and slighted.

"Think about what you're saying. Vienne doesn't even know she's from Mid."

"Maybe she's lying about that."

"She's smart enough to pull off a lie, true. But she loves you. She wouldn't do this to you, let alone East Country."

I think about all the times I lay next to Vienne in our shared bed, the tendrils of her hair mixing against the sharp spikes of mine. How could she have been lying to me that entire time?

"Maybe she didn't know she was being used as Mid's spy," Griffin continues.

"How's that even possible?"

Griffin holds one of Mid's thin forks, tapping it against the metal tabletop as he thinks. "Mid doesn't have very accurate accounts of East. Calix said East has a Technology Faction, but he doesn't know that it's been kept dormant."

"They seemed to know the moment we were going to harvest more Nirogene, though."

"So they have intermittent intelligence," Griffin says. "Getting fed some information but not hearing everything."

I stare at Griffin, an explanation gathering in the back of my head. "Like a transmitter going in and out." I stop pacing and sit on the carpeted floor, my legs crossed in front of me, mirroring the twisted way my heart feels. I think of the nano-sized microchips governments used to plant on unassuming people during criminal investigations. Of how Tomlin said politicians like my great grandfather used that technology to determine if people were guilty, at least until the practice was outlawed by the Accords. The chips fed information back to a communication station continuously, except during bad weather when the signal went out. Since the eco crisis what kind of weather have we had most of the time? Bad weather. Acid rain. Thick suffocating clouds intermingled between bouts of no rain and searing sun. Earthquakes. Floods. You name it. *Bad weather.*

I can almost imagine the static of a transmitter feed crackling in and out. I explain the chip technology to Griffin who nods as I talk fast.

Tomlin relayed an unending wealth of information to me about the past, and I have never imparted it to anyone else. Even as other townspeople in East Country volunteered to teach our children something they knew, that educational ritual was never expected of me. In fact, it was frowned upon. I was taught things about the past that my parents didn't necessarily want others to remember. But now, telling Griffin feels satisfying, like I possess a useful skill.

I picture telling Vienne that she's been a pawn of Mid's for fourteen years. I envision her crumpling face as we stand together on the hills between East and Mid. I see her puncturing herself over and over again to find the lodged chip. I'm repulsed at the idea of Vienne's milky, flawless skin ripped apart. But an angry, dark seed inside me also wants to know the extent of her loyalty. If she agrees to find the bug inside her, it means she's devoted to East. If not, we'll have our answer and the person responsible for East's demise. I swallow thickly, bile stinging the back of my throat again.

Griffin and I go to sleep together in my apartment's small bed, and even though we're finally together and there's an opportunity to be more intimate, the thought of Vienne as a defector and what she'll have to do to extract the chip pushes more romantic thoughts from both our heads. When Griffin finally falls asleep, his hand intertwined with mine, I lie awake, staring at the whitewashed ceiling. Have I grown as callous as Mid's Elected if I'm willing to let my own wife destroy herself to wage war against an enemy country?

As I too start to drift into a fitful sleep, a disturbing childhood song chimes its refrain through my head, setting off a series of dreamy memories.

Lock your strength far away;
Save it for a rainy day.
When the sun no longer shines;
That's when you'll need this little rhyme.

Left in an enemy city that is indeed trying to blot out the sun, the rhyme strikes a chord. Where have I heard this song before? I can almost hear my mother's voice connected to the words, but it's such an old memory and I'm so utterly spent, it's hard to pin down. With my eyes shut, the words circle through my head. This time, I picture my mother tucking me into bed as a child. Her cheeks lift into a smile as the purple pills' vault key inevitably falls forward out of her blouse, as it always did on its long string. It dangles in front of my eyes like a hypnotist's charm. The key clinks against a second charm on the cord, a scalloped medallion. It's a golden disc that glints in the firelight, attracting my attention.

In my mind I'm a three year old again, grasping for the two objects jangling overhead. My mother moves a lock of hair off my forehead, and while I blink to accept her touch, she slips the necklace back within her clothes. I try to hold onto this picture of my mother now that it's clearer. My favorite memories of her are ones from before I turned four and was told to hide my gender. Before she became purposefully unemotional with me.

I wish I had a part of my mother now, something tangible and solid to hold onto like that key or the pendant. But Dorine, our cook, stole the key, and who knows what happened to my mother's jewelry. For a long time now, I don't remember Ama wearing anything else around her neck other than the key to our family's purple pills. I wonder if she lost the medallion or just decided it was too decadent to wear in our plain society.

Or maybe she used the gold for something practical, like tooth fillings or as an arthritic rubbing agent. I can't help smiling a little. That seems like my mother. Frivolity was practically considered offensive in our house. She would have made some more beneficial use of the gold.

Thus, all I have of her are the words she sung me so long ago. I repeat them to myself for a third time, thinking that I need to do just what the song advises. Lock my strength away. I'll need strength in the coming months more than ever before.

7

GRIFFIN SNEAKS INTO MY room to sleep each night but leaves before the skyscraper's tumult of people exit into the hallways at exactly eight o'clock each morning. No need to be conspicuous about our cohabitation.

Griffin learns more about Mid's experimentation with animals and finds that the process of cloning ends up killing off more species than it's helping to save. We've connected with Margareath a few times too, and she's even given me an anti-solar panel I can keep to visit Vienne at the hills every other week. Unfortunately, I missed my first scheduled meeting with Vienne at the two-week mark. The night I was supposed to leave, acid rain beat down on the city, causing everyone to leave work early and huddle in their apartments before the usual hour of six. People were surprisingly testy about not being able to work, exactly the opposite of the euphoria I would have expected with a free day off. It seemed only Griffin and I appreciated the extra moments to lounge intertwined together in my living room.

I continue to work with Mid's engineers, sometimes meeting them with Calix, other times conducting my history lessons without their now officially sworn in Elected. What Calix does when he is not with me in the armory or technology buildings, I don't know. All I can hope is that he's not listening to more radio transmission from Vienne's bug.

I try to remember enough from Tomlin's lessons and salvaged picture books to make myself indispensable to the engineers, but I never give them what they really want. I don't tell Mid's technicians what I know of uranium enrichment. So they proceed only slightly further with their precious nuclear bomb, even with the extra hours each one is granted to work. In a month I've been pretty successful keeping them interested but far enough away from certain tidbits of knowledge to provide any actionable data on nuclear warfare.

As I hoped, I'm afforded a high degree of freedom. I move easily from building to building, helping wherever my services are requested. No one monitors where I'm supposed to be each day, and that's what helps me escape when I finally do reach the one-month mark. By this point I'm itching to see Vienne and East Country again, not only to tell them about Mid's incorrect hypotheses and so Vienne can start the process of exhuming the transmitter, but also because I'm homesick. Having Griffin with me in Mid Country is a blessing I'm thankful for every day, but something about the very soil of East Country calls to me.

The evening I'm set to leave, Griffin stands in my apartment, leaning against a wall, watching me stuff a backpack full of food from the never-ending wall cut-out.

"I wish you'd let me go instead of you."

I've considered Griffin's offer to travel back in my place, but besides my desire to see East, I know he can't get away as easily as I can. We can't risk anyone in East seeing him. He's supposed to be dead, for heaven's sake.

But I don't harp on that last point, as if even saying the words "dead" and "Griffin" in the same sentence is a bad omen. Instead I say, "They'll notice you're not at the animal clinic. And you can't claim to be broken like Margareath did. You haven't been inducted into the monthly medical checkups here yet."

Griffin turns away, his frustration at not being able to protect me written all over his face. He shakes his head, clearly agitated. "You're right. We need to stay off their radar as long as possible. But the thought of you running toward the border by yourself while I just sit here in Mid . . . " Griffin wraps his arms around my neck, staring me in the eyes. The blacks of his pupils grow larger, and the amber of his eyes thins. "Promise me you won't take any unnecessary chances. Only walk at night. Take shelter during the day."

"I promise." I bury my head in his neck, breathing in deeply. His skin is cool to the touch, and I let my cheek rest against him for a long moment.

"Come on," Griffin says reluctantly after a few minutes have passed. "If you're going to go, you have to leave with as much time to travel in the dark as possible.

I nod, grabbing my backpack and the heavy panel we snuck in via the stairs. I simultaneously hand Griffin my fingerprint mashed into a piece of clay. Another reason he has to stay behind is to cover my tracks at the apartment's keypad. Every night at six he'll swipe this silhouette of my finger over the devise. We've already tried it on previous nights, and miraculously, the swirling lines of my fingerprint embedded in the clay's surface engage the door's lock. A few weeks ago, we might have trusted Margareath with the job, but as time passes she seems to become more loyal to Mid and frighteningly more forgetful about East.

Griffin follows me to the hallway, watching as I walk toward the elevator. At the last second before I step through the iron door into the dark, cavernous lift, I turn and look back. Griffin stands stalwart against one of the walls, his eyes never leaving mine. *Please let him stay safe in Mid* I pray silently. If something happened to him, I don't know I could bear being in Mid at all. He's the only thing that provides light here.

I smile at Griffin, as if to reassure him that everything will be fine. He doesn't grin back, but instead raises two arms, bent at the elbows, to hip level. His mouth scrunches together like he's in pain, and then his hands rise up in East's signal for goodbye, hello, and honor, all wrapped into one. Griffin's palms cup in the customary fashion, looking like he's giving a ghost a hug. I keep glancing back for one more second and then turn fast before he can see a tear welling on my lower lid. Griffin's gesture is the same he gave me after Vienne and I got married. A moment when he thought he'd lost me for good. Now I'm going again. Leaving him alone in favor of Vienne and our country for a second time.

I exit the tower easily, informing the turnstile guards that I'm conducting extra engineering work in the evening. They let me by immediately, already recognizing Mid's infamous technology historian who has their Elected's explicit blessing. I walk swiftly toward the main gates of the walled city, and at the last moment when I can't stand the tension anymore, I start to run. I lug the panel close to my side, feeling its thin, plastic surface hitting my hipbone with each step of my right leg. When I'm free of the walls, I sprint, putting all of my energy into getting as far away from Mid as I can before daylight. Even when the sun rises six hours later and my legs burn with the constant pace, I maintain my speed, not even keeping the promise I made to Griffin. I don't want to be a sitting duck, waiting for an airride to spot me. I want to keep moving.

But it's this fervency, which reminds me, with spasms to my midsection and calves, what I almost forgot during the last few weeks in Mid. I'm pregnant. I can't keep up the same rhythm my body endured before. It's painful to keep going. Being in Mid where I never saw children and no one talked about fertility every day, it was easy to forget my predicament.

I stop for a moment, the panel slapping hard against my thigh. *Predicament?* Did I really just think of my growing baby like that? I sidle up to a nearby boulder and drop the panel into the dirt.

What's happening to me? I want this baby more than anything. So why all of a sudden have I characterized my pregnancy in such negative terms? And why am I just now remembering that I'm pregnant? Am I becoming so enmeshed in Mid's technology like the rest of their people, that I'm starting to forget things too?

I think that maybe the sweltering heat is just starting to bother me. I'm not superhuman; I need rest. I sit down heavily and let my back contour against the hard rock, cracking my spine in a long stretch. I grope around into the depths of my pack for something to eat, quickly shoving a piece of jerky into my mouth. Finally, after I eat four slices and drink enough water to bring on a stomachache, I groan my way back to standing.

I punish myself with the rest of the run toward East, albeit at a slower pace, only stopping again to eat a slice or two of a pink orange for its vitamins. Each time a muscle in my leg cramps, I run through it. So I'm not surprised I make it back to the border hills in record time, hours before I'm set to meet Vienne at the appointed midnight hour.

I drop down onto the ground, face first, letting my head be the highest part of me on the hill's incline. In this position I can stare into the distance and see faint images of East without anyone noticing a figure standing conspicuously at the hill's crest. There are a few tendrils of smoke twirling skyward from the evening's dinner fires. Here, where they still cook their own meals, I think about the families all laughing together, enjoying each other's company underneath the same sky as Mid. The two countries couldn't be more opposite. I can almost hear the vivacity of my people in East, and the pull in my heart grows stronger. I almost give in and walk down the other side of the hill into my country, but I know that would be folly.

I look at the stars and know I still have four hours before Vienne will meet me at midnight. I hope she still comes—that Vienne hasn't given up on me after I missed our first meeting. Then I think nastier thoughts. I hope she isn't Mid's willing informant. I don't even know what I'll do if she is. With that last thought pulsing in my mind, I let my eyes close.

"Aloy. Wake up."

A gentle hand pulls at my shoulder. If I didn't automatically recognize the voice, I'd have jumped straight out of my skin.

"Vienne?" I open my eyes and see an angel standing over me. I can't help beaming back up at her face. Blonde tendrils of her hair sweep forward as she looks down on me, and the full, glowing moon behind Vienne frames her like a halo. The moon is the only light peeking through large, full clouds.

"How long have you been waiting here?" she asks.

"Just a few hours." I blink crusts of sleep from my eyes and stand up, not bothering to brush any of the hillside's dirt or grass from my brown shapeless shift.

"You look worn out." Vienne says the words with worry on her brow, but she's smiling widely anyway. I throw my arms around her neck, overcome with how much I've missed her. "Whoa. It's only been a month." But she laughs, relief and happiness at seeing me overtaking her as well.

"I'm sorry I missed the two week mark," I start to say.

Vienne pulls back from my embrace, scanning my face as if she's trying to heal my weariness with just her eyes. "It's okay. I was worried. But I figured you'd come when you could. I've been making daily visits to the hills, just in case you were here at a different time."

"Every night at midnight?" I step back from Vienne and rub my eyes. I take a moment to drink a few long gulps from the water satchel before looking at my wife again.

Vienne pulls an apple from somewhere within her flowing yellow robes. "Yes, every night. But tell me about your endeavors. Do you have enough to eat over there?" She hands me the apple, and I take it gratefully, crunching down hard.

"You have no idea." I can't believe the first exchange of information between us concerns the cut-out in my apartment's kitchen, but I suppose it's a good enough place to start as any.

I tell her about Mid's use of technology; Griffin's role with animals, looking for my parents, the robots with the scary orange eyes, the tall buildings, Calix, Aaron, Margareath, registering, my new job, and how there aren't any children in Mid. I save two important details for later, though. I skip over Mid's intentions against East and the spy they've been using for fourteen years. Instead, I let Vienne have a moment to speak, and I start peppering her with questions about East.

"How's Tomlin?" I ask. "And the Technology Faction? And your baby?"

Vienne laughs. "Okay, slow down. First our baby." She emphasizes the "our". "He's doing fine. I've started to feel kicking. Have you?" She automatically looks down at my belly.

I look down too. Kicking? No, I can't say that I've felt anything inside me unless I count the eruptions of vomit that come at inopportune times. I shake my head.

"Well, that's alright. It doesn't mean anything if you haven't." She backtracks quickly and then changes subjects. "Tomlin is good. We told everyone at the town hall that you'd left to gather information on Mid Country. People seemed to accept that—were actually glad for some action. Even Grobe agreed it was the right thing for you to do."

At this I grumble. "Yeah, he was probably happy because it gets me farther away from things here. Easier for him to make a move."

"Maybe," Vienne says. "But he's been helpful so far. The Technology Faction has put all of their efforts behind making more armor glass. We'll have a few more slabs up by tomorrow." I look to my left, way down the top of the hill. Already I see they've installed not only the pieces from the prison, but three additional slabs as well. They must have reopened the mines, found more Nirogene, and started production.

"Impressive. You're doing great as the Elected. See, I told you." She had been concerned taking over the role in my absence, but it looks like she's doing fine; maybe even better than me if she's been able to corral the Technology Faction.

"I'm not the Elected," Vienne says quietly. "It's still you."

I look over her shoulder at my country. We've been talking for hours, and the hint of the sun's shadow is starting to reach the horizon. Soon my country will be lit up and people will begin their work for the day. We only have a couple more hours.

"There's something you have to hear, Vienne," I say, the seriousness of my voice causing her to look at me with new concern.

"What is it? Are you alright over there in Mid?" Then she stops and puts a hand on my knee. "You're coming back here like we planned, right?"

"Yes. It's not that." I'm trying to find the right words to tell Vienne that our country is doomed and there's nothing I can ultimately do about it. She just stares at me. Not for the first time tonight, I wish Griffin were here. He would just have out with it. Wouldn't waste any words telling Vienne the truth about our imminent future. "Mid is being attacked."

Vienne opens her mouth in shock. "Like us? So it wasn't Mid that bombed our mines? A different country is assaulting both of ours?"

"No, it was Mid that took out our Nirogene harvests." I stumble on my words. "They . . . think *we've* been the ones assaulting *them*. Their attack on our mines was in response, and they're building bigger weapons to use on East."

"Us? Attacking them? But that's impossible. How could they think . . . ?"

This time I break her off. "They've heard we have a Technology Faction. All the aerial assaults they've received, they think it's us. They think we broke the Technology Accord long before they did."

"Well, they're wrong!" This time Vienne's indignant. Her eyebrows are sharp upside down Vs.

"They're pretty fixated on the idea."

"But how in the world did they hear about the Faction?"

I breathe in deeply. We've finally arrived at the point I've been dreading all night—when I'll stare into Vienne's eyes and know whether she's with me or against me. I instinctively clasp onto the concealed knife inside my robes and feel my insides brace.

"There's a spy from Mid in our country." Vienne is about to speak, but I put up a hand to stop her. "It's you, Vienne. They heard through you."

For a second she just stares at me, and I stare back, reading her eyes. For the first time in the entire year that I've known Vienne, she doesn't have the perfect words for the situation. Her cheeks flush a deep red, and her eyes turn from brown to almost violet in the rising cast of the sun's rays. She finally looks down at her shoes and then back up at me.

"No. No. That's ridiculous." Her voice, normally fluid like heavy cream, is cracking.

I don't touch her, though I'd like to reach a hand to Vienne's shoulder to steady her. I have to know the truth. I can't let my fondness for Vienne cloud my vision. I keep watching her closely.

"Who told you that? Calix? Why would he make you think it was me? Why would you believe him? Do you? Do you believe that?"

I stare at her closely one last time and then finally reach out my hand, dropping the knife once again into the folds of my garment.

"I do. Vienne, I think you're the spy."

At this she folds, physically bending at the waist.

"When would I have had the chance? I've never been over to Mid! I . . . I . . . "

I stop her onslaught of reasoning and give her the rest of the story; the child left on the border at four years old, the intermittent nature of Mid's intelligence, the idea of a hidden transmitter. I try to make my words calm to provide an anchor against the hysteria that flickers behind Vienne's eyes. I've never seen her like this. She's always so sure of herself. Now I've told her she's a quisling and has been used her whole life against the one place that took her in.

"Is this what they do with all of their children?" she chokes. "Send them away to spy on other countries?"

I look at her a moment, wondering if she's right about all the other kids in Mid.

"I don't know. But there are no other countries, just Mid and East. West is gone."

"Why . . . why didn't Tomlin tell me how I was found? If I'd known I never would have volunteered to be East's Madame Elected!"

I push my hand down harder on her shoulder. "Yes, you would have. My parents and Tomlin were right about you. You belong in East Country even if you weren't born here."

"But I'm a spy. A turncoat! It doesn't matter that I didn't know. That's what I am! I've endangered our entire country." She's on the verge of sobbing and already tears stream down her face in long lines. This can't be good for her or the baby. I have to stop it now.

"Vienne. Look, you didn't know. None of us did. But now we can take action. We can be careful what we say and when." I look up at the thick clouds overhead and notice that there are spaces in between them. Our very conversation could be streaming directly into Mid right now, but I don't care. I grab both of Vienne's shoulders and pull her toward me, hugging her tightly.

"You're right," she says. "There is something I can do. I can go off into the wilderness by myself. Then no one will hear anything from me about East."

I look back into her face. Her eyes are dry again and they look hard. Resolved.

"No. Not that. There's something else you can do." I glance down at the skin on her arms and Vienne follows my gaze. It takes her only a moment to understand what I insinuate.

"Oh."

"Maybe you can feel it under the skin," I start, hating myself for even suggesting it.

"Right. Of course," she says, nodding her head rapidly. "Whatever it takes."

"Just be careful. You're pregnant. You can't touch the skin around . . . the baby." The idea makes me gag.

"I won't. I'll get help looking for it." We're talking around the idea of Vienne gouging her own skin over and over again to find Mid's intruder. Even thinking the idea inside my own head makes me feel ashamed. Saying it out loud produces queasiness.

I swallow, trying to disregard the growing bubble of anxiety in my stomach. "Be careful what you talk about when the sky is clear. Actually, talk about how we don't have any technology. Talk about how it wasn't us who hit Mid."

"Okay." Vienne looks grim.

"Don't worry," I say. "It'll work out. You'll take out the bug. I'll find a way to prove to Calix that East didn't start the attacks and that we have a common enemy." For the first time ever, I'm the one reassuring Vienne. It feels odd, like wearing a piece of clothing that doesn't fit correctly.

She nods, her head bobbing too many times. "I'm so sorry."

"Don't be." I take her face in my hands as the sun makes its final attempt to rise. It peeks over the horizon, a full semicircle now. "I love you."

She cocks her head and gives me a faint smile. "Two weeks. I'll see you in two weeks, and I'll have good news for you by then. I'll hand you that transmitter and we'll destroy it together." She hiccups once and then says, "I love you too."

I hold her hand a moment longer, both of us looking over the hill at East Country.

"Take care of our country," I say.

Vienne nods again, and then I let her hand fall. I back up, taking small steps away from East, feeling the ache in my heart as I leave it once again.

It takes me longer to reach Mid than on the first leg of my trip toward East. This time I follow Griffin's advice and only advance forward at night. During the day, I crouch down next to boulders, finish the last bits of food in my satchel, and try to sleep. I should have told Vienne to bring me water next time we meet. I only have a little more to get me through the next day, and already my body wants to drink down the last few gulps.

By the time I reach Mid on the second day, I'm soaked in sweat. I hide in the outskirts of Mid's fake forest until nightfall. Then, as planned, I sneak back into the city. Even with ten times the number of people we have in East, Mid Country is quiet as a mouse. Everyone is tucked into their individual apartments, and only the robots and guards are travelling around on the moving sidewalks. I'm the only civilian skirting around, ducking behind buildings, and making a dash for Tower One.

When I get to the skyscraper's front doors, I immediately know something's wrong. The usual two guards watching the turnstiles are surrounded by five others. They're all talking with purpose, alternating between looking at video monitors and receiving instructions through small glass handsets strapped to their wrists. I squeeze my body against the cool metal of Tower One's exterior, trying to make myself as flat as possible. No matter what's going on, now is probably not a great time to trounce into the building with my feeble lie. Even with authorization to work on the weaponry after hours, if there is some crisis, they'll have locked down all the workspaces. Maybe Mid's been raided again.

I decide not to take any chances and instead head to the stairway entrance on the side of the tower. As I guessed, the door is open and completely unguarded. Mid relies so heavily on technology, no one even thinks about using stairs instead of an elevator or as a potential way into the building. Only me. I look up at the dark stairway above. It goes on forever. I sigh deeply, knowing my exhausted body will have to bear a hundred and thirteen floors before it can rest. At least it's cool in here. I don't have the urge to ball up my robe and fling it over the nearest rail, as the heat from outside is completely eradicated by Mid's forced cold air.

In the next two hours it takes me to climb the monstrosity, my mind wanders. I put one foot in front of the other, trying to get the stair climb to become automatic, like muscle memory, so I don't have to focus on how much it hurts my now swollen legs. Instead, I think about my country and our enemy.

I'm convinced Vienne is still on my side, an unwilling player in Mid's twisted style of espionage. And Mid's children—I have a renewed eagerness to find out where they are. Can people in Mid even have kids anymore? If so, are they all sent on missions similar to Vienne's? Where and to what country?

On floor fifty-nine my mind switches to Griffin. One month has already gone by. That leaves me just seven or eight with him. When the last month hits, will I have the courage to leave him in Mid forever? Will we just meet on the border once a month for the rest of our lives? Or can I bring both him and Margareath back to East? I think of Vienne's assurances that Grobe and the Technology Faction are helping her. Will Grobe let a rival back into the country without a second thought? Even if Griffin abdicates the Faction's leadership role, people will inevitably follow him. Grobe might find a way to silence Griffin forever if I bring him back. No matter what I try to imagine, I can't get around the fact that Griffin's safer over here in Mid than in our own country.

I envision an old fashioned scale, like the ones the former United States used to symbolize justice. On one side of the scale my mind sets

Vienne, East Country, and her baby. On the other side I put Griffin and my baby. East Country should at least tip the scale to Vienne's side, but the scale rocks back and forth. It won't settle anywhere. I shake my head violently as if just this act could tilt the scale into a sensible spot. But I can't rid the confusion from my mind. My thoughts are fuzzy in my tired state. The only picture that comes through clearly is Griffin's face, the angled jaw, the dark hair uneven in patterns of half-moons across his forehead. I'll swipe in at my door and then immediately go to Griffin's room. I *need* to see him. The demand inside me grows stronger with every higher floor I reach.

But each individual step sends shooting pain up my calves. I'm sure I have tiny fractures throughout my bones. No one's body should be penalized like mine has been for the past month. I reach floor one hundred thirteen on my hands and knees. I stand, grasping the doorknob like a lifeline. As soon as I peek out into the hallway I'm greeted by a mirage outside my apartment door.

"Griffin!" I can't help calling out his name, breaking the hallway's silence. My legs find renewed energy and I run at him, throwing myself into his arms.

He doesn't have the same lightness in his eyes when we face each other, but his hands find the small of my back and pull me close. His words tumble out fast, even as his fingers brush against the rough texture of the robes we each wear. I can feel the tips of his fingernails dig into my back hungrily, and I want to push him backward against my closed apartment door and kiss him right here. Forget the hallway cameras. My need for Griffin is more urgent. But he halts my onslaught with a rushed whisper.

"It isn't safe. I came to warn you."

I stop holding tight to his upper arms and take the smallest of steps backward. "What's going on?"

"They've been looking for you."

My eyes grow wide. "The clay fingertip. It didn't work on my door?"

"It worked, but the Elected wanted to see you at building thirteen the first day you were gone. They've been canvassing the city for you ever since."

"The extra guards downstairs. They were for me?" I don't have to ask the question. I already know.

Griffin nods, his mouth a pinched line. "It'll be alright. I just wanted to make sure you had an explanation ready for tomorrow morning. You'll have to say you were sick, holed up in your apartment. That you were too *broken* to tell anyone."

I have no idea if the idea will work. We still can't be sure they're not watching us via cameras in each apartment. But it's the only alibi I've got, so I'll have to use it.

"I need to get back to my own room," Griffin says. "It's too dangerous to be out for too long tonight."

I nod in agreement, as our hands grasp each other's tightly for one more second. I feel the familiar squeeze he gives against my palm. He breathes in, as if resolute to finally depart.

"Vienne's not the spy," I burst out before he turns. "You were right."

Griffin finally lets a tense smile peek across his features. "Of course I was. Did you have any doubt?"

And at once we're kissing, the taste and touch of his lips against mine a balm against any worries. He's ice and I'm all heat. Mixed together we fit like hot chocolate sipped on a snowy night. I take in all of Griffin. His hands raking up my back. The front of his hair tickling across my forehead. The dizzy electricity radiating from the skin where our mouths meet. Our kiss is frantic and only lasts seconds, but it is everything I need.

When at last we pull away from each other, I smile back, indulging in this one last moment together. I hug Griffin tightly across the waist a final time, and then he disengages.

I don't stop watching until he's completely gone, the stairway door clicking shut behind his back. I know I should be more concerned about my latest dilemma, but I can't wipe the beam off my face.

It's with this same silly grin flushing my cheeks that I slide my fingertip across the sensor and unlock my door, realizing that I should have been more worried.

Someone sits in a chair in my living room, legs crossed, a drink balanced in one hand.

"HELLO, ALICEN." CALIX'S VOICE is self-satisfied, a fox who's just caught an unsuspecting chicken.

"Elected," I say, trying not to sound surprised or scared out of my mind. "To what do I owe the honor?"

Calix points up at me with his raised glass. "*You* haven't been at work for the past two days."

"Of course I have," I say, slightly changing the story I devised in the hall with Griffin. "But I've had a cold. I didn't want to make anyone else sick, so I just worked at night."

Calix raises both eyebrows. "Oh really? Where did you work?"

My mind races. "At the rocket launcher." Mid is still cleaning up after the attack a month ago, so it's a semi-plausible alibi.

"You didn't go to the doctors. I checked."

I look down, playing up his previous assumption that I'm scared of them after what happened to Aaron. "I . . . I . . . "

"Never mind. That doesn't matter. But I'll have the Surveillors bring up video coverage of the rocket launcher for the last two nights. See if you're telling me the truth."

I merely look at him. His threat gives me just this night and maybe tomorrow morning before he knows for sure that I've lied. This means I have only a few options: concoct an alternate story between then and now, somehow steal the tapes, or come clean right this second. I choose option two, already trying to devise a way to sneak into the building early tomorrow to snatch the video.

"Why are you in my apartment?" I ask, trying to sound polite even though my question could be construed as rude. I'm exhausted. All I want to do is fall onto the bed in the other room, but Calix doesn't seem to be going anywhere. The sooner I help him with whatever he needs, the more likely he is to leave.

"I figured you'd come back here eventually. You know, we've had people looking for you for the last few days."

"I'm sorry. I should have told someone my plans."

"Well, you look like you're feeling better now. I expect to see you tomorrow bright and early." He issues commands like it is his birthright, which I guess it is. I hope now he will leave, and I can finally close my eyes and sink onto a mattress. But instead, he gestures at me with his free hand. "Why don't you have a drink with me."

"Oh, I . . . " I stumble on my words, thinking of a reason why I can't. "I don't have anything to offer you."

"I've brought my own." He pulls out a decanter of golden liquid. "Scotch. The very best. A Macallan. Sold for half a million dollars in 2010." He laughs as he takes a long draw. "Can you imagine how ridiculous people were back then? Trading with pieces of worthless paper?"

I smile tentatively; glad we are at least off the subject of my disappearance. "Did anyone ever tell you what it was like when things "went free"?

"You mean when the world collectively abandoned the concept of money?" Calix asks.

"My father told me the story. People started working for free and then got things they needed without having to pay."

"Things they needed . . . " He gazes at his expensive liquor. "People aren't evolved enough to blot out greed. We're human beings. We'll always pine for more than we need." He takes another sip. Then he pulls a thimble-sized glass from within his robes, pours scotch into it, and hands me the cup. Calix pauses as I taste the drink. "What do you think?"

"It burns a little," I admit, coughing on the alcohol.

"It's supposed to. Feels warm?"

I do feel like someone's just slid a wool blanket through my insides. Kind of nice, actually. "Mmm-hmm," I say.

"So what was your childhood, like, Alicen? Pull up a chair and tell me about those grander times in West when your father gave you those history lessons."

Now we've hit dangerous territory. I have to do what he says, but I don't have to tell him the truth. I don't want to get caught in a fabrication about West either. He probably knows more about that country than I ever will. I pull another chair from the kitchen to the small living room, thinking that if this were Griffin, he'd have had the decency to retrieve the chair for me.

"It was alright, I guess. Probably not like yours, though." I try to steer the conversation back to him, and Calix takes the bait. He seems like the type who's happiest talking about himself.

"Probably not. We had the best of everything, me and Aaron. Anything good scavenged from the ruins was optioned first through the Elected family before making it to the public warehouses."

"Must've been nice." I take another small sip from the cap of golden liquid.

"Didn't teach us to appreciate anything, though."

I realize Calix is exceptionally self-aware for a spoiled monarch, and I wonder how he got that way. How can I use the fact to my advantage? I wish Vienne were here for a dose of her expertise in psychology.

Calix keeps going, "Nowadays kids aren't concerned with expensive toys anyway."

This I grasp onto. "Kids. I've been meaning to ask. Where are they? Don't you have any in Mid Country?"

Calix laughs, throwing his head back hard, like he'll snap it right off. "'Course we've got kids." Then he gets quiet. "Not as many as I'd like, but then that's the price we pay."

"Price we pay for what?"

His eyes cloud over. "Nothing. But sure we have kids. Haven't you been to building fifteen yet?"

"No, that's not one of the tech stations."

"The kids all live and are taught over there. You should go sometime and watch them."

"Watch them? Like in a zoo?" My eyes are round, staring at him with accusation.

He doesn't pick up on my expression. Calix merely asks, "A zoo?"

I've forgotten that Calix probably doesn't know the concept. "Never mind. But I don't understand; why aren't the kids with their parents?"

"People need to focus on technology production and science. They can't be worrying if their kid has come down with a cold or if one is bullying another. We make it simpler here in Mid. A few caretakers cover a bunch of kids at once."

"So the children don't see their parents?"

"If the parents want to view them, it's allowed," says Calix. "Adults are pretty busy here, though."

"Yeah, I've noticed." I can't help shaking my head, not even masking the fact that I think his country's child rearing is absurd.

"It's a beneficial practice for everyone. We get more accomplished as a society this way. You'll see."

The thing is, I'm afraid I will see, just like Margareath. She's becoming more and more a fan of Mid's ways. I wonder if I stay here long enough, I'll also start seeing things from Calix's perspective. I can't imagine I'll change my mind about the children, though. No one would be caught dead taking my child away from me. I'm reminded not for the first time in the last few days that I still need to tell Griffin about our baby.

My eyes close for a half second, exhaustion taking its toll on me again. The scotch, even the two small sips of it, increased my desire to sleep. It's a moment before I even realize Calix is speaking again.

"So you said your parents are deceased?"

I stifle a yawn and look over at him again. "Yes."

Calix leans forward in the chair, his elbows resting on his knees. "Sorry to hear that, but I suppose it's not too uncommon." He reaches up and rubs an eyebrow with the back of one hand. "Mine are too."

"Oh? They didn't just leave when Aaron turned eighteen, like the Elected Accord states?"

"If by 'leave' you mean they were shot by firing squad, then yes." His mouth forms into a crumpled grimace, like he's trying to brush off the idea of his parents' death with some lighthearted, sarcastic quip, but can't quite get himself to say the words.

My eyebrows shoot up. "They were killed by firing squad?"

Calix frowns deeper. "Aaron took the Elected Accord very seriously. It says the Elected parents must be gone for the child to take ownership of the Country. Aaron signaled the shot himself."

I hold my stomach. "How old were you?"

"Fourteen. Four years younger than Aaron."

"Did you know what he was planning?" I can feel a fresh swirl of bile in my empty stomach.

"Not until my parents were summoned to the execution site. Neither did my parents. Obviously."

I pull my chair closer to Calix's. I can see he refuses to shed tears, but it looks like he wants to. "That must have been . . . " I can't find a word bad enough to describe it. "Horrible," I say at last.

"I figured once Aaron became Elected, my parents could finally focus on me. Tell me the same stories about the past they had taught Aaron. I never thought much about what the Elected Accord stipulated. I didn't picture them leaving, let alone being killed." He looks away. When Calix finally turns back a few long moments later, his eyes are dry, and he gives a barbed laugh. "I've never talked to anyone about it, really. Don't know why I did just now." He clears his throat.

"What did you say to Aaron afterwards?" I ask.

"Same thing I always said. Not much."

I nod slowly, trying to picture Aaron, not as a confused engineer with dementia, but as a tyrant leader who killed his own parents.

"You're a bit different, Alicen," Calix continues, setting his glass of scotch onto the table and squinting at me. "I don't think anyone else in Mid will ever ask me what I thought about my parents' execution. No one has up until now, at least."

I look down. He has no idea how different I actually am.

"I like that you're unusual, though," he adds. Calix shifts closer to me, his eyes making their way from the top of my head down past my chest to the ankles sticking out of my robes. I cross my legs, the sudden energy in the room vibrating as I avoid Calix's gaze.

When I don't say anything, Calix stands and pulls me out of my chair with one outstretched hand. "I'd better be going."

I nod, still wordless, watching him as closely as he eyes me. Calix starts to look toward my door, aiming to leave, but at the last second he turns back so that our faces are only inches apart.

"You *feel* more than the others do." As soon as he says the words, I gulp and look toward the brown wall to my left, anywhere but into his eyes. I memorize the lines in the faux wood, breathing in sharply as I concentrate on anything but Mid's Elected searching into the depths of my soul with his deep gaze.

It's in this second that Calix takes the opportunity to move even closer. Too late to do anything, I realize Calix is kissing me. I'm so taken aback, I don't move. I don't kiss back. I don't close my eyes. I just stare at the wall as he pulls his lips off mine and backs up slowly.

"See you tomorrow," Calix says, the words thin and sickly sweet like melting caramel dripping down his lips.

The door clicks shut behind him, and I just stand there, staring blankly ahead. I stay still for a full minute before moving even a muscle. My mouth feels like cotton, and I realize it's been hanging open. I clamp it shut so forcefully I can hear the gnash of teeth on teeth. He kissed me. The current Elected of my enemy country kissed me.

I run a hand through the messy tufts of my hair. They've started growing out in the last few weeks since I haven't had access to scissors and didn't think about hiding my gender anyway. Now that Margareath doesn't seem to care about East, it doesn't matter if she knows I'm a woman. It didn't seem to matter in the asexualized Mid Country. Until now.

Does Calix know I'm a girl? Or does he think I'm male? Does he like men? Or does he not care what gender I am? The questions just keep flying through my head, one after the other, a tumult of quandaries that leaves me even more exhausted than the stair climb.

I feel my insides grow cold, the warm blanket of scotch now completely eliminated from my system. If Calix likes me, I don't just have to stay in his favor. I can take advantage of his feelings to do even more. Already he has given me unprecedented access to the city as his technical historian. If Calix is attracted to me, what else can I get him to do?

I run to a nearby cabinet and ruffle through the clothes I wore when first arriving in Mid. What I'm looking for is right where I left it, swathed in my threadbare scarf. The mechanical bee's stinger is sharp and pointy. With barely a glance in the shiny cabinets lining my living room, I use the thin metal spike to rip at the ends of my locks, leaving my gender a secret yet again.

The only question now is what Griffin will say about my new plan. How can I tell him my latest strategy involves seducing Mid's Elected?

9

THE NEXT MORNING, I jump out of bed as soon as I hear my apartment's digital timepiece pronouncing seven am. Notwithstanding my new plan to distract Calix, I still need to steal the surveillance tapes, which show that I didn't work in the rocket launcher over the last two nights. I slept fitfully all through the night, half expecting Calix to burst in with a set of guards and haul me away. I need to be stationed at the rocket launcher as soon as the Surveillors get there but hopefully before Calix. Since everyone starts work at the same exact time, I just have to be inside the launch building before eight.

Fifteen minutes after I wake up, I'm out the door, hearing the robotic voice from my apartment in back of me as I hurry out. "You still have forty-five minutes. Taking time to eat a good breakfast is essential to the health of the country."

"Whatever," I say back over my shoulder. I want to scream *mind your own business*. Instead, I stop in my tracks. If the tapes are going to pronounce me a liar, I'll need something to defend myself. I step one foot back through the open front door.

"Good choice. Breakfast is the most important meal of the day," says the computer.

"Stop watching me."

"I am not watching you. I am sensing your heat signal through the room."

I ignore the voice and head back to where I left the bee's stinger on the nightstand. I slip it within an inner pocket of my robes and head out again without eating a thing.

I think about rousing Griffin for help but don't want to involve him if I'm about to be discovered. I keep walking ahead, arriving at the dome in record time. There's no one inside except for a couple of guards who look at me with curiosity when I pull back the massive doors.

"Excuse me," I say. "I'm looking for the Surveillors from this building."

One guard looks down at a monitor under the front counter and says, "Floor nineteen. Elevator's been fixed, so you shouldn't have to take the stairs." He raises an eyebrow in the direction of his comrade, and the two guards erupt into guffaws.

"Yeah, the stairs!" The other guard joins in with a grunt.

So they've recognized me, and I'm the brunt of their joke. It seems like everyone now knows the details of Aaron's rescue. I roll my eyes. But I do take the guards up on their offer of the elevator. I've gotten used to the suffocating little boxes, and today I appreciate that they're faster than walking. Plus, my legs still hurt from so much running over the past few days, even the idea of another set of stairs causes me to cringe.

When the elevator pings at floor nineteen, I'm out the doors before they fully open. The surveillance room on this level is instantly recognizable. Behind a set of glass windows is an array of cameras and monitoring equipment. Mid's not even trying to mask the fact that they watch everything. They *want* people to know. I pull on the glass doors, but find them locked. I think about breaking one to grab the camera feed from last night, but I'm sure the guards downstairs have cameras on me right now. They'd be up here in a flash, and I doubt I could outrun both of them, no matter how fast I am. So I lean against the wall and wait for someone to show up.

A half hour later the hum of workers starting their day reverberates around the stark hallway. The elevator opens again and again, dumping people out onto the floor, but no one comes to unlock the surveillance room. Finally around 8:15 when I think no one's coming to work the automated machines today, the elevator dings again.

As the door opens I hear a frightened voice say, "Of course we keep a strict watch on the feed."

"Well, I want to see it," growls Calix. He looks up as the doors slide open, and we lock eyes. He gives me a half-smile, cocking his head to the side. "Ah, what a surprise." I can't tell if he's genuinely happy to see me or upset that I'm obviously trying to get at those tapes. Either way, it seems like the situation amuses him. "Come to view the feed with me?"

I don't say anything. I am lost. I know he is about to see the blank tapes, which will announce loud and clear that I was lying about working the night before. I try to conjure a different story and think of a reason why I lied to him, but nothing sounds right in my head. Nothing is convincing enough. My other option is to run. I instinctively look toward the stairwell door at the end of the corridor, but Calix catches my eye and wags a finger. "Uh, uh, uh, Alicen. I wouldn't if I were you." His tone toward the Surveillor is suddenly sugary sweet. "Why don't we just have a look at those late night feeds?"

The Surveillor glances up, obviously terrified and now confused as well. "Ummm . . . of course. Just a minute." He fumbles in his pocket for the room key, dropping it a few times before the little piece of metal even reaches the door. His hands are shaking. "I'm new. First day on the job, you see," he says into the air, glancing at me nervously. He's too worried to even look at Calix.

"I should go," I mumble. "You know, get back to work. I'm sure there's a lot . . . "

Calix stops me with cold fingers wrapped around my wrist. "Oh, no. I insist. Stay and watch the camera feed with me. This should be fun."

He knows he's about to catch me. I'm a deer, and he's the hunter slowly cocking his gun.

The Surveillor finally unlocks the door. "Right over here, I think," he says, still only looking at me. He doesn't realize I'm the one about to be ousted by these videos. The man places his fingertip on a biometric reader, types in a code, and is granted access to the feed. "What time frame did you want to see, Elected?"

"Six p.m. two nights ago through eleven p.m. last night." He grins, his teeth catching the overhead light and glimmering too white in his mouth. They're almost venomous in their snake-like shine. "Tell the computer to search for heat signals on each floor of the launch building. When you find any, zero in on those."

There won't be any heat signals. No one was in this building after hours, except for maybe Aaron. But even his nighttime escapades were supposedly curtailed after his misadventure on the upper rails.

This is it. I grab onto the corner of a nearby desk to steady myself. I'm visibly shaking, but Calix and the Surveillor don't notice because their eyes are trained on the monitor in front of us. What will they do to me? Does Mid use hemlock here? Will Calix let me live if I tell him I'm pregnant? What will happen to East Country?

My thoughts are a jumble when I hear the Surveillor say, "Heat signal. One person in corridor nine. One a.m. two nights ago."

"What?" Calix's voice is no longer amused. He sounds annoyed. "Bring up that video." He looks over at me and then just as quickly at the screen again.

An image of a woman flashes on the monitor. It's grainy at first, but Calix orders the Surveillor to focus the film. The woman's back is to the camera, but her ear-length, light brown hair transmits through the video clearly. I know it can't actually be me, but it looks awfully similar. I lean my body forward, even though the two men are in front, obscuring my view.

Calix takes one more long look at the screen and then turns on his heels. With gritted teeth he says, "Alicen, it appears I owe you an apology."

The Surveillor looks completely befuddled and tries to busy himself with a stack of papers.

I don't utter a word in response. I might let out a pent up squeak if I dare speak.

"You continue to surprise me." Calix places one hand on his chin, staring at me, his eyes pensive. He purses his lips and licks them once as if contemplating his next move. Then Calix seems to remember the Surveillor is in the room and breaks eye contact with me. "Well." His voice is an octave lower. "Keep up your work here at the launch pad today, but join me tomorrow in building four. I'd like your take on something."

Finally, I open my mouth. "Yes, Elected."

Calix starts to leave but turns back one last time. I think he is about to kiss me again, just like he did in my apartment hours earlier, and I brace myself. But he just says, "Don't call me that. I'd prefer you use my given name, Calix."

The Surveillor looks down at his Elected's bold words but continues to shift papers around the desk, trying to blend into his surroundings. Finally left alone with the nervous man, I stand in the middle of the room, wringing my hands. "Can I see that video again?" I ask.

The Surveillor adjusts his glasses, looking at me with eyes that are too magnified on his face. "Certainly." He clicks a few times on a nearby keyboard and the feed pops up again.

I stare at it, this time with my face close to the screen. "Back up a few moments?" I point to the feed, nudging with my finger as we get to the correct spot. "Right there before you get an initial heat signal."

The man wordlessly obeys, and I see footage of an empty corridor. The feed flickers for a moment and then the image of my body double comes into view. There. You wouldn't notice it unless you were paying attention to the video right before the heat signal registered. There's a slight gap in the footage, as if someone has spliced the film to add in a shot of me. I squint closer. But the thing is, it isn't me. I'm sure of it. The curls on the woman's hair are just a bit tighter than my own. And that's not my walk.

I glance up at the Surveillor. He peers over my shoulder but startles, backing up with a loud bang against a nearby shelf, when I turn my whole gaze on him.

"This is your first day here?" I ask.

The man tries to regain his composure, fidgeting with his robes. "Yes, but I assure you I did a thorough handoff with the Surveillor before me. Nothing slipped through the cracks."

He's afraid for his job. It makes me wonder what exactly happens in Mid if you're found incompetent. Is it a trip to the registration office to become a Holder or something worse?

"I'm sure you did," I say, trying to reassure him. My voice is gentle and wispy, a moth's wing beating against glass.

The man responds to the softer tone I employ. "Spent hours with him. Nice guy. Sometimes had a woman with him. You don't see that too often around here."

I nod, trying not to look too excited. "Do you remember anything else? Any bit of information would help. Like where he transferred to?"

"I don't. I'm sorry. He was just switching to another surveillance post." The Surveillor fiddles with his glasses again. "If he did anything wrong with that feed, you should know it was before my time. I wasn't involved in any malfunction. I can't be held responsible for . . . "

"No, no," I interrupt. "Nothing's wrong. In fact the video's perfect."

I start to walk toward the door, but the bewildered man speaks again. "There was one more thing though, now that I think about it." I stop in my tracks, holding my breath. "When he and the woman were leaving once, they said the strangest phrase. I've never heard it before, but I don't get out much, so . . . "

"Go on," I urge. "What was it?"

"A new morning to you?" He says the phrase like it's a question.

"Day," I say. "Day. Not morning."

10

I KNEW IT WAS my mother in the video. I don't know how they figured out the exact help I would need, but my parents have obviously been keeping close tabs on me. My mom cut her own hair to make it appear like mine in the video.

I'm running out of the building even before I realize where I'm headed. The robots along the moving sidewalks jump to the side to let me by. In my euphoric state of mind, I even think they seem polite. I find myself outside the barbed wire fence surrounding the barns.

"I need to ask a colleague some technical questions," I lie to the front guard.

"Finger please," he says.

I dutifully supply my fingertip and with just a quick glance at his monitor, the guard's eyebrows rise. "You are cleared for admittance to all buildings in Mid. That's unusual. I don't think I . . . "

"Thanks!" I say and keep walking through the turnstiles. I can't waste any more time. I know exactly what I want to do right now.

I find Griffin inside one of the stalls, hosing down a horse. He looks oddly like his father did the last time I met Maran in East's stables, but I am determined to shake off that image.

"Alicen!" he says. Griffin lets the hose drop onto the floor with a clatter, which causes the horse to jump. He pats the animal once in apology and then bridges the gap between us with one step. "Is everything okay?"

"Calix suspected me of lying. He was in the apartment waiting for me last night."

Griffin grabs my shoulder, his eyes flying around us. "Then what are we still doing . . . "

"No, wait. It turned out alright. Calix wanted to see video surveillance of me working nights, like the story I'd concocted. I thought I was sunk, but it turns out there *was* an image of me in the building's video from two nights ago!"

Griffin's still looking over my shoulder, on alert for anything out of the ordinary. He doesn't yet understand that we're safe—that my parents *saved* us. "How is that possible?" he asks.

"My parents are here! They're helping us! My dad spliced in a few seconds of my mom walking down the hallway. It looks like me, and it fooled Calix." My words are bubbles bursting out in thin, breathless gasps. There is so much good news, I can't get to it all fast enough.

"Where are your parents?"

"I don't know. But I mean, they're still in Mid, working as Surveillors. I don't know why they haven't made themselves known to us, but we're bound to see them soon, I'm sure." I lean up against Griffin, placing my head on the top of his chest. I finally allow myself to take a deep breath, burrowing deeper within the crook of Griffin's arm.

"So Calix is still in the dark about your trip back East?"

"Definitely."

Griffin's lungs expand, like he too was holding his breath. His arm relaxes around my back, and his thumb starts a rhythmic rub against the coarse fabric of my robe. I can feel his whole hand through the thin material, the touch of his fingertips causing a shiver to ascend up my spine. I so wish we could go back to one of our apartments in the middle of the day. There is no place here to be alone. Nowhere perfect to tell him what I want to say next.

As if he can sense my frustration merely from the tensing of my shoulders, Griffin pulls back to look at my face. "What else is going on? What aren't you telling me?"

I've been withholding the information about our baby for so long, now it feels like the words are stuck in my throat. I want to say them, but for some reason I just don't know how. What if Griffin's angry that I kept it a secret until now? How can I explain that I almost forgot I was pregnant during the last month we've been in Mid? I don't even understand the momentary mental lapse myself, let alone know how to speak the words to Griffin.

Griffin frowns, his grip tightening on my upper arms. "What's wrong?" He starts looking over my shoulder again, searching for an impending onslaught of guards or other signs that I've been caught in the act of espionage.

I take Griffin's hand and guide him to sit in a corner of the stall. The lab seems so clinical with its white walls and harsh lights, but inside this tiny horse stable, sitting cross-legged on a floor of hay, it feels like we could almost be back at East's White House. I keep my eyes focused downward, trying to pretend I'm with Griffin in the familiarity of our home.

"Vienne is doing well," I start. "She flourishes in pregnancy. Really shows now."

Griffin nods, confused at my seemingly sudden change of topics, "That's good news. But what does this have to do with . . . "

"She's not the only one who's pregnant," I blurt out. My words hang in the air, like rain suspended in a heavy fog. I wait for them to fall, the pause leaving no uncertainty as to my meaning.

Griffin's eyes widen, looking first into my face and then down to the rumple of my robes at waist level.

"I'm . . . I'm . . . ," I can't seem to say 'I' and 'pregnant' in a full sentence.

"With child." The word sounds ethereal coming from Griffin's lips. He stares at me, and for a second, I think he's about to get mad. Or tell me all of the reasons this shouldn't have happened. Instead he reaches forward, hugging me fiercely, burying his head in my neck. Through a grin I can feel against my cheek, he asks, "Are you sure?"

I exhale a sigh of relief. "Yes. Vienne gave me a test."

Griffin smiles wider and holds both of my shoulders as he stares into my eyes. The joy written across his features shouldn't have surprised me so much, but it does. His exaltation is heartwarming. I can almost feel my anxiety evaporating. Griffin probably doesn't even realize how long I've held back the announcement. I'm sure he thinks Vienne just gave me the test at our recent meeting on the hills, and I don't enlighten him on that one detail.

"This is fantastic news!" he says. We sit cross-legged for a few more minutes, our backs leaning against the stable's fake wood paneling. We hold hands and stare blankly ahead, both of us taking a moment to let the news settle. "Another Elected child for East Country," Griffin finally muses, gently circling the top of my thumb with his own.

"Another child for you."

"It's lucky to have one child, but two is unreal!" He shakes his head, the gleam in his eye only accentuated by the glow coming from his cheeks. He squeezes my hand. "How do you feel?"

I purse my lips, not wanting to tell Griffin the extent of my nausea. Last thing I want is for him to worry about one more thing here in this wayward country. "Fine. Just tired."

"Well, I'm going to make sure you rest now. No more saving citizens of Mid who are stupid enough to climb the rocket launcher."

I roll my eyes but lean into Griffin harder, laying my palm against his heart.

After another few beats of silence, he looks down at me with one eyebrow cocked. "How will you pick which baby gets the Elected role?"

I purse my lips and shrug.

"Whichever is a boy?" Griffin asks.

"Not necessarily. Since I've already broken the Fertility, Ships, Technology, *and* Elected Accords myself, why not go a little further? A female leader wouldn't be the most offensive rule I've demolished, certainly."

"You've got a point." Griffin puts a hand to his brow. "So either of my children could be groomed for the position."

I think about how Calix's parents prepared Aaron for the role, leaving their younger son neglected all those years. "I think we'll groom them both."

"And just see who wants it more?"

"I don't know. We'll have to figure that out later. You never know. Eighteen years from now, the world may look a lot different."

"Hopefully not all under Mid's leadership," says Griffin, his lip upturned in a sneer. We let the thought ruminate for a few minutes, and the silence is only punctuated by Griffin's eventual question, "Why was Calix in your room? Why didn't he just corner you at work the next morning? Or get someone else to interrogate you?"

Ah. Leave it to Griffin to sniff out the one sticky part of the story. "He has some sort of infatuation with me."

As I tell Griffin why this plays to our advantage, his eyebrows rise with skepticism. "And you're planning to do *what* with this knowledge?"

I shrug again. "Keep him interested for as long as possible, I guess. Get as much information as I can from Calix before he stops liking me?"

Griffin drops my hand and begins rolling a piece of hay between his thumb and index finger. When I pull his chin so that he's facing me again, I see Griffin's eyes have grown dark. "What?" I ask. "Do you think I'll start liking him during the ruse?"

Griffin's smile is rueful. "No. That's not my concern." He tosses the shredded fragments of hay onto the floor. "You think that Calix will just get tired of you and leave you alone after you've gotten some juicy information out of him?"

"I haven't thought that far."

"Well, you need to think about that." Griffin's voice is a degree louder now. "You don't get it, do you?"

"What?" I sit up on my knees and hold both of Griffin's hands to keep him calm.

"He won't just get tired of you! You are very . . . alluring." I see the tension and desire brimming under his skin, as if it's trapped. My heart races, thinking of what we'd be doing right now if only we were in private. "What's going to happen as this fake love affair escalates? What if Calix wants more from you? How far are you willing to take it?"

I don't say anything. Just look down at our clasped fists. His knuckles clench so that they grow white under the skin.

Griffin keeps fuming. "I'm not okay with you going *that* far with him! Not even to help our country."

"I'm not going to . . . I wouldn't . . . " When I can't find the right words, I say, "Plus, I can't let him figure out I'm pregnant, so there's no chance I'd let him . . . " The end of my sentence trails off.

Griffin nods. He takes a long, ragged breath. "I don't like you putting yourself out as bait, but it's not like you can reject Calix's advances without who-knows-what happening in this insane country." I can see the tension building in Griffin's clenched hands like it's a palatable object. He slams a fist up against the side of the stall, which startles the horse again. I jump, knocking over a bucket of water as I scoot to the side.

"Sorry," Griffin says to both me and the mare. The horse whinnies a disgruntled reply but calms again when Griffin strokes its neck. "I just feel so helpless to protect you here."

I skirt around the growing puddle of water, looking outside the stall to see if any of Mid's countrymen heard Griffin's outburst.

"You know, Calix is letting me evade a trip to the doctor's office because he likes me. That's a plus in the whole situation, right?"

Griffin grumbles under his breath, "At least that's something."

We slide down against the side of the stall again, our thighs firmly pressed against each other. This is as close as we can get, at least until this evening. I can't wait until then. Come six p.m. I plan to unleash all of Griffin's pent up frustration one button at a time.

We sit inside the cocoon of the stall, letting the din and bustle of the workers' afternoon cacophony balloon around us. I refrain from saying what's on my mind, wondering if Griffin's considered the same thing about the doctors. The thing is, the monthly medical visits are mandatory. We've already been in Mid for a month, and soon, like Margareath once told us, the doctors will come looking.

If not for me, then certainly for Griffin.

11

THE NEXT DAY I do as Calix instructed, meeting him at the entrance to building four at exactly eight o'clock. He already stands at the gate, leaning with one arm against the iron fence.

"Have you had breakfast today? Or is it just yesterday that you skipped the meal?" he asks when I get close enough.

I raise my eyebrows, perturbed that he obviously reviewed my apartment's computer records.

"Is nothing sacred?" I ask, my fury building before the day with Calix has even begun. "Do you listen in while I use the bathroom too?"

Calix laughs out loud. "I tapped into your home computer's voice script. It said you hadn't eaten breakfast yesterday. I apologize. I'll respect your privacy going forward." He bows extravagantly, arms out wide.

"Well, aren't you gallant?" I can't help being snide even though I know he is the Elected.

Calix chuckles. "I can be very much so. In fact, I only asked you about breakfast because I brought you this." He pulls out a crisp white box from behind his back. "It's a croissant. I don't know if you have ever had one before, but I thought you'd enjoy it. Freshly baked."

I take the box from his outstretched arms.

"An apology for yesterday," he says. "I should have trusted you, not made a circus out of the country looking for you these last few days."

I bow my head. I can't let him see the deceit in my eyes. "Thank you."

"Alright then," Calix says with finality, like a boy who's just been handed back his broken toy, all shiny and new again. "Eat the croissant along the way. I have something important to show you."

I bristle at Calix's pronouncement, but I follow him through the wide glass doors of building four, past the guards who don't ask to see our fingertips, and up five levels on the elevator. As the doors part, we're in an expansive room I've never seen before. It looks almost identical to the surveillance area we visited yesterday. This space, however, is bigger and packed with equipment. Here, the entire floor is open wide, and teams of people gather around monitors with no walls between them and the next set of cameras. The sounds around us are a steady din of people talking and monitors beeping.

I hold my arms against my sides a little tighter, as if they could protect me from the flurry.

"What's this?" I ask as I follow Calix through the maze of people.

"Our central surveillance hub. It's where we gather all the data, tabulate everyone's food consumption, and document radiation symptom outbreaks. Anything I want to know about my people, the answer's here."

I look around in long, far reaching glances, hoping to see my parents working nearby. If my father is still a Surveillor, chances are he's stationed here.

"Amazing, isn't it?" Calix asks.

I nod, still too focused on looking for my parents to answer him with real words.

"Here we are." Calix holds out a hand to stop me in front of a busy workstation. He directs his attention to three men sitting in front of a large monitor with earphones strapped to their heads. "Gentlemen, you're excused for the next half hour. We'll take over for now."

The three men immediately stand up from their desks. Two of them hand over their headsets, one to each of us. I stare after them, watching to see if they seem displeased in any way by our interruption, but they merely walk away, silent, obedient and impassive like the orange-eyed robots wandering along the city's moving sidewalks.

Calix automatically adjusts the set onto his own head. When I look at my set for a moment too long, Calix reaches over and starts helping strap mine on as well. I can feel his long fingers tightening the earphones so they fit snugly in between the tufts of my hair. A part of me wants to squirm away from his touch, but I hold still, waiting for Calix to finish.

Everything around me is muted when the headphones fully cover my ears. I can barely hear Calix when he turns toward me, gesturing toward a knob on my headset.

"Turn it clockwise so you can hear the feed." His lips move in exaggerated pronunciation so I can understand what he says through the padding.

I fumble with the button, mirroring his actions. At once, there's a scream so loud in my ear that I automatically pull the headset off. It smashes hard onto the floor.

Calix stares at me and then laughs. He pulls his headset off just one ear so he can talk to me more easily.

"You turned it on too loud. Here, let me."

He picks up my headset again and begins adjusting it back on my head. I just stare at him, blinking in shock, thinking that the sound coming through the earphones will cause me to go deaf. This time when Calix finishes lifting the set over my hair, he adjusts the volume knob himself.

I stare ahead of me, hearing the same sound from a moment earlier, now in lower volume. It's a person screaming. The screeches pulsate, like the beat of a heart, in and out, rapidly and then more slowly. After a minute of hearing the awful screams, I turn to Calix. "What is this? Someone's being tortured in Mid?"

He laughs again, obviously amused at my train of thought.

"No, we don't torture anyone here in Mid. This is audio feed from somewhere else."

I look at him for a second, my ears still dripping with the sounds of the yelling coming from within the headset.

When I open my mouth again, my words come out hollow, clipped like a bird whose wings have been damaged. "From somewhere else? Like East Country?"

Calix smiles. "I knew you'd catch on." Then he looks at the monitor in front of us again, turning gauges on the equipment.

I listen more intently, finally understanding what I'm hearing. It's the sound coming through Vienne's microchip. She's near someone who's screaming. The audio is fuzzy for a moment, and I think I was right about how Mid's spyware feed works. It comes in and out, fuzzy and then sharp again like clouds passing overhead in the breeze. The screaming continues for another minute and then finally peters out. The person on the other end of my headset pants.

Calix turns, nudging me in the fleshy part of my upper arm. "Barbarians over there. Listen to how they're hurting their own people."

I strain to hear more, unable to answer Calix. Finally, the voice on the other end speaks. "It's alright, Tomlin. That's enough for today. We'll look for the chip again tomorrow."

At once the blood rushes out of my heart, pooling in my hands and feet. I feel like I will slide off my seat and drop directly to the floor. All of my energy is sucked out, like a balloon losing its helium. The voice through the feed—it's not Vienne listening to someone in East. It *is* Vienne. Doing exactly what she said she would, trying to find the micro-chip under her skin. Without sedatives or the purple pills from long ago, I can only imagine what Vienne must feel.

I sit still as a stone, eyes transfixed to the blank monitor in front of us.

Calix leans in again. "I told you. They're monsters over there. The woman we sent in. They've realized she's the spy. They're torturing her." He purses his lips and makes a grunting sound. "They'll even hurt their Madame Elected. Can you imagine?" I still don't say anything, so Calix continues. "Well, that's not the main thing I wanted you for. Here, listen to this and tell me what you think."

He presses more buttons on the equipment in front of us, and again voices come through my headset.

"I've endangered our entire country."

Calix looks over at me, nodding for me to keep listening. The feed gets fuzzy again, alternating between clarity and a flat roar of static. Then, words come through once more.

"And just be careful what you talk about when the sky is clear. Actually, talk about how we don't have any technology. Talk about how it wasn't us who hit Mid."

I stop still, my hands plastered to the desk in front of us. I can't move a muscle. Any twitch of my face is sure to give me away.

Calix grunts, looking up to the ceiling, still listening to the feed.

My voice comes through loud and clear again.

"Take care of our country."

Calix slams his fist down on the desk, and I jump, my palms making a wet squelching noise as they peel off the metal.

"They've got their own damned spy!" he says.

12

I LOOK OVER AT Calix, my eyes round like saucers and my mouth dry like cotton. Is this how it will end? Has he brought me here to listen to my own voice over the surveillance feed just so he can finally tell me he knows who I am? Or does he not realize that's my voice?

"They've finally figured out we've been spying on them," he says, running a hand through his hair. "Not as much good stuff coming through the audio since they solved that riddle. Can you believe they even thought to feed us lines about how the raids weren't their fault? Outrageous!" He pumps his fist into the desk again, but this time I'm more prepared for it. I don't jump. I just sit in my seat, eyes forward, unblinking.

"Well, what do you think of it all?"

I try to answer him, but my words come out in wisps. I'm not even sure my voice will work. "I . . . I . . . "

Calix jumps back in. "I know. Takes your breath away. So now they have their own spy over here in our country. More than one for all we know!" He pauses his rant, finally turning to look at me square on. He doesn't know the voice in the audio was mine. It was too scratchy over the feed. I breathe a small intake of air, trying to get my heart back to a normal pace.

"I'm . . . not sure . . . ," I mumble.

"Well, of course not. But what do you think about the spy? We've gathered that they meet at two week intervals."

This time I find my voice. It's shallow in my throat, but it does come out. "Then why don't you just stop the meetings if you know about them?" I don't understand why he'd allow my meeting with Vienne to go forward without consequences. Why didn't he blast me to smithereens when they initially heard the audio a few days ago?

"Thought about that. But I'd rather hear what they say instead of shutting down the little operation. Don't you think that's wiser?"

I look into Calix's clear blue eyes. He really wants my opinion. I catch my breath again and then say, "That's probably smart. No sense killing the spy before you get all the information out of him."

"Exactly." Calix grunts again, nodding. Then he stands, planting both hands on his hips. "It's only a matter of time now." He looks away, but I catch the smile blooming across his cheeks.

"What do you mean?"

Calix looks back at me and claps his hands. "Only a matter of months before we test out some of our more sophisticated weaponry on East. Then they'll see what we're really capable of!" He's more animated now than I've seen him all morning. I can see how he sucks down revenge like a child's sugary sweet.

And I can see how I'll have to be so much more careful than before.

It takes all of my willpower not to run toward East Country as soon as Calix finishes with me that evening. I know it's not my designated time to meet Vienne, but maybe I can go in disguise and sneak into the country to find her. I can't let Vienne keep cutting herself to find the microchip, and I have to tell them about Mid's plans for war.

I tell Griffin as much back in my apartment that evening.

"You can't go now," he says. "It's too dangerous for you to disappear again so soon. And sneaking into East is risky. They're so worried about intruders now they're bound to kill you the second the guards see someone descending the hill."

I look down at his words. "But Mid's expecting to hear the spy meet with Vienne at two-week intervals. This will be less suspicious. And Vienne . . . I shouldn't let her . . . " I can't get the sound of her screams out of my head.

"She can take care of herself."

"You didn't hear!" My voice comes out high and raspy, breaking on the end of my exclamation.

Griffin pulls me close so that my head automatically finds his shoulder. "She's strong. This is what she wants to do. Even if you run over there, Vienne won't stop until she finds the chip."

I can't help agreeing with him, albeit with reluctance. Vienne was adamant last time I saw her. Either she hurts herself getting the chip out or she runs off into the wild, pregnant and alone. The second option means certain death. The first option only means pain.

Not for the first time, I wish I wasn't born into the Elected family. I wish I was normal with normal worries, normal friends, and a regular life.

"At the very least I have to get over there to tell them about Mid's plans to attack. East will have to evacuate." I think of my people packing up, never returning to their home country. I can't even picture where they'll go. The environment north and south of us isn't hospitable anymore.

"Yes, you'll warn them. But not until your next designated meeting once we've figured out a better plan to sneak you out and when Vienne will be waiting for you at the top of the border. What exactly did Calix say?"

"That they'll start using the nuclear weapons in a few months." Griffin looks away, staring at the blank walls. "Are you okay?" I ask after a few long seconds of silence.

"We should have been developing a way to fight back this entire time."

"What do you mean?" I ask, my cheeks turning red.

"Weapons of our own. We could have manufactured some way to defend our country; if only we'd started earlier." He shakes his head and pulls away from me. "Sometimes, I think we'd have been wiser listening to my father the entire time."

I stare at Griffin. "Your *father?*"

The muscles in Griffin's back twitch at the inflection. He puts a tight fist around my bedroom door handle, clenching and unclenching the knob.

"Yes, my father. It turns out he was right all along."

"You can't mean that." I try to keep my voice low and calm, but even I can hear the pitch rise. "Your father advocated destruction. He wanted power. If we followed his ideas, East would've been as bad as the warring countries of the past."

Griffin turns to look at me, his eyes squeezing shut as if he's warring with his own thoughts. "And now what? We'll arrive at the same conclusion, but this time East will be destroyed."

"We don't know that. I still have a chance to dissuade Calix. If I could just . . . "

Griffin cuts me off. "My father's solution would have protected our country. Your solution . . . your father's . . . " he tumbles over the last words.

"Our what?"

Griffin looks down at the floor, his hand still holding fast to my doorknob. "By not creating weapons and defenses, you've put East in danger."

This time I stand up from the bed, but Griffin doesn't let me get a word in edgewise.

"You could have followed my father's advice. You had the power to agree with him and create technology," he says.

"I can't believe you're saying this!" I thrust a hand through my hair, closing my eyes for a split second. "I thought you agreed with my methods, my plans . . . "

"I agreed that we should come here and find out information on Mid. Find a way to disarm them. Not start falling for their Elected as the ultimate solution!"

"I'm not falling for Calix! That's not my ultimate . . . "

"You just want to keep *talking* with him. Don't you realize? He's beyond talking. Nuclear weapons will kill everyone we love in East. Brinn, my child, Vienne; they'll all be gone. Don't you *get* that?"

My child. He says the words like he never thought Vienne's and his child was also partly mine. The room is all of a sudden cold. I don't even realize it, but I'm hugging my stomach.

"Yes, of course I *get* it." My voice is low. "But creating technology to wipe out Mid before they wipe us out isn't a good solution. We have to find another way."

"There *is* no other way. Don't you see what's coming? Everything my father predicted is happening. Mid will destroy East. Only weapons and technology, evenly matched up against Mid's bombs, can save our country. And now we only have three more months before Calix pulls the trigger."

"I'll get him to stop. I promise. I'll do whatever it takes. I'll . . ."

Griffin puts up a hand to stop me. "Don't say it. I don't even want to know what you'll do to convince him."

We look at each other for a long moment, our eyes a tumult of accusations. He thinks I'll give myself to Calix to change the Elected's mind. And I think Griffin is blaming me for East's demise.

"I think you should leave," I say at last.

Griffin looks at me for one beat longer and then says. "Fine. Good idea."

I turn my back on him, tears starting to brim in my lower eyelids. He's out of the room so fast I don't even have a chance to change my mind. But as soon as I hear his feet on the hard tile of the kitchen, I want to take back what I've said. There are only the two of us to help each other in Mid. I run into the living room, but the door to my apartment is already closing. All I can see is the sole of Griffin's shoe as he stomps off into the hallway. I fall to the ground and smack my hand hard against the floor. Unwilling to follow him further and unwilling to say he was right about technology, I just sit there, shaking my head.

There is no way that complete and utter aggression can be the answer. I feel unsure about the exact way forward, but I know I'm right on this. Bombs against bombs is the way of the past. We're more civilized now, at least in East. There has got to be another way to disarm Calix, even if it does mean sacrificing myself in the process.

13

TWO MORE WEEKS PROCEED excruciatingly slowly. Each day, I work with Calix or another engineer in the rocket launch building. I try to take them off on tangents, looking at the metal casing of one of the wings instead of moving farther along with their nuclear bomb. They're sidetracked for a little while, but always find their way back to the more menacing technology, focused on getting it ready for an offensive.

Hoping to see Griffin at my door every evening, I almost run back to my room at six p.m., but he doesn't come. I picture him sitting alone in his apartment, fuming. I want to go see him, but I know I'm right about technology. If I try to tell him again how his father was wrong, it'll just push Griffin farther away. He's got to come to the conclusion himself. Until then I wait, getting lonelier as the days proceed.

I start talking to my baby, which feels a lot like talking to myself.

"Don't you want to move around or kick or something?" I ask it. I remember women saying their babies kicked so hard it sometimes hurt. But there's nothing from mine.

I wait, as if hoping there will be some kind of response.

"No? Well, I guess you'll do things at your own pace." I sigh, sitting at my living room table with my second plate of food half-finished in front of me. The light purple drink in front of me is cool and refreshing after a long day on my feet. I wish I had someone to spend my free time with. I'm even contemplating going to Margareath's apartment when there's a knock on my door.

"Finally!" I call out. "I was wondering when you'd . . . "

But as I swing open the door, it's not Griffin who I find on the other side.

"Aaron? What are you doing here?"

His eyes flick back and forth, manic, across the expanse of the outside hallway.

"Are you okay?" I ask, thinking this frenetic creature is a lot different from the picture of a merciless monarch Calix painted.

He still doesn't say anything, just hops from foot to foot, fidgeting in my doorway.

"Do you want to come in?"

He still doesn't say anything, doesn't even look me in the eye, but he walks over the threshold into my living room. His eyes scan the tabletop and he bends so far forward, I think he's trying to look into my hallway without actually walking around.

"Do you want something to drink?" I don't know what else to say. Aaron seems even more foregone than when I saved him weeks ago.

He doesn't answer, but continues to pace. Aaron looks up at my ceiling, poking at one of the drop panels where the time is projected in bright green numbers.

"Up here," Aaron finally says.

"What's up there?" I ask, walking closer to him.

"They're listening here." I know he means the surveillance teams, but I'm not surprised. I know they exist, and I know they have the capacity to listen into all the apartments if they want to. Apparently though, this news troubles Aaron.

"It's okay," I say, reaching out to pat him on the shoulder. When my hands are within an inch of him, Aaron jumps back like I've just tried to poke his arm with a hot iron.

"Listening isn't okay!" Aaron hisses. He paces in tight little circles across my front foyer, and I suddenly think I was wrong to let him inside. He's coming unhinged, and he's in between me and an escape. I can't get past him to safety if he loses control. "My brother is evil," he says.

I wonder if in Aaron's dementia he's mixed up exactly who did what in the "evil" department. I start to back up, working my way toward the kitchen. That's where I've left my knife from East Country. It's a much better weapon, should I need one, than the blunt utensils Mid provides within each apartment. It's even better than the tiny bee's stinger I still keep wrapped under my pillow.

"He's not so bad," I say, hoping to dissuade Aaron from whatever rant he's on.

"I'm looking for him. You're always with him. Thought he might be here."

"No, I . . . " My words clot in my throat as I remember Griffin's words about me getting too close to Calix.

Aaron fumbles with something inside his long robes and pulls out a revolver. It's silver and filigreed, obviously an antique, but still ruthless in its capability.

"Where is he?" Aaron yells up toward the ceiling. He talks to the computer stashed in my apartment. In his crazed state, Aaron's face has grown pink, all the way from his neck to his forehead. With his pink face and equally pink eyes, he looks like one of Mid's neon oranges, ripped apart and bursting with unnatural rosy color.

I back further away into the kitchen, never taking my eyes off my uninvited guest.

"Where? Where? Where?" Aaron yells the question at the projected time and then points his gun and cocks it.

I glance around my kitchen for some space to crawl behind when I hear the bang. I fall to my knees, the gunfire so loud in the tiny apartment that I shake along with the walls.

"No more listening in!" Aaron laughs at the ceiling and then fires the gun at the computer again. The second bang jolts me. I jump back up and find my knife on the counter. I hold it securely in my hand as I see Aaron approaching me.

"You're in on it with him. He stole my Elected role, and now you're hoping to be the Madam Elected!"

I hold the hand with the knife behind my back as Aaron continues advancing. I'll need the element of surprise because I know my knife, sharp as it is, won't fare well against his blazing gun.

"No, I'm not doing anything like that," I say.

"You are! You are!" Aaron's voice is wild, unruly with his rising anger.

When he's inches from the kitchen doorway and about to block me into the room, I make a run for it, smashing into him with a grunt. He loses his balance but claws for me anyway, his long, thin hand closing on my neck. I stab at him with my knife, causing blood to spurt out of his upper arm. But he lunges forward anyway, tightening his hold. All I can do is use my legs to kick at his shins. We struggle together like this, me twisting and reaching for his gun, him trying to get a good angle to fire his weapon while still grasping onto my neck. I'm starting to see stars as my air supply diminishes. I wonder if I'll pass out from lack of oxygen first or if he'll eventually crack my neck in the struggle. I think I'm about to collapse, and I'm gasping for breath, when my front door bursts open and people come rushing in.

Aaron instantly drops me to the ground, aiming his revolver forward instead of at me. I gasp and clutch at my throat, trying to gulp as much air as I can.

"There you are!" yells Aaron.

Calix runs into view, flanked on both sides with two guards. "We've been looking for you, older brother," he says, a half grin on his face.

"I knew you'd be here!" Aaron says, still crazy with fury.

"Only because I followed *you* here." Calix's voice is amused. It doesn't carry any hint of the danger I know to be present. I want to call out to him to watch for Aaron's gun, but my throat feels like someone's stuffed a wad of linen down it. I can't get out any words.

"You're a liar!" screams Aaron, lunging at his brother with the gun set to fire. But the guards step forward, twisting Aaron's arms and grabbing the weapon before he can do any more harm.

Calix just laughs. "And *you're* a menace to society." Then to the guards, Calix says, "Lock him up. Solitary confinement."

The guards look back and forth from Calix to Aaron as if unsure which Elected to follow. Then they make their determination, probably by seeing Aaron's unstable, furtive eyes and hustle him out of my apartment.

I'm still sitting on my kitchen floor, one hand clutching my throat, when the front door closes and quiet once again pervades my living quarters. Calix stays and for the second time we're alone in my apartment. He walks into the kitchen and holds out a hand to me. He sees the knife in my hand but doesn't say anything, just picks it up, rolls it in his palm, and wordlessly drops it onto my counter.

"Here, drink something. It'll make you feel better." He holds a cup of purple liquid out to me, and I sip it, staring into the glass.

"How did you know he was here?" I cough out the words, my throat still dry and swollen.

"We heard the gunshot."

"Good timing. I thought I was done for."

"You wouldn't have gotten hurt," Calix says.

I look at him and manage to roll my eyes.

"He was firing dummy cartridges," Calix continues. "Aaron took one of my parents' antique guns from the museum. No gunpowder in those."

"Well, my furniture's broken. And I don't know what he managed to do to the computer," I say, and attempt my first smile. "So no more listening in on me."

"I already told you I stopped at your request." Calix grins and leads me to an intact chair in my living room, one hand around my waist and another holding my elbow.

"Aaron said you were a liar and that you were trying to steal the Elected role from him."

Calix looks away from me, grumbling. "His recollection is a bit twisted."

"A bit?"

Calix peers toward me again, inspecting the handprints that I'm sure are blazing red on my neck. "He hurt you." Calix sighs, the confident, playful mask finally leaving his face. "No more playing engineer for him. I can't have Aaron wandering around the city."

I nod; satisfied that Calix is going to take this seriously.

"I'm sorry," he continues. "This is because of me. Let me do something for you to make up for your trouble."

I look away. There's nothing he can do for me here in Mid, except decide to stop the rampage against my country. I think this might be the time to come clean and ask for what I really want.

I take a deep breath. "Calix, I . . . " I start to say.

"You've been working hard," he says at the same time as me. Then he stops.

"Go ahead," I say, ever differential, playing my role.

He nods, used to having people acquiesce to him. "You've been working long days. Giving us valuable information for the weapons. But I can see you're tired, and now you're hurt on top of it. Why don't you take a few days off? Take some time to yourself. Go visit the Satisfaction Room or our forest."

I squint my eyes, about to tell him that the last thing I need is more time by myself. But then I think better of it. I'm coming up on the two-week mark to see Vienne in two days and I could really use an excuse not to go to work. So I jump on his offer with zeal.

"Thank you. I could really use a respite."

"Perfect. Well, it's settled then." Calix smiles again, happy with himself for rectifying the situation so easily.

"What is the Satisfaction Room?" I ask, gulping down a few more swigs of the purple drink. I've yet to see this room people mention.

Calix grins broadly. "Ahh, you'll see. Just take a stroll on over there when you've got a few hours to kill."

My eyes start to droop, the adrenaline from a few minutes ago seeping out of my body.

"You're tired," Calix says. "So I'll leave you. And I suppose I won't see you for a few days. Have a good vacation."

If he only knew I'd be taking a true trip.

He starts to walk toward my door, and he's about to leave when I blurt out, "Aaron thought I was going to be the Madam Elected."

I'm not sure all of a sudden why I've said this. I guess I want to see Calix's reaction. I don't know why he's not already paired up—why Aaron doesn't seem to be paired up either. The question niggles at my mind.

Calix stops, one hand on my door to leave, the other resting by his side. His back is to me, but he turns slowly. "An interesting idea, isn't it? Have a good night, Alicen."

14

FOR MY SECOND STINT to see Vienne, I'm well prepared and craving her presence like never before. I have my anti-solar panel, I am rested from a couple of days off work, and I have a backpack loaded up with plenty of water and food. I take two days to walk to the border, which is actually pleasant, and I find myself whistling. I didn't get to see Griffin before I left, but during my walk, I've decided to go straight to his room when I return. I'll apologize, or he'll apologize. It won't matter at that point. I just miss him, and I know he must feel the same.

As I come up on the border sometime after dusk the second evening, I can't help smiling in anticipation. At the crest however, my smile fades, replaced with more of a slight twitch of my cheek. From a few miles away I can see the hill has a line of armor glass snaking across its crest for miles. My countrymen must have been able to manufacture more Nirogene and produce great quantities of the glass in record speed. This means they have more defenses, which is most important, but it also means I won't be able to talk to Vienne. My heart sinks, thinking that she'll have realized this too and won't have come. I'm desperate to see her after hearing her screams over the surveillance feed.

I keep walking forward anyway, intent on reaching the crest to see down into my country at the very least. When I'm just a few hundred yards away, I notice long white robes reflected in the moonlight. Pale hair catches the wind, sending it flying out to the side as if the wisps themselves could defy gravity. I wish I could reach out to Vienne, touch her soft skin, and tell her how sorry I am that she's been in pain. I'm so happy to see her I could let out a whoop. But her back is to me. She doesn't know I'm here yet. Vienne watches our country from up high. I walk up close and look in the same direction.

There are over twenty huge bonfires all blazing in the distance. They look like small lakes of orange dotted across our countryside. I can smell them too. It's a chemical scent, burning plastic and tree sap mixed together. My people are manufacturing armor glass, even now. Albeit a crude method, not using the chemists' ovens, I know they're exhausting the fires to melt Nirogene for production. I glance across the landscape, wondering how they've obtained so much wood to keep these fires going. There's not a tree in sight. Everything's been cut down, even the tree I hid in, listening to Griffin teach the children about animals before my wedding day. I feel ill at the thought that all our greenery has been forested, but I would have done the same thing.

Suddenly Vienne turns, and I'm struck with a different kind of feeling in my stomach.

Nausea.

I stand stock still, unbelieving that the face in front of me could be hers.

Her once perfect features are marred with black lines of clotted blood and manmade stitches covering her neck, chin, cheeks and forehead. She looks like a monster. She's gouged herself in precise inch-long wounds each a meticulous few centimeters away from the next. Vienne has been disgustingly mechanical in her search for the chip.

I bow my head forward so my eyes are downcast and my forehead rests on the glass between us. I have no way of talking to her to tell her how sorry I am and that she should stop. When I look up again, one of her hands is planted on the glass across from me, as if she could reach through and touch my bent head. I know there are tears in my eyes. I can feel their liquid warmth bunching in my lower lids, but I don't wipe anything away. I don't break eye contact with Vienne, but I shake my head back and forth, signifying that she shouldn't go forward with her plans to extract the chip.

Then I think maybe she's already found it. I raise my eyebrows with the question and she catches on immediately. Vienne slowly shakes her head no, shrugging her shoulders as if to say it's okay. She gives a half smile to reassure me, but nothing can make me feel all right after seeing her face. I only wonder now, how far down her incisions go.

I point to her belly, shaking my head no, willing her not to have harmed our baby in the process of her search. Vienne parts her robes and shows me the flawless skin of her bump. At least she hasn't touched that spot. She shimmies further out of her robes to point out all the incisions. They go from her head down to her breasts. Then they start up again at her hips. She's finished looking through three quarters of her body and only has her knees to feet left.

Why in the world did Vienne start with her face? I can hardly look at it with all the marring and crooked scars. I wonder which of the incisions elicited the scream I heard through the monitor back in Mid. A sane person would have at least started somewhere less painful, like the legs. But the face? Why would Vienne feel the need to injure her beautiful face first?

A dull ache wraps itself around my body. She thinks she deserves this. Starting with her face is the most pain Vienne could inflict on herself. She's punishing herself for being the quisling, even though we both know it was an unwitting role. I raise my hand, motioning stop, and point to her legs. She can't keep doing this.

She shakes her head violently in return and I read her lips as she says, "I must."

I look away from her toward the horizon, trying to collect my thoughts. Trying to get the image of her mottled face, her gray skin, out of my eyes.

When I look back, I point to the large expanse of armor glass and give her a thumbs up sign. She smiles in return. We've moved past the microchip onto other topics. I make hand motions for mining Nirogene, trying to ask where they've found more. Vienne points south toward what used to be West Virginia. It's land on the cusp of our country—within our lawful borders but a place few people live.

I nod a couple of times, telling her I get the gist. Then I try to figure out how to tell her the real news. I need to convey Mid's impending air strike. I point to the sky and then spread my hand out wide like blasts raining down on the land. I do this over and over again. Then I put my arms out to my sides like wings, tilting them slightly up and then down. When I look at Vienne her brow is furrowed in concentration. She mouths across the glass to me. "When?"

I shrug my shoulders, indicating that I'm not positive. But I put up three fingers and mouth "Three months?"

Vienne lifts her hand to the glass again and mouths, "We'll be ready."

I nod. Maybe they will be. With all of this armor glass up, at least East Country won't be infiltrated from this spot. Mid will have to fly around the glass, using extra fuel that they might not have factored into their equations. If they do try to fly over the glass, their airrides will be disabled, crashing to the ground with scrambled signals because of Nirogene's wondrous properties. I wonder if Mid will be able to launch bombs from a far distance, sending their destruction careening through the air. I hope the bombs themselves will fly off target because of the armor glasses' capabilities. I make a mental note to study this feature back in Mid.

Vienne breaks my thoughts by pointing to my stomach. She rubs her own in a circle. I look at her bump, which is decidedly bigger than mine even though we should be exactly at the same point in our pregnancies. She puts up four fingers to indicate that we're in our fourth month. I nod. She makes kicking motions with her two hands, smiling widely. I know she's asking whether I feel anything from the baby. I catch the way her eyes light up at the thought.

I don't want to worry her; especially after all she's done to her body over the last two weeks. So I just smile and nod, making the same kicking motions back to Vienne. She doesn't have to know that my baby is as still as a rock. She looks relieved and claps her hands. Then she points two fingers at me and stamps the ground. I know she's saying we'll meet at this spot again in two weeks.

I agree and then wave at her. She puts both hands up to the glass, and I do the same, our palms mirroring each other. Vienne leans forward and kisses the space above our hands. I am again repulsed by the way her skin sticks to her bones across her cheeks and lips, oddly trying to fit back in place after having been ripped apart. Creases web outward from each cut, growing the skin back together. I put the image out of my mind, close my eyes, and kiss the glass back at her. Then we look up at each other once again. Vienne turns, waves one more time, and starts her descent.

I take a moment to sit on the hill, resting after my long walk here. I drink a whole bottle of purple liquid, eat three pieces of dried meat and a hot pink orange, then stand again. I'm tired, but lighthearted knowing East has a better defense than I'd feared. Plus, I'm going back to Mid now, intent on seeing Griffin. I can't wait to tell him about everything East has accomplished in just two weeks.

My two-day walk back to Mid is almost as pleasant as the first leg of my trip. The weather is warm but not so hot that I'm sweating. The sun shines a beautiful yellow color, the way it's supposed to instead of how it sometimes turns red on extremely hot days. My stomach is still knotted from seeing what Vienne's done to herself, but at least I know she can still walk on her own, and her baby seems healthy.

When I arrive back within Mid's city gates, the moon is high, and I know people will be in their beds. I figure it's around nine p.m., but I look at the city's clock projection on a nearby tower just to make sure. I jog back to my apartment, assured that when I enter Tower One this time, no one will look at me strangely. It's like I have keys to the city.

I deposit my backpack in my empty living room, wondering if Griffin missed me over the few days I've been gone. Maybe he'll have found a way into my apartment to leave me a note. But seeing nothing on the living room table or on my neatly made bed, I shake off the disappointment. It would be unnecessarily dangerous for him to have snuck into my apartment. I just need to be brave and go to his door already, even if that means I apologize first.

I change into fresh clothes fast and am out the door again within minutes. The hallways are quiet and empty, and the elevator comes for me almost the instant I press its button. I'm at Griffin's front door just moments later. It's been two weeks since our fight, and I can almost forget what it was about. Almost. Either way, I'm ready to apologize and then fall into his arms, both of us indulging in our perpetual pent-up desire.

I have to knock a few times at Griffin's door before I hear footsteps. When the entrance finally opens, Griffin looks down on me without saying a word.

"Hi!" I say, almost bouncing, I'm so excited to see him. "I've missed you so much!" He doesn't say anything, which I think may be because his apartment still has its surveillance mechanisms intact. I whisper the next sentences. "Vienne is doing fine, and you'll never guess how well East did procuring more Nirogene!"

I'm about to go further, to tell him about the miles of armor glass, but his silence jars me from my monologue. I stare at him. Griffin's face is blank.

"Are you still mad at me?" I ask. "Look, I'm sorry. I didn't mean to kick you out of my apartment. It was a stupid thing to do."

Griffin puts a hand on his doorframe, almost like he's intentionally blocking me from entering. "I'm not mad at you."

"Well, that's good!" I sigh and give him a huge grin. I reach forward to hug him, but the instant I'm close, Griffin jolts back like it'll burn if I touch him. My eyebrows knit together. "What's wrong with you?" I ask, mad now. "I said I was sorry."

"Nothing is wrong with me. I feel great." His voice is robotic and cold.

"Well, then why don't you want me to touch you?" I put my hands on my hips, intent on getting more of a reaction out of Griffin. "Why won't you let me in?" I peer through his bent arm into the living room in back of Griffin. "Is someone here?"

"No one is here. You can come in if you like."

"Fine." I push past him into the small foyer that looks exactly like mine. I listen for a second and know he's telling me the truth. No one else is in his apartment. But that still doesn't explain why he's acting so odd. I sit down at his table and glance over at Griffin as he stands still in the open doorframe.

"You're really not mad at me anymore?"

"No."

I squint my eyes, trying to determine if he's being truthful. When Griffin doesn't blink or screw up his face at me in annoyance, I take him at his word. But his demeanor is completely different from his normal confident nature. At the very least, I thought he'd be interested to know details about my trip to East. Or find out if I'm okay. I start to interrogate him further, to whisper to him about my adventure, and to ask again why he's being strange. But as soon as I open my mouth, I close it again. My jaw feels stuck together as my stomach does a hard flip.

I realize he's not mad.

He's indifferent.

With one hand instinctively clutching my heart, I try a different tactic. "So what have you been up to? How is work?"

All of a sudden his face breaks into a whirlwind of emotion, as if I've just turned on the light in his head.

"Absolutely fantastic!" he says. "You wouldn't believe the cloning they've got going this week. They took a human arm. A real human arm! And they're attempting to create a synthetic one exactly the same."

If I didn't already know something was wrong, I'd be convinced now. Griffin was never a fan of cloning.

"Griffin," I start slowly, the word coming out stilted. I feel like I'm watching myself from overhead, a ghost come back to view scenes unfold, already knowing their outcome. "Did you go to the monthly doctor's checkup?"

He sits down opposite me at the living room table. "Sure did. They made sure I was radiation free." Then he takes a second glance at me. "You know, you look kind of flushed. You should go to the doctors' too."

15

Now that I can finally act like a girl if I want to; sing, cry, laugh in a high pitch, and grow my hair long, it's all lost on me. I'm in a place devoid of emotion. Sure, Mid seems to care a great deal about their technology, but nothing more than that. Griffin has been indifferent for two months now, and every time I see him around the city I want to cry. I don't know what they did to him over at the doctors, but he's not the same. And he's not returning to normal, no matter how much time goes by.

I make a point of venturing into the animal warehouse at least once a day, just so I can look at Griffin and see if there's been a change. But the only difference is how enamored he is about work. He recognizes me. He talks to me. He even laughs. But it's only about cloning. Griffin doesn't reach out to touch me, and after I've tried to hug him three or four times, and he's jumped back at each instance, I've stopped. It's too unbearable. Now when I visit Griffin at his workplace, I just watch from afar, not even bothering to talk to him.

Margareath is the same. When I go see her at the planting fields, she's more than willing to show me her latest crop of orange trees, but she doesn't ask me about East Country at all. It's like she's completely forgotten everything she used to care about. When I ask her what they specifically do to her at the monthly doctor checkups, she just shrugs and says, "Make sure I don't break."

I know I'm over here in Mid for a purpose—a specific mission—but I can't help feeling alone and afraid. Without Griffin to bounce ideas off of and discuss plans, my tactics become muddled in my head. Should I dismantle the bombs in the dead of night? Should I give the engineers the wrong wiring ideas? Should I just make the bombs explode inside their launch building before they can be sent over to East? I can't seem to see my way to the best option.

On top of all that, I still can't find my parents. I've been to almost every building in Mid now, and each place I go, I comb the surveillance rooms looking for them. No one except that first man remembers a woman with curly ear-length hair. Even the first Surveillor denies remembering them now, furtively glancing over his shoulder when I dare ask. Maybe they've left. But I still don't understand why they wouldn't have come to see me first.

The only time I feel slightly less alone is when I'm running to see Vienne at the country's border. I don't have Griffin to cover for me or tell me if anyone has caught on while I'm pretending to be broken from overwork, so I try to make my visits as short as possible. I run through the night, making it to the border in less than a day. Then I run back, not even stopping to sleep. Since Vienne and I can't talk through the glass, we just shrug our shoulders at each other; nod our heads side-to-side for no and up and down for yes. It's a crude method of communication. Unfulfilling. I yearn for more meaningful personal contact.

Surprisingly, the only person in Mid who *is* willing to bestow me any kindness is Calix. He's taken to asking me for a drink in his apartment at least twice a week. We drink old, expensive scotch from his crystal goblets, and I've even started enjoying his company.

"You've got to be kidding me!" I laugh, as he pours me a third glass. I've been in Mid Country for three months, and my tolerance for drinking is still low. I hiccup in between gulps.

"No, really, the guy thought the time projection was magic!"

He's telling me about a new man in Mid who stumbled in from the wilds. All the technology is new to him, and the poor man thinks it's unworldly.

"Cut him a little slack," I howl. "He's probably never seen even half the things you have here."

"True enough!" laughs Calix. "More chocolate?"

He hands me a silver plate piled high with square pieces of dessert. The chocolate melts on the tip of my tongue, and I savor it going down my throat.

I still abhor Calix's reliance on technology and his disregard for my people in East, but I can understand why he's angry at them. He thinks they started a war. I'm starting to appreciate his dry sense of humor, especially when he regales me with tales of his upbringing as the Elected-in-waiting. It's becoming clearer to me that his whole childhood was affected by his family's role in the country, much like mine.

"So tell me again. What did your parents say when you wanted to invite a friend over?" I ask.

Calix spits out a whole mouthful of scotch, splattering the table between us. "Friend, that's rich! They said, 'no one here wants to be friends. Be friends with your brother if you're so interested in playing around'." He mimics a high voice of his mother.

I laugh hard again, the scotch having gone straight to my head. We are both drunk, and I stop to wonder if this is bad for my baby. But no one has ever told me the rules of pregnancy before, so I just keep drinking. I'm not about to tell Calix I can't drink with him because I'm carrying a child.

"You have a nice voice when you talk in that register," I joke. The drink sloshes in my glass as I fling my arm out.

"I'm a regular Shakespeare!" Calix says. He moves his chair a few inches closer to me, and I don't even care. It's nice to have someone trying to get closer to me for a change. "Tralalalala!" Calix sings, going further with his Shakespeare impression. "I can even sing!"

I laugh so hard the scotch runs out my nose and burns. "Ow," I moan. "That feels like fire in my nostrils."

Calix leans forward to look up my nose. "Here," he says, wiping a bit of scotch off my top lip. "It's spilling." I blink when he's so close to my face our eyelashes could touch. This time when our lips touch, it's not just him leaning in. I'm an active participant. When we finally back up, my eyes are wide and Calix's smug smile is more tame than usual. He looks surprised.

I stare down at my drink, watching it swirl in circles as my hand shakes. I can't believe what I've just done. This time when I felt his lips on mine, I enjoyed it.

I glance up at Calix for a split second, almost afraid to catch his gaze when I ask my question. "Why do you like me?"

Calix looks into his drink for a moment too before responding. He gives a little laugh, but it's not like his others. We are still drunk, but our kiss sobered us up enough to talk about more serious matters.

"Because everyone else in this country has their emotions turned off. You're not like them. You're still interested. Passionate."

I nod, still staring into my goblet. It is a viable reason. I may not be his first choice, but I'm the only one left. I guess I kind of knew he'd say that. Everyone in Mid is more like a robot than a person. Calix and I are the only two left who seem real.

"I know you're avoiding the medical checkups," he says quietly. I look up, worried now that he'll make me go. I'm about to object, but he interrupts. "No, no, it's okay. I don't mind that you don't see the doctors. In fact, I prefer it."

This time I meet Calix's eyes. I refuse to leave here tonight without some answers on that subject.

"Calix, what do the doctors do to people? And don't tell me nothing, because I know they do something so people forget they ever wanted personal interaction."

Calix nods. "It wasn't my idea. It was Aaron's. He came up with it when he was only twelve years old. A prodigy. That's what my parents called him."

I listen closely; finally ready to hear what Mid has been doing to its people.

Calix sighs. "Aaron called it optogenetics. He read something about it from the past and took it to a new level. Apparently it was being tested at the turn of the century, but it was abandoned because people thought the practice of mind control was immoral."

"And Aaron didn't," I say, hitting the table harder than necessary with my crystal glass.

"Not at all. In fact, he said it was the *moral* thing to do to save our country."

"What is it exactly?" I ask.

"I don't understand all of it, but the idea started in the nineteen seventies when some guy named Crick suggested that neuroscientists could control brain cells. Imagine being able to turn the neurons in a human's brain on and off from the outside."

"You make people do what you want."

"Sort of, but it's more complicated than that. Optogenetics involves inserting fiberoptic tools into the brain in order to control the target neurons using pulses of light as a trigger."

"Light?"

Calix looks sheepish. "Like the light we project on the sides of all our buildings to tell everyone the time."

I gasp. "You're controlling people with the light from the clocks?"

"Learning to shine light on a neuron isn't the whole answer. In order for the method to work, the neurons have to be re-engineered so they'll react to the light. That was made possible by inserting a protein that can be used to turn neurons on and off in response to light. We do that part at the monthly checkups when people think they're being cured of radiation poisoning. And we double the protein through our drinking water. Put it all together, and you have genetically engineered neurons that you can turn on and off at will, inside the brain of a living and freely moving person."

"You're making your people over into robots." My voice is low. I can hardly believe what I'm hearing, and my heart feels like it'll break in half. Griffin might never recover from this.

"It's not as bad as you make it sound. We really are curing people of the radiation by making their neurons reject ultraviolet material. Their cells won't grow cancer because we've figured out a way to tell them not to."

"It's grossly genius," I say, my head falling into one hand.

"Exactly. So genius that my parents decided everyone in Mid should get the treatment. They started it to rid everyone of radiation, but then once the attacks came from East, we needed people to concentrate fully on technology production. So Aaron and my parents used optogenetics to amp up that side of everyone's personality. Make them want to work extra hard on research and science."

"I don't understand."

"It's like they've made everyone really smart at science and math and really bad at social interaction. Love was a distraction so they extracted it from everyone's sense of need."

"So people could focus on building up your offenses to strike at East?"

"Yes. See, optogenetics isn't so terrible when you realize it's the one thing that'll save Mid."

I look down at my hands. That is the ultimate piece of this entire puzzle. Mid wants to save its people just like I want to save my country. I can almost understand how far they've gone to achieve the goal.

"There has got to be some side effects, though, right?" I ask.

"Of course. Our population is declining significantly. People don't want to be intimate with each other, so fewer children are born. But we have to deal with the most dire problem first. We'll take out East Country, and then we'll figure out how to increase the population again."

"But what if you can't?" I say. "What if people can't go back to normal? What if no one cares about love or personal relationships anymore? What if you've messed with their minds so much, they're altered forever?"

Calix shrugs, looking down into his drink again. "That's the risk we have to take."

I want to tell Calix right this second that I'm East's Elected and that he has to stop hurting his people. We haven't done anything to him. We need to band together to stop whoever else is the aggressor. But I can't risk endangering my position here. Not before I've figured out a way to disable Mid's nuclear capabilities.

"So now you think I am a cruel leader, don't you?" he asks, one blonde eyebrow raised.

"No," I say, licking my lips. "I can understand why you do what you do."

"Good." Calix leans toward me again, kissing me for longer than earlier. His breath tastes like liquor and chocolate, and I don't automatically hate it. He pulls back and looks at me without blinking. "Because if you and I are attached, you will never have to see the doctors. Just remember that."

It's a threat. And it's one I won't forget for as long as I'm here. If Calix wants someone to show attachment, I can play the best Shakespearean actor he's ever seen.

16

"I CAN'T BELIEVE YOU haven't tried it yet," says Mac, thumping me on the back so hard it hurts.

I rub my shoulder and shake my head in his direction. "Why won't you just tell me what it is?"

Mac and I are working side by side in the rocket launch pad, screwing in a few bolts. He's especially jovial today because of all the progress he thinks we're making with the weaponry. Little does he know that for every bolt he attaches, I come by later and detach two more. But he is yet to notice the degradation. Every day I damage their plans little by little, giving the engineers wrong information or leaving out the most important parts so there are gaping holes in their knowledge. I'm surprised people in Mid know so little about past technology and are so wholly at my mercy on the topic.

"Because ya' have to experience it for yourself!" says Mac. "You've earned it. For every hundred hours people work, they're allowed to spend one hour in the Satisfaction Room. For all the hours you've put in, ya' could spend all day there!"

"Maybe I'd go if someone would just tell me what's inside the room already!" I'm sweating while lifting a piece of the rocket propulsion system. Mac just laughs and grunts as he gives me a hand with the other side. "Fine. Don't tell me. I don't care," I say.

"Ya' probably noticed people here ain't married, right?"

At this I stop, setting down my side of a metal socket and squatting on the ground. "Sure, it's a lot different here than in West." I'm careful to maintain my cover.

"Just 'cause we don't want the nuisance of relationships here, don't mean we don't crave a little physicality from time to time. You know what I mean? Get it out of our system so our bodies can get back to work without any distraction." Mac bursts out into huge guffaws, his whole stomach wobbling.

I have no idea what he means. All I know is that whenever I've tried to touch anyone besides Calix, the person jumps back like they've been scalded. "No one wants personal contact here."

Mac raises an eyebrow at me from over his piece of rocket wing. "Did I say anything about *person*-al?"

"I don't underst . . ."

Mac cuts me off, laughing again with his back toward me. He carries a chunk of metal out of the room. "Just go try it already! Ya' won't be disappointed!"

I balance in my crouched position, letting my ankles and calves rest for a moment before standing again. I stretch my arms behind me so my shoulder blades almost touch. In this position I can feel a small bump forming on my stomach, but even at six months, I'm still hardly showing my pregnancy. The dress-like robes cover whatever I do have in that area. But my legs and feet hurt like never before, and I can't help noticing small blue lines snaking up my calves when I undress by myself at night.

So far I've been successful keeping Calix at a respectful distance. He seems satisfied with kisses and my undivided attention over dinner multiple times a week. He doesn't reach for me or try to lead me into a bedroom, and for that I'm grateful.

But I do feel lonely. Even though I've denied it a few times, I'm starting to wonder what actually goes on in the Satisfaction Room that involves some kind of touching but no people. So at the end of the workday when the clocks' projections all read six p.m. and everyone begins closing down their workstations, I leave the rocket launcher with a certain determination.

I eat dinner in my apartment alone, knowing that tonight Calix is planning to visit his brother. I change into a fresh set of robes and then start the short walk to building sixteen where the infamous Satisfaction Room is housed. When I'm just a few buildings away, I see a long line twisting from sixteen's front door around the side of the building. There must be two hundred people all waiting for whatever is inside. I contemplate turning around, wondering how they'll possibly get through the line before people have to be at work in another twelve hours. But a shout stops me in my tracks.

"Alicen!" It's the registrar from months ago when Griffin and I first arrived in Mid. This time he isn't looking down his nose at me. In fact, he's standing by the Satisfaction Room's front door, beckoning me over with large waves of his hand.

I step through the crowd, which passively parts for me.

"So you've come at last," he says.

I turn to my left to look at the people around me. They don't seem interested in our conversation. They just stare ahead, slightly swaying on their feet from standing in line so long.

"Sorry," I say. "I didn't know it was a requirement." Sarcasm, learned from Calix, drips off my tongue easily.

The registrar chuckles. "It's not, but we keep tallies of who's been in."

I scrunch my brow. "I'm sure you do."

"The Elected asked me to specifically watch for you. Wanted to know when you'd been here."

I almost slink off then and there. I hate being scrutinized like this. But another part of me wants to see what's inside and why Calix wants to know when I tried it.

I snort. "Well, you can tell him I've come tonight. I'll just take my place in the line, if you'll excuse me."

"No, no. You don't have to wait in line. Come in." He opens the front door and gestures grandly with one arm extended.

I look again at the people who I'm supposed to be passing in line. No one seems bothered that they've waited for two hours and I am about to sidestep them all. I follow the register through the glass doors and into the almost black interior of building sixteen. My eyes have trouble adjusting to the lack of light. All I see are red lights on the floor leading us down a corridor.

"Just through here," says the registrar. "Since this is your first time, I'll go inside with you and explain the process."

I shiver, but he can't see my nervousness in the darkness. I follow the registrar obediently, passing by a few rooms. I hear nothing coming from within and ask if anyone else is here.

"We have five other rooms all going at once. Soundproof walls. You won't have to worry about a thing. Complete privacy."

I almost snort out loud again. Privacy. Yeah, right. The surveillance team is probably jotting down everything that happens in these rooms.

"What kind of place is this?" I finally ask when we're standing outside of a shut door at the very end of the hallway.

The registrar doesn't laugh this time or tell me it's a stupid question. "Beyond that door you'll be able to choose whatever physical satisfaction your body requires. Anything you need to get your physical needs out of the way in a timely manner without any messy talking or emotional attachment. So you can get back to work feeling refreshed." My eyes open wider, but the registrar doesn't notice. "You can have any pleasure from your wildest imagination." He opens the door, and the room is a stark contrast to the dark corridor. It's a gleaming white box with nothing inside except a large monitor and a touchscreen. "Here we are," says the registrar, guiding me toward the equipment.

I look at the blank screen, trying to discern how it's supposed to work when the register reaches down, flips a switch, and the monitor revs to life. The screen beams out a yellow background with the word SATISFACTION across its face in black.

The registrar types in his code and the one-word image is replaced with a series of questions. "Just read these and fill out your answers by touching the keys you see on the screen. You can write in answers or if you can't think of something you'd like, just use the drop down boxes for ideas."

I stare at the screen and look back up at the registrar.

He smiles at me indulgently. "Take as long as you like. First-timers are allowed an extra hour." He starts to walk out, and all of a sudden I'm nervous to be left alone in the eerie white room.

"Wait!" I call. "What if I don't want to choose anything?"

The registrar laughs, but it's not condescending, just assured. "Oh, you will."

Then he turns on his heel and the door clicks shut behind him. I am alone. I run to the room's entrance to see if the door locked me in. It opens easily, though, and I breathe a sigh that I'm not a prisoner here. I slowly walk back to the glowing screen and look down at the first question.

Do you like men or women or both?

I cough out loud, embarrassed already by the first line. Uneasily, I put my fingertip out to choose an answer and then stop. It's funny how just a year ago I wouldn't have known how to answer this question. Now as I place my finger on "men", I'm surprised how easy it is to respond. I still don't understand what will exactly transpire in the Satisfaction Room or how it'll be accomplished without another human being, but I keep proceeding through the process.

How would you like to be touched?

I have no idea how to answer this question. I don't even know what would be sufficient. One word? A whole paragraph of explanation? It's such a convoluted question for me, I almost laugh out loud. If I write "I'd like a hug from my mom," I wonder what would happen. Instead I punch the key for the drop down box and turn a deep shade of red as I'm allowed to check as many of the options as I want. The options range from things like, *'Tickle my feet.'* to *'Tie me up and spank me.'* I punch in four of the answers and then press enter.

Describe your ideal romantic atmosphere.

For this question I decide not to pick from a drop down list but write in the answer myself. A forest completely surrounded by trees. An open space within the pine trees with soft needles under our feet. A warm evening, but not humid, with a crescent moon in the sky for light.

I press enter and am rewarded when the room around me is transformed into the very images I just described. The walls become vibrant green pictures of a forest. Sounds of birds chirping and owls hooting quietly leak from hidden speakers. The scents of pine and cedar hit my nose. The only things they haven't been able to create are the pine needles. But fake plastic grass shoots up from the floor in front of me as if it's been growing there the whole time. I look down at the screen again.

What color hair would you like your suitor to have?

I choose "dark brown" from the drop down box.

Hair type?

I look at the suggestions and click "straight".

Eye color?

I type in "brown the color of maple syrup."

Body build type?

At this, I feel a chill run down my spine, but I keep staring at the screen to type in "Tall. Lanky. Wiry muscles. Strong enough to wrestle a wolf and win." I smile at my last written words, remembering the lone wolf we had in East Country's animal sanctuary.

After a dozen more questions, some of which send my knees shaking, the screen returns to a yellow background. It now reads, *"Please wait while your robot is created."*

I twirl a piece of my hair with two fingers, squeezing my lips together. So this is it then. They can make robots look exactly how we want, and the robots will please us exactly how we wish. I bite off all of the nails on my left hand as I wait.

Finally, an almost invisible door opens in the far right corner of the room. My robot glides forward, long legs, dark brown unruly hair, and a crooked smile.

"Pleased to meet you, Alicen. You look lovely tonight."

I bow my head, surprise and a touch of shame causing my cheeks to tingle. Without knowing it, I've made my robot look almost exactly like Griffin.

The automaton walks closer and immediately puts a hand on my shoulder. Its touch is surprisingly warm. It's skin realistically smooth and flesh-like. He runs a fingertip across my cheek and then bends down and kisses me softly on the lips. I don't move a muscle, but the robot kisses me more deeply. It feels so real I squeeze my eyes together. If I just forget where I am and that it's a robot, I can almost make myself think I'm back in East Country with Griffin.

The robot slowly pulls at the laces of my robes and one of my shoulders comes uncovered. He starts kissing me there and then easing lower so that my collarbone and chest are exposed to his lips. I breathe deeply, the air catching in my throat, a mixture of embarrassment and lust. I want this so badly I can hardly admit it to myself. In this enclosed room with this robot who will never tell my deepest desires, I let my inhibitions go. I kiss him back, feeling his tongue brush mine. He wraps an arm around me and gently lays me on the grassy floor. I see the fake moon projected on the ceiling in back of his head as the robot continues whispering in my ear. He tells me how beautiful I am, how much he wants me, and what he will do with me. I can feel the blush creeping from my face down to all parts of my body, the heat spreading like syrup.

When the robot is completely on top of me, having divested me fully of my robes, I can't help whispering back to it. My voice comes out in a soft moan. "Oh, Griffin."

As soon as I say the words, my eyes fly open. I stare at the stars above us and realize what I've just said. I want Griffin. The real Griffin. Not this haphazard machine that's trying to take the place of the person I love. I push on the robot's chest softly, then harder so that it moves off me.

"Would you like something else, Alicen?" it asks, a sweet, coaxing smile unwavering on its face.

I stumble up, trying to grab at my discarded robes. "No . . . I . . . I can't . . ."

"Yes, it's okay, my love. You can do this." The robot soothes me, reaching a hand out to touch mine.

I almost falter at its enticing voice, but then I back up, putting more space between us. "No, I can't. You aren't my love. My love is out there." I point toward the door. "I can't let something fake replace who I care about."

I pull the cords of my robes together and walk toward the door in long, quick strides. I glance back just once and see the robot standing in the middle of the room, still smiling easily, like it doesn't matter if I stay or go. I know I'm right. This isn't real, and I'll only be satisfied with the real thing.

I fling open the door, which hits the side wall with a thud. I'm determined to see my Griffin, the one made of flesh and blood. This time when I find him, I vow not to leave his apartment until he remembers exactly what I mean to him.

I step out into the black hall again and practically sprint down the long expanse. "Registrar!" I call out when I'm near the front doors. But no one responds. The lobby's empty. I pull back the front doors of building sixteen, expecting to the see the same complacent citizens still standing in line, waiting their turns for indulgence. But what I see instead causes me to stop in my tracks.

In front of me is complete chaos. There's smoke wafting from a dozen spots across Mid Country. People are running in all different directions. I try to stop a couple of townspeople as they sprint by, but they're too crazed to stay still. They pull out of my grasp and keep running. I push my way through the crowd, intent on getting to Griffin. I'm like a salmon battling against the current. People bump me, not even looking me in the eyes as their shoulders crash into mine. But I fight through. I hope to find Griffin in Tower One but before I can get to the front doors I see that a section of the skyscraper has been crippled. A whole chunk of the top is missing and people are piling out of the tower into the streets, completely unorganized and frantic. I look wildly around, hoping that I'll see Griffin among the throngs, but already knowing that it would be like finding a needle in a haystack. I'm barely tall enough to see over anyone's head, let alone find a specific person.

But I do see Calix barking orders to a mix of military-looking robots and two dozen armed guards. "Assemble Airrides One to Five!"

I push harder through the crowd, knowing that I can at least get answers from him. When I'm yards away from him, I yell to get his attention. "Calix!"

His head spins, and at once his eyes lock onto mine. There's a fire there, sparking behind his heavy lashes. I know something big is happening. But the moment his eyes find mine, I can tell he's relieved to see me. He immediately parts through his circle of guards to grasp me through the crowd. People make way for him and before I realize it, I'm swallowed up within his powerful group. I look around at the circle of guards and then back at Calix.

"What's happening?"

"We've been attacked by East's bombs again. Worse than ever before."

"What did they hit?" I try to conceal my fear as I look up at Tower One again; counting the floors to make sure Griffin's wasn't one of the ones splintered into bits.

"Our nuclear building again!" Calix is yelling over the crush of the crowd's voices.

"Did they take out all our offenses?" I cross my fingers behind my back that all of Mid's weaponry is vanquished.

"The uranium deposits were taken first, but they continued bombing multiple buildings. Don't worry, we still have enough non-nuclear firepower to wipe East to the ground. We just have to get it back up and running. We will attack as soon as we can."

My eyes open wider and I swallow sharply, already feeling bile back up into my throat.

"We'll strike as soon as possible!" Calix continues. "You'd better take cover in one of the bomb shelters. Try Tower Two. It hasn't been hit." Then he grasps my shoulder, giving it a hard pat, trying to send me on my way. But this time I don't follow his wishes. I stay still, my feet rooted to the ground.

"I don't think that's a good idea!" I cry over the squall of voices.

Calix shakes his head like he didn't hear me right. When I don't move he says, "What? Of course we'll strike back. Tonight if we can muster it!"

I bite my bottom lip. "Shouldn't we try to negotiate or find out exactly who's ordering the bombings?"

He looks at me like I'm crazy. I know Calix still won't believe that East isn't involved, so I try another tactic, something speaking more to his military prowess. "I mean, what if all of East isn't involved? Don't you want to launch a precise campaign?"

"The time for precision is over, Alicen. I repeat, get to cover! Now!"

I look at him one last time. His whole body seems to vibrate with aggression. He won't back down. In my heart I know no matter what I say, he won't stop. Even if I tell him exactly who I am, he'll keep gathering his forces for an attack. He needs someone to blame for the smoke filling Mid's air. With one more look toward Tower One I come to another conclusion. I won't stop either. I turn to leave him, but I don't head toward the bomb shelters.

Instead I start running, faster than I think I've ever run before. It's not time for my regularly scheduled meeting with Vienne, but I need to warn East Country. They don't have months to evacuate like we thought. They have maybe just a couple of nights, if that. I don't bother finding an anti-solar panel or even water for my trip. I know the run will cost me, but I have no other choice. If this is the last thing I do for my country, at least I have to do it in time to make a difference.

So I run like my heels are burning with fire. Strange thoughts pour through my mind as I go. I remember Tomlin telling me about ancient civilizations. One of their gods, Mercury, had wings on his feet so he could deliver messages faster. I feel like my feet have these same wings, practically flying over the barren landscape. Even with their belief in these amazing gods, the superpower Roman Empire wasn't immune to warfare. It kept on warring until the conquered people they kept within their walls struck back. Will we ever learn? Are human beings destined to keep fighting each other, replaying the same cycle over and over just under different circumstances in different times?

I wonder how long it'll take Mid to recover from the attack and start launching airrides. I imagine Mac frantically gathering equipment for the deluge, if he made it safely out of the bombings. I don't know who was hurt in Mid. My mind crystallizes on Griffin's face, willing him to have been one of the lucky ones. But I push that thought from my head, no matter how hard it is to do, concentrating not on what I left behind me but on what is ahead.

I feel like my lungs and legs are about to give out as I finally reach the border hill. I haven't slept. I've just kept pushing forward, sometimes running but more often walking as fast as I can bear it. Now, I have to go another ten miles out of my way to get around the armor glass. Five around the left and five back toward the middle again. No one is waiting for me on the hill's crest like previous times. I pick up my robe and begin a half-run half-tumble down the hill. The terrain is filled with holes, and I think I'll twist my ankle in the process, but I keep moving just as fast, holding the train of my robes with one hand and keeping another arm under my aching stomach. At six months pregnant, I have an awkward bump that doesn't like the constant impact of my feet on the ground. I inwardly pray that my baby holds on. *I still can't feel you, baby*, I think to myself. *But just give me a little more time. I promise I won't be so harsh on you after this.*

As if the baby can actually hear my thoughts, I instantly feel a sharp spasm inside the sensitive innards of my belly. I almost stop my frantic pace forward, so surprised at the kick. *Hello there! Hold on!*

At the bottom of the hill I run toward the first person I see.

"Guard!" I yell. The lone man turns toward my voice in the dark, raising a long stick high in the air.

"Stop there!" he shouts.

"It's your Elected!" I keep running forward, unafraid of his club.

He peers at me as I approach. "You are not! Our Elected is a man." He sees me clutching my stomach, the robe pulled snuggly against my protruding bump. "And you're pregnant!"

"Yes, but it's me, Aloy."

The man steps forward when I say my given name, leaning in to look at my face more closely. Behind my now ear length hair and the long flowing robes, he seems to recognize me. He jumps back as if I have just hit him with lightning. His eyes are wide, confusion and shock thrown like splattered paint across his features. I'm about to tell him more, but a stabbing jolt rips my stomach from within. I instantly fall to my knees. The man doesn't know what to do. He looks down at me as I grip the ground on all fours.

"It can't be. The accords say a woman can't be . . . "

"I don't care what the accords say!" I yell. "I am your Elected!"

He stumbles over his words. "Shall I get you some help?"

"Yes. I need to see Vienne and Tomlin now! Run please." I choke on my last words, feeling my stomach squeeze again.

He nods and wastes no more words on the fact that I'm a woman.

It takes the guard over an hour to return with people, but when I finally see a horse galloping toward me from the horizon, my body is relieved. I've been sitting on the ground, holding my stomach and gently rocking myself back and forth. I should have thought to ask for food and water.

Even though I'm still in pain, I stand at the sight of the horse in the distance. It's only one horse, but maybe Tomlin is busy and can't come with Vienne. It doesn't matter. As long as I get to tell one of them, they can begin preparations to save our people from Mid's impending attack.

But as the horse gets closer, I see it's not Vienne riding the stallion. It's not even Tomlin.

It's Grobe.

"I asked to see Vienne," I say as Grobe jumps down from the animal's back.

"Ah, but you get me!" His eyes are dark with unveiled hatred. "Well, well, look at you. So this is why you left the country." His eyes stop on my stomach. "The guard told me, but I could barely believe it."

"We don't have time for this. Where's Vienne?" My voice cracks as I try to get out the words fast.

Grobe leans on the horse's side, taking his time with the conversation. "You look like you need some water. Lucky for you I happen to have some." He reaches into one of the horse's bags and pulls out a flask.

I reach for it fast, my body reacting at the sight of the liquid. I almost ask him if he has food too, but I refrain, focusing instead on the task at hand.

"Now that your gender is revealed, you can't think your baby will be the next Elected. Or Vienne's for that matter. Who got her pregnant?" Grobe laughs, elation covering his features. When I don't answer he continues, "The people will demand an election. Your family's line is finished!"

I swallow another gulp of water and look back up at Grobe. "None of that matters now. Mid is coming to attack East sooner than I thought. They were bombed tonight and they're going to retaliate in the next day or two."

Grobe's face falls for the first time, the lines around his forehead growing deeper at the same time. "Are you sure? But I thought we had . . . Vienne said . . . "

I cut him off. "Months. I know. But we don't. Vienne will have to evacuate everyone tonight. Where is she?" I can't help looking out into the darkness ahead, imagining she'll come riding up just a few minutes after Grobe.

"I've taken over the country. She's in my custody as a traitor."

If I wasn't already completely exhausted and didn't need Grobe to warn our people, I would hit him across the face. A traitor?

"You can't possibly be serious," I say, my voice going stiff like brittle paper about to tear.

"She's a figurehead. While you've been gone, I've been the one spurring our people to make armor glass as fast as possible. I am the true leader." Then he looks at my stomach. "Even if you return now, the country won't mobilize behind you. A woman!" He scoffs, his voice catching on the last two words as if they're poison on his tongue. He shakes his head like he knew all along I wasn't fit for the Elected role and he's finally been proven right.

"And Tomlin okay'd you imprisoning Vienne and stealing the Elected role?" I ask, knowing that couldn't possibly be true.

"Your precious tutor is sick." The way he says it, I think a smile will erupt across his gray face again.

"Sick with what?" I bark my question, attempting to mask the feeling of fear making all the hairs on my arms stand straight.

"What do you think he's sick with? The same thing everyone here contracts without those precious little pills."

Cancer. I know it even before he insinuates which disease. I find I can't even look at Grobe. I hate him for telling me like this. For not even acting sorry that Tomlin is sick. For not bringing Vienne to me like I originally asked.

"Where do you have Vienne? Is she alright?"

"She's locked up, but she's fine."

"I swear, if you touch a hair on her head or harm her baby in any way, I will personally execute you. Forget the honor of drinking hemlock yourself. I will rip your heart out and let you choke on your own blood as you're forced to swallow it whole."

Grobe sneers. "I have nothing to fear from you." Then he raises a hand, waving it casually in the air. "But Vienne is of no consequence. I am leader now and everyone follows me. Nothing will derail that. I won't harm her if she behaves."

I try to imagine Vienne "behaving", sitting casually by while Grobe takes over the country. She won't behave, but hopefully she has the wherewithal to act out in concealed ways.

"You may not have to fear me, but you should fear Mid. They're sending in bombs anytime now. Evacuate my people, Grobe." Then I stop, looking back up at him. "Your people. Evacuate them or in a few days you won't have anyone left to follow you."

This seems to faze him appropriately. "They're really coming with bombs? They have the capacity?"

"You have no idea. They won't just be arriving with one airride to steal Nirogene this time or blast a bit of our mines. They're coming to destroy East. For vengeance."

Grobe thinks about this for a moment, as if contemplating this is all a ruse by me to get the East's Elected role back. "Fine," he finally says. "I'll get our people out of the epicenter. And what will you do? I don't want you coming back into East now."

I squint my eyes at him. "I'm not coming into the country. I'm going back to Mid. I'll see if there's anything else I can do to calm down their Elected." I can't help picturing what exactly I'll have to do and how I'll be able to make Calix listen to me. I shudder, thinking there may still be something from me he wants that will make him lie still.

Grobe nods and gets back onto his horse. My horse. I feel vomit brimming in my throat as I see him ride off with *my* Elected title on *my* father's stallion.

My walk/run back to Mid is excruciating. Shin splints slice through my legs, and I wonder if my leg bones are actually breaking under the strain of running all this way. My stomach squeezes in on itself over and over again. I alternate between being so sick that I vomit in dry heaves and being so hungry that I even eat a tuft of grass along my path.

I try to go without sleeping again, but by the end of the second day of running and then at times practically crawling back to Mid, my body falls beside a large rock, exhausted. I sleep soundly, not even caring that my head rests in an awkward position against the inflexible rock. It's not until I hear the sky above me roar that I open my eyes and come back to the land of the living. I think maybe I'm in the middle of a thunderstorm; the ground even reverberates with the sound. I wait for a crack of lightning to follow the thunder. If I get hit with an acid rain storm now, I'm sunk. This rock won't provide enough cover to save me from the horrible droplets. But instead of lightning or even a gush of rain hitting me in the face, I'm hit with a familiar, sickening smell: tailpipe fumes.

As soon as I identify the oily mechanical stench, I see an airride zoom by. Instinctively, I crouch closer to the rock, cowering under the ear-blasting roar. When the airride flies by without slowing down, I stand up, staring into the distance toward Mid. What I see hits my stomach like a punch.

A murderous line of eight airrides flies so close together their wings almost touch. They fly with precision, an awe inspiring, frightful line of death, moving steadily closer to my country.

I run. I don't have the luxury of waiting another moment, of even thinking how I will seduce Calix to distract him from murdering my people. The attack on East has already started.

I'm close to Mid now, but I think I'll still be able to hear the bangs of bombs going off over East. I'm screaming as I run, almost falling over my legs trying to get inside the city gates as fast as I can.

I hear the blasts one after another as I get to Mid's gate. I'm in a frenzy now, looking wildly for Calix. I will throw myself at his feet to plead for my country. Tears stream down my face, and I don't care who sees me. I must look like a wild animal, my sweaty hair set against my face like a wet blanket. But no one stops me. In fact, there's no one around the gates of Mid Country. No robots slowly buzzing by. No people milling about, doing their work obsessively. Instead I see a huge crowd in the distance, surrounding the front of the half-destroyed Tower One. The building has a chunk missing and is still black and smoky from the assault three days ago.

I run toward the group, screaming Calix's name, not even caring about using his given name instead of his Elected title. Maybe it will make him look toward me faster. When I get to the front of the tower, it hits me that this is the middle of the work day for Mid. Why isn't everyone inside the buildings, putting together more bombs or even cleaning up from the assault? There are still obvious pieces of concrete and broken structures for people to fix. But in front of me is what seems to be the entirety of Mid. There are maybe forty thousand people all standing around the tower in a semicircle. People crane their heads to see over the citizens in front of them. Some even climb on top of each other's shoulders, oddly touching each other without wincing.

I have to see what they're looking at, and I'm sure Calix will be here. I scream his name over and over again, and like magic, the crowd parts for me. Slowly, like sand dripping out of someone's barely spread hand, the people move back, making a ragged line for me to move through.

I spot Calix before I can even see what everyone stares at. He's on a crudely constructed stage, pointing toward the front doors of Tower One. His brows are knitted together. He looks so angry I can picture thunder ripping through his eyebrows and lightning piercing us from his eyes. I look to his right, following the line of his arm as he points.

A row of ten guards are lined up, holding menacing looking guns. The firearms are long and straight, not like the semi-automatic weapons I've seen the robots carrying recently. I know these guns are called rifles.

Then, like my head is on a spike and someone turns it for me, my eyes move toward the left, this time following the pointed guns toward their target. I know someone is going to be killed even before I see the perpetrator. My tongue goes slack in my mouth, becoming big and spongy. I can no longer call out Calix's name.

"The sentence is death by firing squad!" Calix yells. "The crime is espionage for East Country!"

Please Heavens, don't let it be Griffin. I have a terrible feeling in the pit of my stomach that it will be him. They will bring out the perpetrator, and I will see Griffin's brown, messy hair falling forward into his face. And I'll die. Right here in the middle of the crowd that's parted like water for me.

" . . . hiding in barren land between Mid and East!" Calix's voice rings out clear, bursting through my thoughts.

As my head swivels all the way to the left and the front doors of Tower One open, I see not one but two perpetrators being led out with their hands tied behind their backs. They're quickly pushed up against the metal backdrop of the tower's outer walls, and the guards holding them move aside, leaving the two people by themselves.

I feel the scream starting in my stomach before it even reaches my lips.

"Mother! Father!" I rush forward, wild, intent on saving them. I'm ready to tell Mid's Elected everything so that he will take me instead of my parents. At the sound of my voice, my parents turn, startled. They see me, but their eyes don't register the same crazed fear that mine do. My parents' eyes are resigned. They just look at me and raise their elbows up in the air, as if they are giving me a hug. It is our customary goodbye gesture in East Country.

"Stop!" I yell, the spittle from my own words erupting out of my mouth onto my own outstretched arms.

But I'm too late. Even though the crowd turns to stare at me, to see who has called out at this most inopportune of times, the guards don't lower their weapons.

I can't get to the tower wall fast enough, but I can feel myself running anyway. My legs are limp, and I swim forward like I'm encased in a suffocating fog. The whole world stops still as I hear Calix give his order, and I realize I'm about to lose my parents again. This time permanently.

"FIRE!"

The blasts of each gun go off in my right ear, and even though I know the weapons weren't aimed at me, it's like an airride has just barreled through me. I see both of my parents' bodies drop like ragdolls, and then I'm falling to the ground too. The last thing I think is that I never got a chance to thank them for helping me maintain cover in Mid. I never got to tell them that I came here to bring them back home.

I can feel my knees hit the hard ground in front of me. Then my hands. My whole body falls forward, my face smashing against the dirt as the shock of seeing my parents die is too overwhelming to comprehend.

Then there is just black.

17

I CAN FEEL MYSELF transition between lucidity and sleep. There are flashes of pain and then nothingness again. I grip the edges of a flat table, my knuckles surely turning white as I hold on with all my strength. I'm lying on some sort of metal slab, but I can't seem to open my eyes to see exactly where. I keep trying to come out of the fog, but feel like I'm being held underwater. My thoughts are like pudding. I think I see my parents ahead of me, facing Tower One, their hands not cuffed but held softly by their sides. I try to run at them, to warn them about the firing squad, but as soon as I reach them, they turn and it's not them. Part of me knows it's a dream, yet each time I find myself back in the same spot, standing in front of the shadowy tower, I try to reach my parents again. Every time they turn and it is a strangers' face on their bodies, the whole scene evaporates like steam. I'm constantly frustrated, crying out, trying to grasp at them over and over.

Then one time when I wake up, I hear people in the room around me. Their voices are rough and cloudy. I can hardly make out what they say except for fragments.

" . . . her . . . sedated already, dammit!"

In that moment, I feel an intense ripping through my torso. This time I can place my own voice as it screams out. I can almost hear the tearing of my flesh as the searing pain propels through my stomach down my legs and up through my fingertips. Every part of me vibrates with the sensation of my insides being gutted. I screech again, a high animal noise that I wouldn't even recognize as my own if I couldn't feel my mouth moving.

Then I hear another high-pitched cry, but it's not my own. It's a yelp, small and plaintive. I instinctively stop screaming even though the pain still ripples through me. I listen with every fiber of my being, trying to focus my attention on the small cry. But it stops as soon as it started, and I hear scurrying close to my head again.

"Get him in here! The baby's lungs are collapsing!"

I feel faint again, a chill encasing me. My cheeks go numb, and I can't help shaking. Then I'm out again.

The next time I wake up, I grip the table again, this time finding that my hands move with more ease. But when I try to pick up my arms, they don't budge. Either they're not working or I'm tied down. I can't open my eyes to see, or maybe I don't even have eyes anymore. I don't know, and the thought of never being able to see again scares me. I try to say something, but the words feel thick in my throat.

"Ba..by?" I croak.

This small word takes all of my effort, and when no one answers me, I black out again, my head falling heavily against the metal slab.

Finally, when I wake, my eyes open automatically and I'm relieved at the fact I can see but at the same time startled at the sight before me. Men and women in white coats stand all around, looking at screens in their hands, punching buttons, and flipping switches. No one seems to notice I'm awake.

"Hello?" I ask, my throat less parched than before but still prickly like I've eaten thorns.

No one answers me, and just one woman glances up. She registers that I'm awake, makes some more notes on a tablet, fumbles with some straps around me and turns away.

"Hey," I say. It's a feeble call for attention, but it's all I can manage.

The woman doesn't turn to me again, but she angles toward another man. "He'll want to know she's awake."

The man nods wordlessly and exits the room, presumably to tell someone I'm alive. I strain on the table, trying to sit up or even to move my arms.

"Where's my baby?" I ask.

This brings a small response. Another man in a white coat looks me up and down, pursing his lips. "Wish he'd have let me manage her brain cells," he says absently, talking to no one in particular. "Told him it would be dangerous to let her remember the baby."

I squirm on the table again, trying valiantly to move within the somewhat stretchy rubber bands tying me down.

Then the man clucks his tongue, looks toward me one more time and says, "Nurse, the drug please." A woman hands him a long needle with liquid squirting out the top.

I scream again. I won't go willingly into the ether of Mid's sickening mind-meld. "Griffin! Griffin! Help!" I shout his name even though most of me already knows it's useless. There's no one left in this country who cares about me or who at least remembers they care about me. The doctor injects his needle into a tube hanging nearby, and I helplessly watch the small bubbles snake their way toward my arm. The icy coldness of the liquid pinches and then floods my vein in one rapid pulse. I'm asleep again in a matter of minutes.

I don't know how long I'm out again, but when I wake the room feels different. The lights are dim above me, and the area is silent. I can still feel restraints holding me down, but they're only on my wrists, not across my whole body. The wires and machines, which pulsed near my head earlier, are all gone. I try to sit up in bed, but as soon as I make a move, the metal table I'm lying on magically starts to rise by itself. In a moment I'm sitting up, staring straight into the cold, oceanic blue eyes of my captor.

"Well, hello, Alicen. I'd love for you to meet my baby."

Calix holds a small bundle in his arms. The infant moves within its blanket, crying out at the sound of his harsh voice. It's the same cry I heard earlier, but this time the yelp has more energy to it. I have no idea how much time has passed, but that is my baby. I can feel it in my bones.

"You have no right to take him from me."

Calix smirks and then looks down at the baby. "How are you so sure it's a boy?"

"I . . . I'm not. But it's mine. The gender doesn't matter."

This time Calix laughs. "But it does. A boy will be successor to your reign as Elected in East Country. A girl will be nothing." Then he locks eyes with me, a hole boring through the space between us. "Unless she deceives everyone just like her *mother*. So you were a woman this entire time." Calix's words almost carry an echo of awe. He looks away again, releasing me from his harsh stare. "But yes, it's a boy. Congratulations." He laughs again, and the sound reverberates around the stark room.

"You can't have him," I say, the four words angrier in my head than how they come out.

"I can. This child, like all others, will go into the pool to be raised by the nannies and caregivers who can devote time to him." Then Calix looks down at my boy again, running a finger across his cheek. I strain on the bed to see more of my child. I want a good look at the baby I've made, but Calix holds him back from me like a present I'm not allowed to unwrap. "Or maybe," Calix says, the words dripping from his mouth slowly, "I'll raise him myself to be Mid's next Elected."

I gasp, the air catching in my throat, rocking me back against the small pillow they put behind my head.

"It wouldn't be so far-fetched," Calix muses. "We were seen together quite a bit. I could easily say the child is mine."

"I will *never* be your Madam Elected!" The words burst from my lips, vicious and snarling, even before I can attempt to hold them back.

Calix laughs, seemingly unfazed. "I never said you would be, my dear. But the baby—he is innocent. Unlike you, he did not lie. He didn't deceive me with an unknown pregnancy. He didn't spy on my country!" Calix stands up now, the fury in his face building. I want to tell him to take it easy, to sit down again while he holds my baby, but he keeps coming closer to me. I pull on the restraining straps again. If I could just free myself, this might be my only chance to get at Calix and wrench my baby away from him. I pull harder as Calix approaches.

"You betrayed me, Alicen. The other spies I shot were your parents. All that time I thought it was East's former Madame Elected's voice on the tapes, talking at the border hills with the current Madame Elected, but it was yours. Here I was pursuing your parents when I had the real

Elected right under my fingertips. I was blinded by my affection for you. My brother was right all along. Caring for others gets in the way."

"Aaron isn't right," I say, trying to buy more time. "Your technology is damaging your people, not helping them."

"You think so?" Calix stands over me, my baby balanced precariously in his arms. "My technology is what saved your premature baby. Do you even realize that your baby was born three months early? In your country, this baby would have died. Its lungs weren't fully developed. Without me and my advancements in cloning, your child would be stillborn."

I gulp at his words. Not just at the disgusting way that he talks about my baby's death, but also at the passage of time. I've been unconscious for three months here?

"That's right," Calix says, turning the proverbial knife in my side by caressing my baby's cheek behind his blanket. "Because we are in my country, this boy has a set of perfectly working, cloned lungs. Do you *still* think that technology damages my people?"

His eyes glower down at me. I pull at the bands around my arms again, furiously trying to loosen them without Calix seeing. But he notices my efforts.

"Don't bother," he says. "They won't break. Another one of my wonderful technological advances. Rubber Nylon that won't tear unless cut by diamonds." He flashes a ring encrusted with large carats on his pinky finger. Calix wiggles his hand close to my eyes so I won't miss the knowledge that my key to escape is so close, yet so far away. I want to reach out and chop off his finger to get at the ring. I picture cracking his pinky at the joint, using the ring to free myself, and then grabbing my baby and running toward East.

Whatever is left of East, that is. I still don't know the extent of Mid's assault on my country.

"So you're just going to keep me here, restrained in this hospital room? Why don't you just go ahead and have my mind erased like you do to everybody else? Or kill me like you did my parents?" I want to cry, the frustration building in my stomach and heart.

Calix places my baby on a nearby table. I watch, fascinated, as the boy's legs rise within the blanket, bunching the material. I strain to see a face within the folds of the fabric. The baby coos gently, and my heart aches.

Calix walks back to me, leaning in close, his breath hot against my neck. "That wouldn't be any fun, would it?" He runs a fingertip up my restrained arm from the elbow to my shoulder, staring at my skin as his finger seems to lick the surface. "I'd rather you didn't get the ease of forgetting all that will be taken away from you. Your freedom. Your country. Your parents. And now your baby."

I try to look away from him, but he grabs my chin in his hands.

"Not so fun playing spy now, is it?"

"It was never *fun*! I did it to help my country so you wouldn't obliterate it."

"Come now. We had some good times." He sneers at me. "And I'm sure you enjoyed yourself in the Satisfaction Room. What did you pick? Let me try to remember." He places a mocking finger on his lips. "Ah yes, you like to be touched softly behind the ear." He moves his finger along the back of my neck up to my ear, lightly brushing the lobe. His touch feels like a snake wrapping itself around my neck. I instinctively shrug my left shoulder to get him off me. But Calix wraps a hand around my throat, holding it there so I can't move.

Instead of turning my eyes to the floor, I look back at him straight on. "You're just as bad as your brother. *Worse* even."

Calix laughs, but I can tell it's hollow. He doesn't want to be like his brother, and I've poked him in a place that hurts. Calix drops his hand from my throat, instead walking back over to my baby.

"Maybe I am. You know, I've never told anyone this, but I could have stopped Aaron from performing the optogenetics on himself. You see, I knew what it would do to him." He looks up toward the ceiling, half-smiling, half-grimacing. "The doctors said their latest research showed that anyone who took large quantities of the purple pill all their life shouldn't risk the procedure. Something about chemicals mixing with the proteins. Said it would make the subject mad. They asked me to pass this information to Aaron because he wouldn't listen to any reasoning from them."

I breathe in deeply. "But you didn't."

"I was about to tell him. We were sitting together over dinner, and Aaron was telling me yet again how superior his intellect was. How he was coming up with new, amazing inventions every day. I couldn't get a word in edge-wise. And I decided right then. I'd just keep quiet and let him go through with it. See what the procedure would do to him."

"Well, you got your wish. He's completely demented."

Calix looks at me hard. Then he slowly nods. "Yes, I suppose I did get what I wanted. In my family, being number two was hard to stomach. I just didn't imagine that being number one would still feel . . . so unsatisfying." There is a slight wistfulness in his voice.

When I hear it, I take my opportunity. I feel the tears already brimming in my eyes, so when I plaintively utter my next words, I don't even have to fake sincerity.

"Please, Calix. You can still be a good leader. Just please let me go. Let me have my baby." I strain against the nylon cords, reaching my hand toward my child. My longing to hold him is excruciating. So much so I think my heart, which has already been damaged by watching Griffin slip away and my parents die, will break the rest of the way. I don't even know what my child looks like. I wouldn't be able to point him out in the pool of other kids at the nursery. Even if I escaped, I'm not sure I could identify him.

Calix looks at me, his eyes flicking back from me to the baby. I think that maybe he'll soften, remembering that at one point he did actually like me. But his next word cuts through me like a knife peeling back the skin of an apple.

"No." The word doesn't come out harsh or loud. It's soft and final.

Then Calix turns on his heels and leaves the room with my baby, not looking back.

I yell after him, screaming for my child. "You can't do this! No! That baby will *never* be yours!" I scream at the door until my voice is hoarse in my throat and two thick guards come into the room to knock me out. One of their fists connects with my cheek and before I know it, everything goes black once again.

18

MY DAYS IN THE hospital are long and tedious. With nothing to occupy my mind and only white walls surrounding me, I think I may go insane before Mid Country decides to put an end to me another way. That is why I am immensely grateful when Calix allows the doctors to unleash me from my bed. My limbs are stiff and my muscles have shrunk down to almost nothing. It's hard to get up from the table, but I do. I have trouble walking too, and no one offers me a hand or even a cane. I force myself to exercise, moving around my room in a tight circle as though I'm a circus performer locked inside a one-ring show. I think back to the stories Tomlin used to tell me about the olden days; how they had plays and movies and other delights to entertain people. I wonder if we all weren't so busy trying to survive if we could have concocted similar pastimes to make the days go by.

I tell myself stories to fill the time, imagining make believe worlds filled with healthy animals and lots of green grass. I wonder what the rest of Earth looks like now. I even let my mind wander onto the subject of my brother. He's the only family I have left now. I wonder if he would even care that Ama and Apa are dead. If he thinks about us, or was just glad to get away. I suppose East's Elected position turned out to be exactly the disastrous role he didn't want to take. Look at me now. Locked away in an enemy country, inside a small room as their prisoner indefinitely.

I did this to myself, though. Maybe if I'd stayed in East Country things would have been different. Maybe I could have somehow saved my people from the bombings, moved us all out of the city center into the remote swampland. If I wasn't so set on following the ridiculous Accords, maybe we would have had some defenses other than just armor glass in time for Mid's onslaught.

I corner myself into these depressing thoughts over and over again through the next days. Even when I try to think of something pleasant, like one of the old fairy tales, my mind circumvents the happy stories and finds its way back into the pool of despair.

One day, I'm walking in my familiar circle around the room when a doctor briskly pulls open my door.

"Ah, you're up," he says.

I nod, blinking slightly at the bright florescent light seeping through the open doorway behind him.

"Get yourself cleaned up. We need to perform a test or two on you. You have ten minutes."

"My baby . . . " My voice is thick from disuse, and I cough as I speak. I ask to see my child every single time someone comes into the room. I've given up hope now that one of the orderlies will feel sorry for me and bring in the boy. But it's become habit now, and I can't seem to stop asking.

"I wish you would refrain from inquiry, Alicen," the doctor says, running a hand across his brow like he's tired. Everyone in Mid still calls me by this name, even though they now know I'm Aloy. "It's upsetting my staff that you are so keen on your offspring. They can't understand why."

I cough again, intent on getting my words out. "They would understand if you just stop flooding their brains with . . . "

"Eight minutes now. You'd better hurry with that water before the test starts."

Before I can even open my mouth to ask a question about what kind of test, the doctor leaves, slamming the steel door closed so fast the freestanding sink in my room reverberates. I look over to the clean water in a porcelain basin he left by the sink. I rush toward it without any dignity. A whole basin filled with warm water to wash myself! They haven't withheld water from me, by any means, but they haven't exactly afforded me any luxuries like a warm bath. I quickly pick up the washcloth lying against the basin and rub water all over my arms before anyone can come back in and change their minds. When I finish pulling the cloth across my face and neck, I give myself a chance to breathe again. What kind of test are they going to perform on me? Will it hurt? Is it a punishment?

Just a few minutes later, I hear the door clanging open again. I'm about to protest with the fact that surely ten minutes haven't passed quite yet, when I look over and gape. My words are lost in my throat, and all I can manage to hear is my own heartbeat filling up my ears.

The orderly sent in to perform the test is Griffin.

"I can't believe it!" I finally speak, exhaling like the clouds have just opened up to reveal a perfect blue sky.

Griffin looks at me warily with one eye as he continues focusing on his work, carrying a few instruments to a nearby medical table.

"Griffin!" I rush up to hug him and then catch myself as he automatically takes a step back from me. "What are you doing here?"

"I need to extract some of your marrow for your baby." His voice is a clang of acid raindrops on a sheet of metal. Hollow.

"For the baby? Why, what's going on? Are they hurting him?"

"Hurting? No." His voice is still deadpan, in sharp contrast to my increasingly urgent tone.

"Have you seen the baby?"

"Of course."

"Why have they sent you?" My voice falls to a whisper. "Don't they remember we came into the country together? I've been so worried what they would do to you after realizing who I was."

"They aren't concerned about me."

I take a longer look at Griffin. He's completely monotone, not just in the off-white clothes he wears, but in his whole physique. No wrinkles alight across his face as he speaks. His mouth hardly turns up or down as it moves. His brow doesn't furrow. He is almost like a statue.

After a moment I say, "I can see why. You're not the same at all, are you?"

"They've fixed me. Just like they're fixing your baby." His hands brush over his silver instruments with care. Almost like he was touching something fine and rare. Almost like he was touching me. I put the thought out of my head swiftly.

"They're going to do optogenetics on the baby?"

"No. They don't start those procedures until a child is a bit older."

I gulp at the thought.

"Then what do you mean? What kind of fixing?"

"We need marrow from the baby's mother to keep the body from rejecting its cloned lungs."

"Alright, whatever they need." I hold out my arm willingly, prepared to give Griffin anything he needs to help our baby. "But why have they sent you?" All I can think is Calix is torturing me by showing me Griffin in this state.

"I clone body parts."

"Animal cloning, I know."

"Human cloning too. It's the obvious next step." Griffin walks toward me with a long needle in his hand. I scrunch my eyes at it but deftly hold out my wrist to Griffin anyway.

He waves my arm away. "Not your arm. I extract the marrow from your spine. Turn please."

Griffin doesn't even pay attention to my fearful expression. He's fixated on the instruments in his hand and on the nearby table. I obediently turn so I'm facing the white wall ahead. If they wanted me to be docile for the procedure, Mid Country knew exactly how to play me—just tell me it's to benefit my baby and have Griffin administer the test. Brilliant. I almost laugh out loud, but I stifle the crazy euphoria I have at seeing Griffin. Instead, I stare at the wall and bite my bottom lip in anticipation of the needle's penetration. I smell astringent before I feel the slightest prick. Then all of a sudden, a piercing pain erupts across my entire back, racing outward like it has legs. I can't help arching backwards, my shoulders thrown back.

"Be still," says Griffin.

I bite my bottom lip harder until I taste the metallic iron of my own blood. I suck in my breath as I feel Griffin's needle pull out of my back. Its exit is so slow and excruciating, I almost call out, but I keep silent, squeezing my eyes shut. Griffin swabs something soft against one of my vertebrae and covers the puncture hole with gauze and tape. If the pain in my back wasn't such a strong throb, I'd probably be happy to feel Griffin's touch. As it is, my body involuntarily leans one shoulder toward him like I'm hoping for some sort of embrace. But he doesn't comply in the slightest.

Griffin walks away from me toward the side table. He starts wrapping up his equipment, head down. I realize this might be the last moment

I have to say anything to him. I struggle against the pain to think of the right words to make our last minute worthwhile.

I grimace and speak through clenched teeth, licking a few droplets of blood off my bottom lip at the same time. "Don't you remember who I am at all?" My voice is forceful, buoyed by the sharp pain in my spine.

Griffin looks up at me for the briefest of moments. "Of course I do."

My eyebrows rise. "Who am I then?"

He pauses a moment. "A traitor to the country who took you in."

At this, I do finally laugh the high-pitched guffaw caught in my throat from before. "You can't be serious." He shrugs. "I'm not a traitor to my country! I'm from East, as are you. If anything you are the traitor! Or have you forgotten where you were born?"

In contrast to my sharp tone, Griffin's voice is subdued. "I know I'm from East. But I've come to my senses. Mid is the place to be now."

"The place to be." I grumble at him and place a hand on my back, putting pressure against my spine.

"Yes," he says like I was asking a question. "Mid has superior technology. The future is here, not in East." He fiddles further with the gadgets in his hands.

"Don't you even care what happens to your countrymen?"

Griffin looks at me again and then away quickly. "You mean my father?" I flinch slightly and Griffin goes on. "Whom you killed?" Even these words are dull and said without feeling.

I suck in a sharp breath through my teeth. I want to get mad at Griffin and tell him he's lost his way. That his memory is ridiculously selective. But I realize it won't matter. Maybe this is what Calix wanted in sending in Griffin—for me to get upset.

I won't give Mid the satisfaction. I try a different tactic with Griffin instead. I look toward the white wall and count to five before opening my mouth. Then I turn around so I can watch Griffin as I choose my next words carefully.

"I appreciate your expertise. For the baby's sake."

Griffin gives me a slight nod, curt but conciliatory. "You're welcome."

I go on, looking at Griffin hard in the eyes. He stares back at me, straight on for the first time. "The father would have been so proud to see his baby born," I say.

Griffin nods slowly. "Hmm." His response is cordial but still distant.

I push one step further, not even blinking. "Thank you for saving *our* baby."

We stare at each other for a second longer, and for the briefest moment I see a flash of uncertainty wash across his slack features. His brow creases for a split second, but it's enough to send shivers through my stomach.

I lean forward, my arm outstretched to him. "Griffin, I . . . "

But as soon as I get the start of my sentence out, the hospital door bolts open, and Calix stands in the frame glancing back and forth from me to Griffin. He looks worried more than angry, sizing up the situation. I don't pay him any attention, though. I continue to bore holes through Griffin with my eyes. I won't waste a moment of the last time I may be allowed to see him. My heart beats so fast, I almost allow myself to jump off the medical table and grab him into my arms. I think about shaking Griffin until he remembers that he wanted to marry me and that we have a child together. But I don't want to put him in danger, especially now that Calix is eyeing him up so suspiciously. I stay rooted in place, gazing at Griffin, trying to get through to him.

"Go," Calix instructs Griffin. "Your work is done. The marrow is collected."

Griffin nods at Calix, slowly, seemingly perplexed. But then he turns and without even a glance back in my direction he walks out the door.

I fall forward against the medical table, all hope running out of my body like seeping blood. A groan escapes my lips.

"I really thought you'd have given up sooner," Calix says. His words are cold, but his tone is actually soft. I can hear pity in his voice, but there is a touch of something else too. Respect. I lie still, face down. "Come now. It isn't all that bad. I haven't hurt your former lover. I haven't hurt your baby."

At this, I give a small sob into my pillow. I feel a feathery light finger against my hair. Calix caresses me, trying to soothe me with a soft click of his tongue. I want to fling his hand away, but instead, I let him touch me, feeling guilty that I long for even this sick kind of intimacy from someone.

"Here, I brought you something," he says. I glance backward at the small bottle enclosed in his fist. "It'll subdue the pain."

"No, I . . . " I start to protest. I don't want to owe him anything.

"Oh, don't be so stubborn." Calix rips the bandage off my back, sending another searing sting through my nerve-endings. "Just take the damn stuff before I change my mind." He dabs the liquid on my skin, and at once my back feels delightfully numb. I can't help sighing.

"You're welcome. I won't wait for any thanks, as I don't expect you've forgiven me for anything yet." He says "yet" like he thinks there will be a long future ahead of me.

This gives me an ounce of hope, and I sit up straighter.

"I brought you something else, too. Wait here a moment," Calix says.

I pull my knees up to my chest, sitting in a tight ball on the medical table, thinking how perverse it is that Calix asked me to wait. Where does he think I'll go? He's back a second later with a tray in his arms. "Just a few things to nibble on." He pulls back a white cloth on the food, and I see a bowl of the delicious bright pink oranges I like so much. "Here." He thrusts the tray onto my lap.

I'm forced to grasp onto it in a hurry, otherwise the whole thing would have clattered to the floor. I immediately bite into one slice of the fruit, letting the sweetness linger on the tip of my tongue before taking a full swallow. I take another slice and another until I realize I've been eating so fast most of the fruit is consumed. I look up angrily at Calix. I didn't want to give him the satisfaction of seeing me enjoy anything he offers, but the moment has already passed. He stares down at me with a look of amusement across his whole face.

"Seems you were hungry."

I thrust the last few pieces of orange in the bowl back to him. "I don't want anymore."

"Oh, come, Alicen. I'm the one who's supposed to be mad at you."

"It's Aloy. And *you* killed *my* parents and bombed *my* country to smithereens. I think mad is an understatement," I say through gritted teeth.

"What did you expect? Your parents were spies and your country started this war, not mine."

At this, I lurch forward, getting right up in his face. Calix doesn't flinch.

"We did *nothing* of the sort. Don't you know by this point? We have nothing over in East to bomb you with. Nothing!" I'm angry at myself for forgetting who I am, for having eaten his sweet pink bribe, and for having taken the blissful pain medicine. I hate this man.

Calix steps back and sits in a chair on the other side of the room. He crosses his legs comfortably and rests one elbow on his knee. "About that . . . " He seems amused again.

"About what? That you killed my people for no reason at all?" How can he be so cavalier when talking about all the people he's annihilated? My words spit at him.

"Now that you mention it. My guards haven't found much of a weapons cache, but we're still looking. Surely, they must be somewhere. An underground facility with fighter jets on an assembly line perhaps?" He leans forward. "Where are you hiding them?"

This time I laugh at him, so bitterly and for so long that the orange slices I just inhaled start coming back up. I cough a few times before stopping my insane laughter.

"Fine," says Calix, standing. He starts to walk toward the door. I realize I can't let him leave now that the subject of East's technological abilities are up for discussion. This may be one of my last opportunities to explain how wrong he was to suspect my country.

"I'm sorry," I stutter. "Please sit back down."

Calix turns slowly, assessing if I am serious or not. "You'll stop laughing long enough for us to have a real conversation?"

"Yes."

"Alright, then tell me." He smoothes his robe as he sits again. "Where do you have the weapons hidden?"

"There aren't any."

He purses his lips and starts to stand again, exasperated.

"I swear on my parents' bodies," I say, placing a hand on my heart. "We have nothing in East except for armor glass." I know I'm giving up all of East's vulnerabilities now by telling him exactly how very defenseless my people are. But I don't even know if I have any people left.

"How did you come by armor glass? If you had the technical ability to make the miles long wall on the border, surely you created other mechanisms of war."

I tell him in excruciating detail how we chose to break the Technology Accord when I saw the kind of weapons Mid was manufacturing. But that was the only technology we created.

"You're going to sit here in my prison and lie outright?" This time the amusement is gone from Calix's face. "You're telling me Mid bombed itself all those times?"

At this, I'm quiet. I don't have an explanation for the numerous times Mid was attacked. When Calix continues to stare at me, I finally open my mouth. "All I know is, it wasn't East."

He turns, fuming visibly. I think I can even see clouds of his breath in the damp coolness inside the hospital prison. I wrap the thin gray robes they've given me closer to my body, waiting for Calix to finally understand that East isn't his enemy.

Instead Calix faces the wall, and I hear him mutter low, "I know you're lying to me."

"I'm not. I swear it," I offer quickly.

"Do you swear again . . . on your parents?" His sarcastic words are thin like ice cracking.

My voice is low, unsure of where Calix is heading. "Yes."

"Then family ties must be as weak in East as they are in Mid because I know for sure you're hording weapons in your country." He pulls out a portable screen from the lining of his robes and pushes the instrument in front of my face. The screen lights up and shows me the border between East and Mid countries. I think it's a mere picture until the frame starts moving. A man scales Mid's side of the border mountain at night, a shovel in his hands. He descends to the bottom of East's side, and then gets on his hands and knees to begin his work. He digs for a few minutes before letting the shovel move on its own. I realize exactly what I'm seeing.

"Bullets, Aloy. I know you horded bullets," he says, using my real name for the first time ever.

19

MY MOUTH IS OPEN as I watch a few more seconds of the video. It's the exact scene I saw in the Mind Multiplier all those months ago in East Country. Calix snatches the screen from my hands and retreats from the room as I try to get in my defense.

"You don't understand . . . I . . . we . . . never . . . "

"Don't even try," he interrupts, disgusted, standing in the doorway of my room. Then he waves an arm and lets the door thud closed behind him.

I don't expect to see him anytime again soon, so when he walks in a few days later, I'm almost happy to see Calix. I've been rehearsing how to explain the existence of the bullets, and I think I found a way.

"You're here!" I say, smiling like an eager puppy.

"My, but hasn't your tune changed." Calix paces the room while I sit on the table, legs crossed.

"I didn't think you'd return, and I very much wanted to explain that video."

"Ready to admit where everything in East is hidden, are you?" Calix's eyes are open wide, obviously waiting for my blanket admission of guilt.

I ignore his question. "Your parents collected relics, right?"

He raises an eyebrow. "I don't see what this has to do with . . . "

"Just . . . hear me out. There was a device that showed up in the hills right after I was granted the Electancy. My tutor called it a Mind Multiplier. It was from long ago, and I never learned how it arrived in my country in perfect condition. I thought I would see copies of the thing here in Mid. When I saw how much technology you created, I assumed you made Multipliers, too, and a stray one was deposited in East along with other things you left along the border." At this Calix leans forward, about to speak, but I rush on. "But I haven't seen anything like it here. If a copy does exist here, it would be in your parents' museum. And you'd know what I was talking about."

When he doesn't say anything, I urge, "Do you?"

He's exasperated, but I see that I've at least piqued Calix's interest. "You haven't even described what this technology does."

"It's a helmet that increases brain activity by tapping into a person's unused brain waves. I tried it on, and it made me see things I wasn't even present to witness. Like an extra sensory perception."

"Even if I did know what you were talking about, my parents' antiques are older than they were. Nothing from before the Eco Crisis works anymore. We certainly wouldn't have handed over something that unique to your country. Where is this going? What does a Mind Multiplier have to do with your country hiding weapons?"

I pull my legs out of their twist and jump off the table. "I can prove to you those weren't East's bullets because of the Multiplier. I can tell you things only you would know from that video."

Before Calix has the chance to utter another objection, I explain what I saw in the Multiplier. The man with the automatic shovel who crossed the border from Mid into East. The bullets with ship insignias. The airride that killed the spy. Even the robotic box that mopped up his blood and carried away his body. When I'm finished with the story, Calix stares at me.

"So you're saying that man wasn't a spy from East?"

"I thought he was from Mid. Readying for an attack by stashing bullets near the border for when you came to invade us. I thought maybe he'd done something wrong so one of your airrides killed him."

"Interesting stories you concoct. I shouldn't have given you so much time to think up this grandiose of a tall tale."

"But you've got to believe me!" Now I'm pleading. I even venture across the room and am posturing myself to Calix in a kneeling position. "We don't have any weapons. Not even those bullets. I ensured even those were destroyed."

"You're a crafty storyteller." He looks up at the ceiling, and I give him a moment to contemplate everything I've said. Even though his words call me a liar, I can tell I've placed doubt in his mind.

After another minute, Calix says, "That was my airride and my robot, but that wasn't my man."

"But you killed him, thinking he was a spy from East?"

"Yes."

"Then why didn't you just leave him in East for us to find the next morning?"

"We needed to check his face in our databases. See how long he was in the country spying on us. Watch what direction he came from."

"And what did you find?"

At this, Calix covers his mouth with one hand, rubbing his chin in contemplation. I give him a full minute to reply.

"Nothing. He never was in Mid."

"Anything else?"

"He doesn't seem to have arrived in Mid from any direction. Just showed up on our side of the border for that one instance."

"Then don't you see? There is another party to blame for the bombings of Mid. They bombed your country and horded bullets in mine."

Calix eyes me for a few minutes and then stands from his seat in the corner. "Those still could have been your bullets." I reach out to him with one arm, willing him to come back and let us talk about other possibilities. But Calix just turns in front of the door to stare down at me. "Kneeling before me doesn't suit you."

And then he's gone again.

Every time I think it will be his last visit, Calix comes again. As the days go by, his frequency increases to once a day. Cooped up in this room, his visit is the only thing between me and another long day. I chide myself for starting to enjoy them, but I can't help it. Even the doctors who consistently monitor my vitals and the nurses who change my bed sheets don't talk to me as much as Calix does, and I know for sure the doctors aren't under any mind meld. I ask about this the next time I see Calix.

"Aren't you worried they'll revolt?"

"The doctors?" he asks. He sits in his usual chair in a corner of my room, peeling back the rind of a pink orange.

"Yes. They haven't undergone optogenetics. Aren't you afraid they'll stop performing the procedures on your people and will tell everyone what you've done?"

Calix laughs. "Not in the least. They're the ones who devised the procedure along with Aaron. They believe in it as much as he did. They're more adamant about it than even I am!"

"Speaking of Aaron, where is he?"

"Still locked away for his own good." Calix looks away.

"Is it still for *his* own good? He's still a threat?"

"What's it to you? Do you still pity him after everything I've told you?"

I lie back on my bed, staring at the ceiling. "Not exactly. But the procedure ruined him. Do you think it's right to keep a mentally ill patient locked up in solitary confinement?"

"He chose his own demise, remember? He has to deal with the consequences."

I'm silent for a moment, still staring at the blank white ceiling above me. "Kind of like me," I say, blinking hard.

Calix doesn't answer, and we sit in silence for a few clicks of the mechanical clock hanging on a wall in my room. I've gotten used to the whirs and ticks of technology all around me. I don't even bat an eyelid at the clock anymore.

"Being the Elected sucks," I say at last.

Calix laughs out loud. "It does." He lifts up a glass of liquor that he's been balancing on his knee. "To being Elected and having the entire responsibility resting on our shoulders!"

I raise an empty hand into the air, clinking his glass with an imaginary one of my own.

"Oh, come have a drink of mine already," Calix urges.

The doctors vehemently prohibit Calix from giving me any liquor on his visits, as they say it will affect the quality of my marrow that they keep harvesting every few days. Griffin doesn't conduct the procedure anymore, but I didn't expect he would.

"Can't. Remember?" I say.

"Just a sip. It won't kill the baby. He's doing fine."

At this, I sit up. "You've looked in on him?"

Calix takes a long draw from his glass. "I have."

"How is he?"

"Healthy. He's still hooked to an air purifying system, but he's doing well. You'd never know those weren't his original lungs." I sigh and look away from Calix in case my eyes are about to shed any unexpected tears. I don't want him to see me cry. "Maybe you'll get to see him again one day." It's the nicest thing Calix has said to me since I've been in this prison, so I take a deep breath and plod forward to grasp the opportunity.

"Can I ask you a question?"

"Maybe. Depends on the question."

I swivel my legs off the side of the bed so they almost touch the ground. I look at my hands resting in my lap. I bit the nails down days ago. "How many of my people did you kill in the bombings?"

Calix puts down his goblet and locks eyes with me. As if he knows the tone of our conversation is now serious, his voice lowers respectfully. "Many."

"Do you have a count?" I hold my breath.

"Not exactly. Your country doesn't keep records like Mid. But the best I can tell is thousands. Three hundred are all that remain in our custody under guard in East."

My head drops at the enormity of what Calix said. I add up the numbers he's just quoted. Three hundred in captivity. That leaves about three thousand, seven hundred dead. I can hear the moan welling in my throat even before it escapes. My hand instinctively clutches my chest like the news will bring on an attack. I sit there, looking toward the wall, allowing the physical reaction to the news of East's obliteration to overtake me. My stomach lurches, and I think I may throw up, but nothing comes up when I do heave.

Calix allows me the privilege of silence for longer than I expect. Finally he clears his throat and says, "A not-so-inconsequential population loss for the planet."

When I swivel back around in mild surprise at the conciliatory tone of Calix's voice, I see his eyes are downcast. I stare at him, my eyes burning like tiny suns.

"I didn't like doing it, if that's what you think," Calix continues, meeting my eyes. "*Is* that what you think?"

I lick my lips, feeling a bubble of accusation starting in the bottom of my belly. "Well, don't you? You've killed thousands of people, not to mention my parents. You ordered their deaths without blinking an eye."

"Remember, it is not me who started this war. East broke the isolation accords."

I just look away, knowing yet again how futile it is to refute his belief when my earlier attempts appear to have been fruitless. Instead, I stare at the wall and ask, "What did you do with my Madam Elected?"

"Ah, the one with all the scars?" I can hear Calix's appreciation for Vienne's still prevalent, albeit diminished beauty in the swell of his voice. "She is there with the other captives. I told the guards to ensure her safety. After all, she unknowingly helped us for so long."

"Is she hurt?"

"We haven't tortured your people to find any weapons, if that's what you're getting at."

It's partially what I meant, but I want to know more—like if Vienne holds a baby when the guards talk to her. If she seems like her spirit is broken. But these are questions I don't dare ask. I can't tell Calix there's another Elected baby back in East. If the baby didn't make it, I don't even want to know right now. Instead, I shift the conversation away from people to inanimate objects. I can handle hearing about the demise of stones and sticks more so than that of my countrymen.

"What else was destroyed in your onslaught?"

Calix shrugs and his forehead furrows. "Your house is gone."

I think of the beautiful half of the White House still standing after the wars in 2100. Now that side is a pile of ash too. I take a second to mourn the structure, but I don't waste tears on it. The house is just a thing. My country has lost a lot more than that.

"The other structures weren't much," he continues.

"We constructed homes from leftover rubble. Whatever we could find."

"Your city was hit hard in the Eco Wars, wasn't it?"

"That's what you get for being the capital of the free world," I say. I try to keep my voice light. If I think specifically about which thirty-seven hundred of my people perished on Calix's orders, and how East Country was blown to bits twice in one century, I'll wring Calix's neck with my bare hands. I go so far as to sit on my hands to stave off the temptation.

Even if I took retribution on Mid's leader right now, I won't be let out of this dungeon, and Griffin and our baby might be killed in revenge. Assassinating Calix isn't a good solution.

Calix is unaware of my train of thought, and he keeps the conversation on history going like it amuses him. "We used to be the most powerful nation, but even the United States couldn't force Mother Nature to her knees."

I picture monster hurricanes ripping holes through our buildings, the Capitol building crumbling after eighteen consecutive lightning strikes to its dome, and people falling into ground fissures the size of five Ellipses. What a mad, insane parent, Mother Nature turned out to be. Not too maternal after all. "Do you think we were wrong back then to create so many man made technologies that ruined the environment?"

"If you're trying to guilt trip me into abandoning technology here in Mid, you can save your breath." Calix folds his legs one over the other in finality.

"No, I know you're not likely to change your mind. I was just asking if you think we brought all the devastation over eighty years ago on ourselves. If we deserved it."

"Humankind deserved a reset?"

I nod.

He shakes his head. "No one deserves to be turned upon by his own planet."

"But isn't our plight kind of like what happened millions of years ago to the dinosaurs?" If anyone will know what I'm talking about, it's Calix. The word dinosaur probably isn't in anyone else's vocabulary. I lean my head on my hand. "Is it all just a long cycle with resets destined to occur over and over again, no matter what we do?"

"You think humans are just one more creature for nature to extinguish to make room for the next life form?"

"Probably," I say.

"I don't know, but this is all getting too thoughtful for me." He rubs his eyes with both fists. Calix smiles. "You can always be counted on for interesting conversation. I'll say that much for you, Aloy. I'm going to turn in. See you tomorrow."

I nod goodbye, marveling again that Calix is so casual with me as to promise a return visit for the next day. I stretch out flat on my back. Calix makes the doctors administer pain relief after every marrow procedure now. I hardly feel a thing as I roll my shoulders and reach underneath to feel the vertebrae where their needles constantly penetrate.

Maybe I've done a good enough job of endearing myself to Calix. Maybe he'll free me and let me see my baby as he said tonight. Maybe I can even convince Calix to return me, and I can rebuild East with three hundred of my people in peace. Maybe he'll even let me take Griffin and Margareath home with me. Perhaps Griffin won't love me again, but I can still get him away from here. It's with these cautiously optimistic thoughts in mind that I turn onto my side and fall fast asleep, too numb to let East's obliteration penetrate my consciousness.

20

NOTHING IN MY LIFE has ever been one hundred percent easy. When I wake up the next morning, there are people bustling around my room, different from any day before. Three nurses and one doctor shake my shoulders to wake me up. One of them pricks the heel of my foot to draw blood before I'm even fully awake.

"What's going on?" I ask, fear clouding my head.

No one answers me, and I'm forced back onto the bed while they hold me down and stick more needles under my skin. "Where's Calix?"

Finally one of the nurses leans toward me over the bed and says, "Tower One's complete."

I just shake my head at her. That's all well and good, but I don't have any idea what it has to do with my current predicament. The nurses wrap me up in clean white robes, take a few more samples of my blood, and then leave as fast as they arrived.

It is not until later in the day that I get my answer. Calix opens my door six hours after the doctor's visit, and I immediately sit up.

"Do you know what that was all about this morning?"

Calix takes his usual seat in the corner of the room but doesn't meet my eyes. "I'm afraid I do."

I tap my foot fast, holding onto the side of the metal table with clenched fists. "Well, what is it? What's the matter?"

"Tower One reconstruction is done."

I roll my eyes at Calix, but he doesn't see. "I heard. What does that have to do with . . . ?"

"I told my people we wouldn't kill East's Elected until reconstruction was complete."

Oh.

When I don't say anything, he continues. "And reconstruction is now complete."

I wrap my arms protectively around my chest. "Can't you tell them what you know now? That East isn't responsible for the bombings? That I'm not guilty of anything?"

"Do I really know that, Aloy?" Calix looks up at me finally, his eyes soft and sad. "Ever since you've been in here—ever since we invaded East—we haven't had any attacks on Mid. My people want vengeance for the wrongs against our country. I have East's leader sitting right here, and I promised my countrymen justice."

I snort and look away from him. "And if you back down now, you think you'll look weak."

"You know better than anyone. Perception is everything. If the Elected family falls—if we're not followed, chaos reigns again."

"You're repeating the mantra as some kind of justification. But under your leadership chaos already reigns!"

Calix stands and rubs a hand across his brow. "You have a right to be upset. I'm sorry."

I'm incredulous. "You're *sorry*? That's all you can say? I'm to be put in front of the firing squad, just like my parents?" Calix doesn't answer me, so I know it's true. "I don't want to go like that. At least honor the traditions of East Country as you kill its leader. Use hemlock."

Calix shakes his head, looking weary. "I don't have hemlock in Mid."

"Manufacture it then!" I yell. "Just like you do with grass and animals and every other living thing! Or take some from East!" I can't keep my anger bottled up any longer, not after hearing this latest decree. I won't be going back to East to rebuild my country. I won't be here to bargain information in exchange for Griffin and my baby's welfare.

I want to throw something. I look around the room and find the porcelain basin from the first time they extracted my marrow. I pick it up and smash it on the floor. Pieces fly everywhere, hitting the sides of the walls and the metal hospital bed. A set of guards burst into the room, but Calix puts up his hand. He just shakes his head at them, and they warily back up, closing the door again.

"Fine. I'll order some hemlock brought back from your country."

"And how long will that take?" I ask, vitriol oozing from my lips and thoughts.

"A few days."

"So, I only have a few days to change your mind?"

Calix looks up at me from under his blonde eyelashes. The fluorescent light in the room catches the flick of his lashes and makes his face seem shiny, like it's covered in glossy paint. "Aloy, I won't change my mind. As much as I want . . . if we were other people . . . "

I shut him down. "I don't want to hear your excuses."

There's a moment of silence between us. I continue my manic pace around the room, again feeling like a lion trapped in a circus ring.

"At least let me do something for you in the last days. Is there anything you would like in here?" Calix asks.

I think about the four white walls bearing down on me. I can't end my life this way, without seeing the sun and feeling earth between my fingers one more time.

"I want to go outside for one last walk."

"I can probably arrange that."

I plunge in with more requests. "And I want to see my baby. I want to see his face."

Calix looks to his left, avoiding my gaze.

"All right."

"And I want to see Griffin."

Calix looks at the ground, shaking his head from side to side. "I don't know why you still care for him. You know he doesn't remember you the same way you think of him." He stops, but then proceeds again abruptly. "But he did ask me about your child." At this, my back straightens. I look toward the far wall so Calix won't see my eyes. "Do you want to know what he asked?" I nod, silent, my breath caught in my throat. "He wanted to know if what you told him was true. If it really was his child."

My heart swells, suspended in time, not beating until I hear more. "What did you tell him?"

"The truth. That DNA proved it was his."

I can't help clutching my chest and leaning forward expectantly.

Calix cocks his head, a mixture of pity and confusion on his face. "You can't possibly think it matters that he knows, though. All is still the same."

"I don't believe you!" I think of weeks earlier when I reminded Griffin he was a father. I saw the shift of his eye. "What did he say?"

"That the child could, of course, stay in the common nursery. He doesn't even visit it, you know."

A small sound escapes my parted lips, like an animal in pain. I manage to say my next words, but it's like my throat is closing. My mouth can hardly make the right sounds. "I . . . want to . . . see for myself."

Calix looks toward the ceiling. "It won't be popular, but I'll see what I can do. Would you be willing to give up a glimpse of the sun in exchange for the sight of Griffin? I could maybe arrange a twilight outing after my people are secured in their apartments."

"Fine," I say, my speech still subdued and raw.

It's not until Calix leaves that I find the full strength of my voice again. I scream and scream until my own ears ring so loud I can't tell when I've finally stopped.

21

EACH TICK OF THE clock feels like my life is slipping away. The more clicks I get, the better. Three days pass with nothing. No doctor or nurse visits. No more procedures to extract my bone marrow. No more late night conversations with Calix. It's lonely, but I use the time to reflect on my last eighteen years. I relive memories, knowing it's the last time I'll be able to dwell on them. I spend a lot of time thinking of my parents while also blocking out the details of their demise. I don't want to remember them in front of the firing squad. I'd rather think about the many ordinary days when we ate breakfast together across the big oak table in the White House.

I also half-heartedly think of ways to escape. I desperately want to get away, but if I did thwart the execution, Mid might take out its anger on Griffin or our baby instead. So my plans are mostly a way to stay occupied. I don't intend to act on any of them. Yet, it's still satisfying to think of strangling Calix the next time he walks through my door to grant my last request. I can't help looking around my meager room for anything that would do the trick. A piece of the bed sheet, cut into a strip. A wire pulled from within an electrical socket, thin and black against Calix's white neck.

I'm in the middle of such a fantasy on the fourth day when my door finally creaks open and the image of Mid's Elected becomes a reality in front of me.

"Why are you smiling?" he asks, one eyebrow raised. He wears a white linen robe with embroidered gold swirls across the chest. They

195

are not unlike the red marks my countrymen painted on my nails for my wedding.

I think about fabricating an answer and then decide it won't hurt to tell him the truth. "I was just thinking what it would be like to kill you."

Calix clears his throat. I've obviously startled him. "How very . . . blunt . . . of you."

I smile bigger. "So what's the verdict? Will your people allow me a moment to see the outside world again before they murder me? Have you procured the hemlock yet?"

Calix is back to business fast. "Yes to both. My people think it's strange I afford you any pleasantries, but they don't care as long as the execution occurs."

"Your people are saints." I've become sarcastic and bitter in my last days. I think of the innocent girl who was afraid to take East's Elected position over a year ago. She is long gone, replaced instead by someone older. Someone with anger and hatred fossilized in her heart. I've seen too much now. My heart must be a slowly pulsing stone made of cracked clay and blackened volcanic ash. I wonder if I'll even feel anything when I drink the hemlock. Maybe I'm so dead inside already, I'll just close my eyes and extinguish, pain-free.

Calix ignores my comment and instead starts to walk closer to me. "Hold your hands behind your back."

I do as he says, watching two burly guards standing in the open doorway ready to aid their leader should I decide to act on my impulses for Calix's blood. He grasps my wrists and constricts them with a thin piece of material.

"Don't try to break out. This is more of the Rubber Nylon." I remember the last time I tried to lunge at him and was unable to rip the bindings holding me to the medical table. But he doesn't have to worry. The thought of Griffin and our unnamed baby keeps me polite and controlled.

"Wouldn't think of it." My voice is a low sneer.

"As this is your last wish, I suggest you try to enjoy yourself. I've had to go to some pains to arrange for your visit with Griffin and the baby."

I don't say anything, but my chest does lighten when, for the first time in four months, I'm led out of my cell. The corridor we walk down is long and deserted. Closed doors line our path on each side. It's just like every other floor in Mid's buildings. No creativity in the architecture and nothing lining the walls. It's just white, like the inside of my prison room. When we come to the end of the passageway, three small steps lead us up to the ground floor. Calix nods to four more guards, and they part to let us through the final glass door.

I can hardly contain my gasp upon seeing the outside world again. I want to fall down to my knees in the dirt, rubbing my palms through it. But I conceal the emotion, instead sucking in a huge breath of air. I take in as much as will fit through my nostrils and throat before opening my eyes again and exhaling. Then I look up at the sky. It's twilight with just the moon positioned above us for light. But it's a bright night, and I can see more clearly in this state than under the harsh fluorescent lights of my cell. The air is cool and dry with a small breeze pulling at my now shoulder-length hair. I stare into the sky, trying to guess what position the sun would take in the afternoons. I try to imagine the fiery yellow ball and feel its rays on my pale skin. Who would have thought I'd relish the sight of that burning sphere again? The sun was a point of much consternation for us in East Country, with its ultraviolet rays perpetuating skin cancer. But now I yearn for it, and I'm slightly sorry I relented so easily. I should have insisted on coming outdoors during the day. Part of me even despairs that I didn't choose the firing squad over drinking hemlock. The first option would have taken place outdoors, probably in the daylight. Instead, this truly is the last time I will see the outside world. I'll most likely be forced to drink the hemlock indoors.

Calix lightly holds onto my left elbow and leads me forward while I continue to take in my surroundings. I stare up at Tower One, which has been constructed anew. The entire building glows like a polished knife in the reflection from the moon.

"We're visiting your baby first," he says.

I don't utter a word, just walk next to Calix as he serves as guide. I'll finally get to see the slope of my baby's forehead, the color of his eyes, the angle of his chin. I can hardly contain my excitement. My whole body is shaking in anticipation.

When we arrive at the doors to what must be the common nursery, I drink in the image. This is where they have kept my boy. This same view is what he will see long after I'm gone. I wonder when they'll start their mind bending processes on him. If he'll be allowed to stay himself long enough to remember what it was like to revel in emotion, indulge in a fragrance, and even appreciate beauty. I wonder if he'll have enough of me in him to rebel.

We walk down another stark corridor. A nurse pops her head out of one door only to stare for a second and then flit away. Other than that, the building is quiet.

"The children are all in bed," Calix says as if to answer my unspoken question. "Your son will be asleep too, I'm sure."

I hoped to see his open eyes and play with him for a moment. But maybe seeing him asleep will be easier on both of us. Maybe if he never sees his mother, his subconscious will have less to forget when the memories are unceremoniously ripped away.

"He's still in an incubator," Calix continues. "His cloned lungs are almost fully grown now, but he'll be under observation for a few more weeks."

I'm glad that Calix warned me before I saw my baby. We turn one last corner and through a glass window I see a stretch of empty carts each holding a white blanket. Only one of the carts is filled with a small human being, and I know instantly that he's mine. Tubes are stuck into his nose and through his mouth, but I can still see a version of my own face behind all of the equipment. The baby lies still except for a slight flutter of his chest with each intake of air. His arm rises in sleep, stretching and settling again above his head.

I feel Calix's hand tighten around my elbow. "Can I hold him?" I ask, my voice quiet and polite as I practically beg for this additional favor.

"I would let you, but no one can pick him up yet. The nurses only touch him with gloves through the armholes there." He points to two plastic sleeves angled into my baby's bubbled cart. "He's still too fragile."

For a second I wonder if this is a lie meant to keep me away from my baby, even in these last moments. But I do think Calix is telling the truth. My boy is so small; his features are as slight as the nail on my thumb. I sigh heavily, and it's enough to make Calix remove his grasp.

"You're getting more of an opportunity to see your baby than other mothers do."

"Yes, but they don't care like I do. You've made sure of that."

Calix clicks his tongue and looks away. He affords me ten more minutes of precious time staring at my son. Then he places a soft hand on my shoulder and says, "Your last request is scheduled now. He will only be waiting a few minutes, so if you want to see him, we must go now."

I contemplate disregarding the last stage of my tour. I think of leaving Griffin to wait out the appointed time by himself. I can spend the extra few minutes with my baby. Griffin won't remember me anyway. He's a shell of the person I once loved. My baby is still wholly the same as when he came out of me. But the idea only flickers across my brain for a moment. I can't go back into my hole without seeing Griffin one last time. If only to see that he's changed from the man I used to love. At least then I won't feel I'm giving up as much when I drink the hemlock.

I nod at Calix, and he and the two guards usher us back out. I turn one last time to my son, arching my neck backward to catch one more rise of his chest. I see his tiny stomach grow bigger on an inhale, and the idea of leaving him once again threatens to crush me. The last time we parted, I didn't realize it. Now the thought of leaving him courses through every particle of my consciousness. I can't help the tears that brim in my eyes. Calix looks away, almost as if he's embarrassed. His guards don't pay me any additional attention, keeping their eyes on Calix or toward the deserted hallway.

I try to gather myself as we step back out of the nursery into the darkening evening. I take big gulps of air, staving off my cries, but a few moans escape my lips anyway. Calix once again holds tightly to my shoulder, and I feel like falling against him only because my sadness threatens to push me down.

"What will you name him?" I ask the question into the air, not looking at Calix as I say the words.

"Name him?"

"Yes. What will you call him? Will you pick the name or will you let one of your nurses do it?" I hear myself saying the sentences, but it doesn't sound like my voice. I sound deflated.

"I hadn't thought about it."

"He will have a name, right?"

"Naturally."

"Think of it now and tell me before I die."

Calix stops mid-step and puts a hand out toward the guards. "Give us a moment, please." They walk a few feet away, close enough to still rescue Calix but far enough away not to hear us. "What do you want to call him?"

"Me?" I am dumbfounded by Calix's question.

"Yes. You pick the name, and I'll use it."

I think for a moment, my mind racing with possibilities. "I . . . I don't know." But as I utter the words, a name crosses across my mind like a flag waving. So bold and bright, that I have no other option but to say it out loud. "Glory. I want you to name him Glory."

Calix considers this a moment and then nods. "So it shall be." Then he turns again, moving his heels one hundred and eighty degrees in the dark dirt. I stand behind him for a moment, unable to put words together to express my thanks for this one small but meaningful gesture.

The guards look at me hard, and I automatically pick up my feet to fall in line next to Calix. He reaches for my elbow again and this time I don't shudder at the touch. We walk in silence. I roll the baby's new name over and over in my mind, saying it silently. It's the perfect mix of Griffin's and my name. Glory. One day it's what I hope the baby can bring to East Country.

It's with this thought in mind that I see a lone figure standing beside one of Mid's fake trees in the distance. The man has his back toward us, and he looks up at the moon above. It's the same casual stance I remember when Griffin stood near our oak tree in East Country, surefooted and at ease. I feel like running toward him and wrapping my arms around his waist. I imagine him turning around, a grin etched across his face. But even as I picture these things in my mind, the real Griffin turns, a scowl lodged in his cheeks. He stares at us and clasps his hands together at waist level. He doesn't look at ease. He looks angry.

When we get close enough he says, "You took me away from my work for *this*?"

I shudder as he looks down on me, moving his chin in my direction on the last word.

"It was her final request," says Calix. Mid's leader directs his next words to me. "I didn't tell him why we were meeting."

"I can see that," I say.

"What do you want?" Griffin says to me.

I stare up at him, my eyes wide, willing him to be the person he once was. When his features don't soften I say, "Mid is executing me tomorrow. I wanted to see you one last time." If I was hoping for some kind of reaction, I am not rewarded. Griffin doesn't move a muscle or look vexed at all.

"Is that all?" he asks.

I nod, but after a moment of awkward silence, I say, "Don't you feel anything toward me? After all we have been through? We had a *baby* together, for goodness sake!"

Griffin turns but then looks back down at me, glancing for a moment at my bound arms. "I don't feel anything for you. I yearn for my work, for the advancement of my country. That is all."

I can't look at Calix as Griffin utters his words. I don't want to see if Mid's leader looks satisfied or not. I just continue to stare at Griffin, hoping some part of my earnestness will get through to him.

"Yes." My voice is hard. "You would do well to remember that. Advancement of *your* country. Don't forget where you came from, Griffin." Before he can say anything else, I finally turn to Calix. "I'm done here."

"Are you sure?" he asks. "We have a few more minutes."

"I'm sure. Let's go and let Griffin get back to his *work*." Coldness seeps into my heart again. I turn without even sparing one last glance at Griffin. I've lost him for good, and he doesn't even care. He won't look after our baby when I'm gone, and he definitely won't keep my memory alive. Now that I know the facts, I actually feel relieved. When I'm saying my mental goodbyes tomorrow, Griffin's will be one less name running through my head.

22

MY LAST NIGHT IN the cell proceeds like every other evening, but this time I see my baby's face when I lie down against the pillow and close my eyes. I let silent tears escape, dripping down my cheeks in streams. I imagine Glory with his eyes open, playing on a bed of soft feathers, laughing as sunlight hits his bare head. I can almost hear him coo. Maybe his eyes are azure blue. I force the picture to change like pages of a book flipping. Now his eyes are grass green, the edges of his eyelashes dewy with sleepiness. I see him stretch, both hands raised high in fists. I lean in, touching him in my imagination. The top of his head reminds me of a summer peach, fuzzy and sweet-smelling. Now I am leaning over him to sing a lullaby, encasing him in a circular waterfall of my hair. I sing slowly at first, then faster as I picture him listening intently. "Lock your strength far away; save it for a rainy day. When the sun no longer shines, that's when you'll need this little rhyme." He beams up at me, innocence spelled out in his bubbling laughter. "Your grandmother sang that to me years and years ago," I whisper to him in my thoughts. I picture my parents bouncing Glory on their knees. Apa would have loved Glory—a real boy to take over the Elected role. I will see my parents again soon.

My imagination slowly morphs into a dream as I sink into the start of sleep. I must fall into a deep slumber because it takes me a full minute to realize there's someone in my room.

"Hurry!" says a voice in the darkness.

I'm groggy, but that doesn't stop the beads of anxiety from forming on my forehead. It's happening. They are pulling me out of bed in the middle of the night for my execution. I thought Calix said I'd drink the hemlock in the morning, but perhaps this is a better way. Like pulling a band-aid off fast, getting it over with.

"Come on, Aloy! Get up!"

The exclamation isn't what I expect. It's not a harsh guard or a doctor or even Calix. I peer into the blackness, blinking hard to see without the luxury of any lights.

"Rise and shine! We've got to get a move on!"

I pull the sheets off my body and swing my legs over the table's side. The owner of the voice stands in front of me, his arms coming to rest on my shoulders.

I'm now fully awake, my heart picking up its pace to the speed of a revving engine. My eyes adjust so that I can clearly see the grinning face in front of me. "What . . . what are you doing here?"

"You don't know how long I've wanted to do this!" Griffin leans down and kisses me hard, holding me in a tight hug. Flashes of light go off inside my head as the realization that Griffin is here and that he's himself wash over me.

My arms hang lifeless and unbelieving at my sides. In my wildest fantasies, I never thought Griffin would snap out of his altered state in time to save me. Maybe I'm still dreaming. The thought flashes like lightning, quick and abrupt.

"We disabled the cameras and other sensors, but only for a few minutes, so we've got to run now," says Griffin, pulling at my arm.

I cling to the shirt sleeves around Griffin's upper arms. Now that he is here, I hold on hard to ensure myself he's solid, not an apparition I've fabricated.

"We?" I ask, my voice a tiny squeak of unabated hope.

"Margareath is helping, but she's gone ahead."

I stutter out my response, simultaneously jumping off the bed and pushing my feet into shoes. "Margareath is . . . cured . . . too?"

Griffin nods, pulling me forward and holding my hand tight. I can feel the muscles in his whole arm twitching. He wrenches open the door to my cell, and I half expect it all to be a joke. Guards will run in, laughing as I'm thrown back against the bed. *"Escape?"* they will guffaw. *"This was just one final trick before we hold open your mouth and pour in the hemlock!"*

But the corridor ahead of us is empty. I run behind Griffin. He doesn't let go of my hand, squeezing harder as we near the exit, and it's a good thing, because I'm still so dizzy with relief and thankfulness that my knees might buckle underneath me.

"I thought you hated me," I say.

"Not since I evaded the doctors. You're not the only one who is good at playing a part!" He laughs into the darkness ahead. I remember once before when Griffin fooled me. He pretended to drink hemlock in East Country at his own execution.

I think of tonight's jaunt in the moonlight. Of seeing Griffin under the moon and the callous way he spoke to me. I'll never again underestimate Griffin's acting skills.

Running behind him, I allow myself to feel hope for the first time in months. There's no one around. We might actually have a chance of escaping. I soak in the sight of Griffin's smile as he turns back to glance at me every few seconds. Now that we're together again, neither of us wants to take our eyes off the other.

We find the set of steps leading upward and burst into the outdoors without any sirens tripping or guards stopping our progress.

"When did you get cured?" I gasp out my question as I keep running behind Griffin.

He looks back at me with a mischievous smile. "Stopped those god-awful doctor visits right after you reminded me I was a father."

"How?" My words are short, as we spring behind buildings to stay within the shadows.

"I scheduled two doctor visits, and then cancelled each one at different times. Made them think I'd already gone to the other. I kept up my cover so well, no one ever reviewed video feed to check on me."

"And you're . . . " I choose my words carefully. "Okay now?"

Griffin leads us between two close buildings, dodging a robot gliding along the conveyer walkway. Its blinking orange eyes pass without seeing us.

"It took a little while to wear off fully, but yes, I remember everything; who you are, our baby, East Country."

I swallow. This is too good to be true. "And Margareath? How did she circumvent the checkups?"

"She was trickier. I kidnapped her, told her supervisor she was sick, stashed an unanimated clone in her apartment bed for the video feed to see, and then locked Margareath in my apartment until she snapped out of it."

I can't help smiling at the image of one of Griffin's Frankenstein-esque clones propped up in Margareath's bed.

"It must have been hard to secure her when she was unwilling."

"Extremely difficult until I realized how to make her stay on her own accord."

"How did you do that?"

"I told her Mid needed her to do research on small apartment gardens that grew under florescent lights. Worked like a charm."

"What is she doing now?" I ask.

"She's breaking our baby out of the nursery." He makes it sound like an easy trip into the forest to gather mushrooms.

"Glory," I say, my voice lower. "I named our baby Glory."

Griffin glances at me, his cheekbones bathed in dim light from the moon. "I like it."

He squeezes my hand within his. I want to kiss him again so badly my chest hurts. But we don't have time, and there are more important things to think about now than just the two of us. We have a child to consider. "Where are all the guards?" I ask, still not understanding how we've gotten so far without being caught.

Griffin is quiet for a moment and then says through the dark, "Cloning isn't the only thing I learned in Mid's medical labs. I can program computers now too. But we've got to hurry. Margareath was only able to turn off the main hub of cameras for one turn of the system."

From working with Calix in the surveillance rooms, I know this is exactly fifteen minutes. The feeds need to refresh their store of solar charge after each quarter hour. As soon as the cycle rejuvenates, Surveillors will realize there's a problem.

"This is crazy! Even if we do manage to get to the gate before surveillance kicks in, Mid will send airrides to apprehend us from above as we run for East."

"Who said anything about *above*?" Griffin chuckles out loud.

I don't understand, and I'm about to ask for more details, but we've already arrived at the entrance to the common nursery. My heart beats so wildly; I can feel my lips quivering with each fast pulse.

"Did you do something to get the nurses out too?"

"No. What I learned only affects the guards. We'll have to take our chances with the nurses, but there shouldn't be a lot of them at night. In the first weeks after you gave birth, your bone marrow was administered to Glory every four hours. People work during the day, but it's mostly robots taking care of the children at night. I taught Margareath how to disable those."

Again, I think to myself that Mid is a strange country. What if the children wake up from a bad dream in the middle of the night? Who is there to comfort them? An orange-eyed monster? These kids probably welcome the idea of optogenetics just to get robot nightmares out of their heads.

We weave through the doors and the maze of empty corridors. We're so close to Glory now, I shiver in anticipation. Everything is quiet. Only the steady ticking of multiple clocks in the hallway welcomes us. I can't wait to wrap Glory in my arms and touch the dark hair on the top of his head. Just like in my dream.

But then a terrible thought clouds my vision. "Griffin, wait . . ."

"Don't slow down." Griffin continues to pull me along, but I force him to turn.

Griffin has visited Glory to administer my bone marrow, but nothing was taken from me in past three weeks. He must not have seen Glory since then.

"He's still in the incubator," I say, pressing hard on the skin around Griffin's arm. "How will we take him with us?"

"You won't." An unfamiliar, cold voice stops us dead in our tracks.

Griffin drops my hand, suddenly on the offensive. An overhead light turns on, flooding the hallway so the shadows disappear instantly. A uniformed nurse holds Margareath around the neck, a surgical knife held sharply against her flesh.

"I'm so sorry," Margareath croaks. "I thought they were all gone."

"Be quiet!" The nurse jabs her knife more forcefully against Margareath's neck, and our friend immediately ceases talking. "Back up slowly."

"There are three of us," Griffin says. "We can overpower you."

"Maybe so, but you still won't get that baby." The nurse's face holds a look of triumph. "I'll be rewarded handsomely for keeping the baby.

Maybe an extra shift or even two!" Her workaholic glee is horribly on target for one of Mid's citizens.

"Take Glory with his incubator or unhook him altogether," I say toward Griffin. His brow furrows, but in a split second he's off, madly dashing toward our son. I tear in the opposite direction, lunging for the nurse without any hesitation. She screams, and there's a scuffle as we clash against each other, my body shoving into the woman as hard as I can. Margareath helps too, wrapping her hands around the nurse's torso to hurl her backward. But the nurse still has the knife's advantage, and she swipes frantically in the air. The metal makes contact with my arm multiple times, and I can't help yelling as blood spurts from the slashes. Nevertheless, I keep pushing forward. Any moment, surveillance will reboot and view this scene. Guards will descend upon the nursery in droves.

As if reading my thoughts, an alarm way in the distance starts to sound. Within seconds, a cacophony of sirens blares from all directions. The nurse flashes me a grin and halts thrashing against us long enough to emit a throaty laugh.

"Griffin!" I shout in the direction of Glory's room. "How much longer till you have him?" Margareath and I abandon the nurse, running into the incubation room. Griffin's poised over Glory's crib, his hands deftly working to unhook our baby's oxygen lines.

"He's turning blue," Margareath says peering over our shoulders.

"Every time I unhook the oxygen from the main line, Glory stops breathing," says Griffin.

"Isn't there any kind of mobile unit?" I ask, my eyes searching.

Griffin's voice is strained for the first time tonight. "No, there's nothing portable. The entire monitoring unit for his lungs is encased in this wall." He slaps his palm against the metal boxes. I walk over to them and try vehemently to pry a box from its spot. Nothing budges.

"We don't have time!" Margareath whispers, her eyes bulging.

More sirens seem to be turning on outside the relative quiet behind the incubator's glass walls. The guards will find us in moments.

I look at Griffin and then down at my baby. "I'm not leaving him."

There's a deep crease forming between Griffin's eyes. "I'm sorry, but you can't stay behind. We tried to take Glory, and it didn't work. We don't have any other choice but to leave him."

"That is my *son* in there!" I point a shaking finger at Glory's incubation bubble. Already tears are choking my speech, and my words only come out as a hiss. "If he is not coming, then neither am I."

"I've never made you do anything against your will, but listen to reason, will you? You can't stay in Mid where they'll kill you." Griffin picks me up over his shoulder with one swift movement.

I squirm, kicking him in the back. "Put me down! I won't leave without Glory!"

"Taking him without medical equipment while we're being chased down isn't an option. He'll die if he comes with us. What good will you be to him here if you're dead? He's staying but you're not!" Griffin's words sound final.

I cry out as I feel Griffin moving the both of us forward away from our son.

"They'll kill him!" I scream.

"They won't," says Margareath in a low voice behind us. "You heard the nurse. They need babies. They won't sacrifice your son just for revenge."

"I can't leave! I can't abandon him!" I scream it as loud as I can, trying to get through to Griffin and Margareath. Maybe they don't understand. They didn't give birth to him. I did, and the connection can't be severed like this.

"He's safer here. But you're not." Griffin doesn't give me any other options. I feel the world going out of focus. What is all of this for—the running, the sacrifice—if I can't even guard over my own offspring?

"Let me touch him at least," I say in a guttural groan. I know we only have seconds, but I won't willingly leave like this.

Griffin hesitates. "We don't have time."

"I won't leave without holding his hand just once."

Griffin and Margareath look at each other over my head. I know what they're thinking. Heavy footfalls pound the nursery floor, growing nearer to us as we argue over how to leave. It's now or never.

"Fine," Griffin says, planting my feet back on the floor with a thud.

I immediately run toward the bubble of Glory's incubator. I tug my hands through the plastic gloves and place four fingers on Glory's forehead, lifting a spiral of his hair. At the touch Glory wakes up and stares through the glass right into my eyes, as if he knew I'd be right there and he was waiting for me. I keep eye contact without blinking. For a second it feels like the whole rest of the world is candle wax, dripping away, leaving me and Glory alone and at peace.

I feel a hand on my shoulder.

"We have to go now." Margareath's voice is gentle but urgent. I hear people growing closer to us, slamming doors and looking in adjacent rooms before they find us in the incubation area.

I whisper goodbye to Glory and nod to Griffin. Pulling my hands out of the gloves and away from my son is the hardest thing I've ever had to do. It hurts more than the bone marrow extractions and the nurse's knife on my arm.

"We'll come back for him," says Griffin. "I promise."

I think 'if we make it', but I don't say the words. I just pick up one foot after the other and start toward the door of the incubation room.

Glory picks up his head to look at us. "I love you," I whisper across the room to him, not even knowing if he can hear me through the bubble.

As we start to run back through the corridor with a powerful stream of yells catching up to us, I think of only one thing.

His eyes are blue like mine.

23

"I swear when you're safe in East, Aloy, I'll come back for Glory. He's my son too. I won't desert him."

I nod, staring straight ahead. If I look at Griffin too long, I'll break down and go back. Glory looks an awful lot like his father. Plus, I can't afford to take my eyes off the floor in front of us. One stumble or fall will land us in the clutches of the chasing guards. I can hear them running only one corridor behind. In moments, they will round the corner and see us. I feel like a mouse stuck in a maze, scrambling to get away from the hand reaching down to pick me up and feed me to a waiting snake.

"This way!" says Margareath, beckoning us with one arm. Griffin tugs on my hand, and we're both running after Margareath into yet another white-walled corridor. I hear crying in front of us, and I don't like running toward it.

"Where are we going?" I ask.

"Through the children's sleeping quarters. That is the last place the guards will come. They won't want to deal with the children's crying after being woken up."

I see the ingenuity in her statement, but I also don't feel comfortable being part of these kids' nightmares. I don't have a choice, though. Griffin pulls me along, making me run faster than I'm used to after having been held prisoner in the hospital for the past four months. In moments, Margareath opens an unmarked door and we stumble in. A light immediately flicks on, and the room is bathed in harsh fluorescence. Standing with his hand on the light switch is a young boy, maybe thirteen years old. Around his sides, grasping onto his arms, hands, and shoulders are younger children ranging from toddlers to others almost his same age. The youngest ones hang from his pajama cuffs.

"We heard the sirens," he says. Before I can utter some kind of apology for waking them or ask them to go back to bed so we can continue on our run, he says, "You're the Elected from East, aren't you?"

I shake my head yes, eyes wide with surprise that this group of young children recognizes me.

"We want to come with you."

My mouth drops. Margareath, who's been silently looking for a place within the rows of metal beds for us to crouch, stops in her tracks and glances at the boy. Griffin lets go of my hands to walk closer to the child. "Impossible," he says.

I walk toward the children's obvious leader, wonder coloring my eyes like haze. "They haven't changed you yet." I stare at him, my head tilted to one side. I know we're still being chased, but I can't help sparing a moment to wonder why these kids haven't received the optogenetics procedure yet. "You know what's happening to your people, don't you?"

"They make us help."

I gasp, but the boy's words make sense. The doctors need assistants who can help them perform optogenetics but aren't receiving the procedure. Any other aids would guess what was happening each month.

"Once we're old enough, they'll change us, and we won't remember helping them," the boy says. "Are you going back to East? We want to come with you."

"Look," says Griffin, brushing the back of his arm across his forehead. "There are too many of you. We can barely get Aloy out of here, let alone twenty others."

"There's twenty-four of us," says the boy, all fact. His small face is still, but determined. He doesn't beg us, but he doesn't back down either.

"What's your name?" asks Griffin.

"Ty."

"Okay, Ty. I'll make you a deal. You help hide us from the guards, and when I come back here to rescue our son, I'll figure out a way to get you out too," says Griffin.

"All of us. Not just me."

I like this boy. My chest aches for him. But it's not just pity I feel. He would make a great leader.

Griffin looks to his left, avoiding the boy's eyes for a moment. Then he looks back. "Okay, you hide us now and help keep our baby safe, as much as you're able, and I'll come back for all of you."

This seems to satisfy Ty. He stands aside, motioning a hand to us. "Hide in there." He points to a long trunk off to the side of the room. "Don't mind the smell."

We run over to the trunk. Margareath pulls back the lid and immediately rears back. A sickly stench of urine hits me in the face.

"Some of the kids have challenges keeping their beds dry at night," he says.

"Where are the robots that watch you at night?" I ask, all of a sudden worried one of them will open the door to check on the children and find us before we hide.

"We disable them at night when there aren't any nurses here to see."

Griffin grins at Ty. "Well, I'll be. Maybe I'll take you with us tonight after all. You're a smart one."

"I'm not leaving the rest of the kids behind," Ty says, hands on his hip.

"Of course not," I say, my voice soft. I give Ty a small smile and then step one foot into the trunk. My foot squishes within the children's discarded, wet sheets.

"How do you know the guards won't look in here?" asks Margareath, looking back at Ty.

"Would you? The guards know what's in the trunk. In the daytime when the nurses come to clean it out, they sometimes get the guards to beat the kids who've soiled their sheets. As a warning not to wet the bed again."

I glance down, realizing I was wrong earlier. The robots with the orange eyes aren't the ones giving these kids nightmares. It's the nurse we encountered earlier tonight.

"Hurry," says Ty. "I hear them coming."

Margareath ducks her head down and closes the lid over all three of us right as we hear the click of the bedroom door opening.

"Did you children see anyone?" asks a gruff man.

"No sir," says Ty. "We woke up 'cause of the noise. What's going on?"

The man doesn't offer an answer. "Guards, search the place. And all of you," he says, speaking to the children again, "get back in your beds and don't move out of them again!"

We hear the scurry of little feet obeying the order and piling once again into their tiny cots. I can see flashes of dark and light through small holes in the wicker trunk. I hold my breath as the men begin their inspection.

"We're wasting time," says a high-pitched woman I recognize as the nurse with the knife. "They'll get away while we're puttering around in here!"

"I'm not leaving until each inch of the place is accounted for!" shouts the main guard back at her.

The woman humphs, muttering under her breath about ineptitude. Then she walks toward our hiding place, the soles of her pumps clacking on the tile. She places her hand on the edge of our sanctum. Griffin squeezes my shoulder hard. Up against my own, I can feel Griffin's leg muscles tense as if he's readying himself to jump if she unearths us.

"Has this trunk already been examined?" the nurse asks one guard.

"No ma'am, but you needn't concern yourself. It's the kids' soiled bed sheets."

"Disgusting brats," she says, slapping the top of the lid. She hesitates for a moment. I hear Margareath take a dangerously loud intake of air. I put my hand on her thigh as a warning, and Margareath doesn't make another sound.

The nurse steps away, instead directing her attention elsewhere. "What happened to your caretakers?" she asks the children, her voice too loud.

It's Ty who answers. "Broken down."

The nurse says, "Not unexpected given the level of overuse they receive waiting on you lot."

"All clear!" yells out the head guard. "Get a move on!"

"I'll stay here and keep an eye on these brats," the nurse says.

My hand squeezes Griffin's harder. If she stays, we're stuck in this trunk until she's gone. But by then the morning shift of people will seep back into the nursery. Either way, this nurse is a thorn in our sides, and part of me wishes we had taken the time to finish her off outside of Glory's incubation room.

I'm becoming more like the people of Mid, I realize. I don't mind killing someone now. I shudder, feeling droplets of cold sweat start at my brow line.

"We can't afford to take anyone off the hunt. Keep looking through the building. These kids aren't a priority right now."

"Fine. As you wish," says the nurse with obvious resentment.

Griffin exhales the breath he was obviously holding, as do I. A steady stream of boots stamp past our hiding place. When the room is silent again, I hear a final guard addressing Ty. "Make sure no one gets out of bed again, you hear?" Before Ty can reply, there is the thud of a fist pounding into flesh and Ty's unmistakable gasp as the wind is knocked out of him.

The guard chuckles, and we hear the nursery door slamming shut. Griffin, Margareath, and I wait a full minute and then gingerly step out of the trunk. My eyes fly across the room to where Ty is sitting on a cot, holding his head.

"Are you alright?" I ask, running to him.

"I'm okay."

"You sure? You're bleeding," says Griffin. He grabs a bed sheet and starts ripping a section to serve as Ty's bandage.

Margareath, in turn, holds a little girl three cots over who's crying with loud, sloppy sobs.

"This happens all the time," says Ty. "The heavier dose of optogenetics given to the guards makes them mean. We'll be fine. Just make sure you honor your oath." Ty looks hard at Griffin and then points to a door across the room. "Just go already. They left through the front. There is only one other exit."

I look around at all of the wide eyes staring at us from their cots. These children are yet another set of people whose safety is now on my shoulders. Another group who has protected me in return for the feeble hope that I will ultimately save them. I close my eyes for a split second, swearing to myself that I won't let them down. "We'll send a team to extricate you. Griffin always keeps his promises," I say.

It's the first semblance of a thank you I've yet to give Griffin tonight. I look at Griffin, trying to silently convey my gratitude for the rescue he engineered and for keeping his promise to look after me in Mid Country. He has never let me down, and what I tell the children isn't a lie.

"Ty, how long do we have until Mid gives you the procedure?"

Ty folds the makeshift bandage around the side of his head, looking up at me from beneath one of the gray bunches of material. "Seven months. I'm almost fourteen."

I look around at the other children, and one little girl's stare stops me. Thick black hair surrounds her face in waves. Her almond shaped eyes show up shockingly blue against her darker features. "They took my brother a few weeks ago," she says in a low voice. "They take everyone at fourteen." Her eyes are imploring. "His name is Liam. Have you seen him?"

Pity for this waif of a girl overwhelms me. There are thousands of people in Mid, yet she hopes I saw her brother. "I haven't," I say. "But I'm sure he's . . . fine."

Griffin turns toward the children. "We need to leave now, but you have my word that even if the three of us are captured, someone from East will come back for you."

I don't know how he can make such promises, but I know Griffin will do what he says. I wonder what other plans he's not sharing with me yet.

Ty nods. "We'll watch out for your son in the meantime."

"Thank you," I say, my voice starting to crack. If we don't leave soon, I may not have the gumption to abandon Glory and all of these kids.

"Come on," says Margareath, pinching my shoulder lightly. She pushes me forward toward the exit.

This time when we leave the room, I don't glance back. I know twenty-four pair of eyes will be on us, silently praying that we keep our end of the bargain. I can't bear to think about how the number of people relying on me keeps multiplying by the day.

24

WE EXIT AT AN intersection of three hallways. "I don't know which way to go," I say when we're a few paces away from the nursery.

"This way." Margareath points to the darkened corridor on our right. "It's the quickest exit toward Tower One."

I stop in my tracks. "Tower One? That's within the heart of the city! We can't go back there!"

"Trust us, Aloy," says Griffin.

A niggle in the back of my brain has been growing ever since we left Glory behind. At Griffin's words, the throb pulsates harder, and I finally understand my irritation. "How can I keep blindly trusting you?" I hiss into the dark. "I'm tired of plans being made without me." I can feel the rush of heat inching from my neck to my cheeks. Griffin says he believes I'm the best leader for East Country, but he doesn't even think I can handle the details of our escape. I'm always last to be included in his plans. Like the fact that he was leader of the Technology Faction and that his father was the assassin in East. Even the acting job he performed at his own fake execution. If he would only share his schemes with me sooner, maybe I'd be in a better position to help.

I can feel this small annoyance growing, licking at my feet like a thick fog curling up from the floorboards. If Griffin told me about his role in the Technology Faction earlier, we could have staved off the riot at the town hall together. If he'd given me any hint of tonight's escape plans, I could have warned him about Glory's reliance on the incubator. Maybe then we could have figured out a way to rescue our son.

Griffin and Margareath exchange a look, but I keep prodding. "Why are we heading further into the city instead of running for the gate?"

"Griffin's got a plan," says Margareath.

"I realize that," I say, my hand on my temple. "But why won't you clue me in?"

Margareath comes to stand in front of me. Her look is shatteringly clear. She's the image of the woman she once was in East, smart and self-assured. "Because you'd be the first of us captured if they do find us."

"So what? So, I'm captured. It's not like I wasn't already in captivity."

Griffin's voice is low. "Yes, but this time they might torture you to find out how we planned to escape."

"They'd do the same to you to get the information." My voice is scratchy as I say the words. I look away from Griffin, instead staring into the dark expanse of space in front of us.

"We won't be captured," says Griffin. His voice is low and rumbly—that same resonation I fell in love with back in East. It's the kind of voice you listen to even if you are not initially paying attention. But this time his low tone signifies something dangerous. I glance back at him, fast enough to see him start to reach toward me but then thought better of it, placing his arm at his side once again. "If they find us, they will shoot me and Margareath on sight. You, on the other hand, still have to endure a public execution. That would give them time enough to extract the escape plan from you."

"I'd never tell," I say, stubbornness overtaking any resignation I feel.

"I know you think that," says Margareath. "But who knows what kind of techniques Mid would use. You don't know how they'd break you. If you do tell, it would endanger everyone in East."

"You just have to put faith in me," says Griffin again.

I place my hands on my hips. I can see their logic, even if I don't like being left out. I do have faith in Griffin. It's just hard to let go of control after I've been trained my whole life to take charge. "Fine," I say, my lips pursing with the discomfort of the acceptance.

Griffin nods. He starts walking forward, assured now that I will follow him. Margareath follows in back, as if they're building a wall of protection on both sides of me. We creep through the hallway and then down another deserted corridor, until a few minutes later we reach a large steel door.

"How do you know there won't be guards waiting for us on the other side?" I ask, still skeptical.

"I don't," says Griffin. "This part is the most risky."

I hold my breath as he pushes the door open and the night sky is illuminated. No guards stand by the entrance, but I can hear their yells in the close distance. In fact, as the door opens a crack wider, I'm taken aback by how many people are outside at this time of night.

"They must have woken everyone," says Margareath through her teeth.

"Robots are everywhere," I breathe out, staring ahead at the hundreds of orange eyes zig-zagging around in the dark. "There's no way we'll get out of Mid."

"We just have to make it to Tower One," Griffin says. "It's not that far from here." He pulls me by the hand again, luring me out from the semi-protection of the interior. "Stay up against the buildings for as long as you can."

We press ourselves against the metal exterior. Floodlights in front of us scan around the city center in circular sweeps. Sirens blare in alternating tones. I can almost smell the metallic tinge of Mid's anger as the whole country looks for us. When we finally reach the end of the building, Griffin turns to both of us. His brow is creased, but his eyes are clear.

"This is it. Keep your head down and run."

Margareath nods silently and then plows ahead. Upon her first steps, Griffin looks at me. I know I'm supposed to go next. I swallow fast and then make my own dash into the open space. I do as Griffin instructed. I run like my legs are on springs, even though I know they will hurt later. My jellied, atrophied muscles stiffen and cramp with each bound forward. I don't look left and right to see if any of Mid's people or guards notice us running. When one of them starts to get close, I dodge to my left, keeping Tower One in my vision the entire time. It's only a total of maybe two minutes, but out in the open without any other protection makes the seconds seem to pass incredibly slowly. Every time I hear a shout I think they've recognized us in the dark and are descending. But I keep running and finally I fall in line behind Margareath as she slams up against the side of Tower One's smooth exterior.

"Thank the heavens," she exhales.

"The door," says Griffin, joining us.

Margareath gropes in front of us, feeling for some kind of handle. I hear something click within her hands, and a small door opens. It's not a tall door beckoning us up and into the lobby of Tower One. This door is half way in the ground. Descending stairs reveal themselves as Margareath pushes the metal door open.

I follow, blind, as Griffin vanishes into the darkness first. We're about to enter the bowels of Tower One, and for the first time I think they might be right. We won't run. We're hiding with enough food and water to last us for months in Tower One's bomb shelter.

I should be thankful that Griffin and Margareath thought of a brilliant plan. We'll hide for the next month and then sneak out again when Mid's countrymen have abandoned their hunt. But the thought of going back inside again makes my heart ache. I want to flee. I want to get out of Mid. Not stay in its belly for one more second.

Each footstep down into the bomb shelter feels like being pulled under water. We walk silently, not daring to turn on an overhead light and hit some sensor by accident. Instead, we watch our feet on the concrete with full concentration.

It makes perfect sense. Griffin could case out the bomb shelter once he was in the Tower for the night. He could prepare our getaway from inside Mid's sleeping quarters.

When we reach the heavy door to the shelter, it takes two of us spinning the tight dial to thrust the door open. Griffin walks to a hanging light bulb and pulls a small string, shedding some light on the room.

I immediately sit down onto one of the thousand cots in the room and start pulling off my boots. My feet and calves are screaming.

"What are you doing?" asks Margareath.

"Getting comfortable. If we're going to be here awhile . . . "

Griffin interrupts. "We're not staying more than a second."

I look up at my two countrymen with real confusion on my face. "But earlier you said we weren't running."

"We're not." Griffin's face breaks into its first full-fledged grin of the evening, reminding me of his more natural, devilish character. "We're going to take a nice, leisurely walk back to East."

"They'll have airrides scouring for us. It'll be dangerous for us to run out in the open back to Mid. But walk *leisurely*?" I ask. "Now I know you've lost it."

Margareath rubs some dirt off the wall in the corner of the room, and a few wooden boards come into view. "We're walking underground." I can see pride bloom across her cheekbones.

I look over to Griffin for more of an explanation, but he just says. "You'll see."

He and Margareath start pulling boards and nails off the wall. Little by little, a hole emerges behind their work. I start to smile wider, realizing their full ingenuity. I watch with wide eyes as Margareath disappears into a narrow but tall tunnel.

"Isn't it amazing?" Griffin asks. "It goes from here almost all the way to East Country."

I nod. "But how did you find it?"

"Didn't find it," says Griffin. "We made it!" His eyes sparkle like the light from the purest of suns.

"Griffin, where do you want these boards? Inside or out?" Margareath's voice calls from within the dark space in the wall.

"Just hold on a sec," Griffin says, holding a finger up in my direction. He disappears into the cavern, and I stare after him at the big black hole they've just excavated.

Calculations start to flood my brain. Griffin and Margareath have only been cured for what? Two months? All the work on the tunnel had to be done at night after work, and Margareath doesn't even live in this same Tower. How could Griffin have dug a tunnel all the way from Mid to East on his own in such a short time? I think maybe my people in East dug the tunnel, but how would they have known to head exactly toward this spot? I'm utterly perplexed, caught up in deciphering the logistics.

When I see a face other than Margareath's or Griffin's staring back at me from the entrance of the tunnel, I don't register it at first. I blink a couple of times and then open my mouth wide into the shape of an O.

When my mind finally makes sense of the image, I scream into the silence, staring at the man who's just walked out of the tunnel and into the empty bomb shelter with me.

Calix.

Tomlin once told me there are two instincts: fight or flight. I've been taught my whole life to fight, and I don't curtail my training now. At once I run at Calix, fists up, knee poised to slam into his stomach. I get in a solid blow, ramming into him with my body, knocking him down onto the packed earth. I sit down on top of his immobile body, ready to smash his face to a pulp. He will *not* stop our escape, no matter what. I completely give in to all my pent-up anger and let it rain down on Calix, blow after blow.

I feel large arms behind me, wrenching me off his body, but still I fight.

"Stop! Enough!" Griffin wrestles me against the side of the shelter. Meanwhile Margareath comes running out of the tunnel's depths. To my complete surprise, she bends down and cradles Calix's head in her arms.

I'm so ferocious, I spit out the next words. "Are you on his side now? Has this all been a trick?"

I think of the way we just happened to make it through the children's quarters without being apprehended. How we ran from the nursery building to Tower One without anyone recognizing us. How we escaped my hospital prison without intervention from any guards. Maybe it was all a set up.

"Of course not!" says Griffin while I struggle against his hold. "Just stop for a minute."

I don't want to stop. They told me to trust them, and here they've brought me face-to-face with my worst enemy. I watch as Margareath helps Calix back to his feet. Mid's Elected stands in front of me, his hands clasped, long fingers interlocked solemnly. He wears a plain brown outfit of linen pants and a peasant shirt, nothing like his garments above ground. His face is strangely blank except for a benign smile sitting upon his lips. You'd think he would at least be angry at me for fighting him. Calix doesn't even bother to wipe the line of blood off his forehead.

"He's a clone, Aloy. Not the real thing," Griffin says, still clutching my squirming wrists. I stare at the man in front of me, not really comprehending Griffin's words said until he voices it a few times. "*This* is the latest technology I learned in Mid." Griffin holds out one hand to the fake Calix, and the clone walks forward.

"Hello. How are you?" it asks me, two arms extended and bent inward in East Country's standard salutation. "My name is Cole. What's yours?"

My mouth hangs open. The robot doesn't hold any hostility for me, even after I fought it. I ignore the clone's questions, instead speaking to Griffin. "How did you get it?"

Griffin looks over the clone's body. "I made *him*." He emphasizes the last word, in contrast to how I described the clone as a thing.

"It's a little dangerous to create a clone in the exact likeness of Mid's Elected, don't you think?" I stutter, still getting over my initial shock.

"Creating clones is sanctioned by the country, but Calix's image is the only one we're allowed to recreate."

"There's more than one Calix clone?"

"My name is Cole," says the man again, tilting his head as if he's trying to give me the most pleasant of reminders. He doesn't seem to understand why I don't use his name. He doesn't realize I hate him just because of his face.

"So there's more than just Clone Number One here?" I repeat.

Cole squeezes his eyebrows together, but then backs up against the side wall again, now watching me with a slight wariness.

"Be nice to him," says Griffin. He pulls me over to the other side of the shelter, standing so close that our stomachs touch. "While we've been working and sleeping, Cole's dug the tunnel continuously. I just gave him the direction, and he's done it all."

"How do you know he won't turn us in?" I ask, pointing accusingly at the clone inched up against the cave wall.

"Because I programmed his mind from scratch and then stole him from the lab. He only does what I say." Griffin grins. "It's kind of fun to have Mid's Elected do whatever I want."

"I bet. But how could you just take him?"

"I stole Cole off the production line before he was equipped with a tracking device. I finished him here." Griffin draws his hand across the air to encompass the bomb shelter.

"What is he made of? I ask, inspecting Cole's face and neck with interest.

"He's not *made* really. Cole's all flesh and blood. He has real lungs, grown just like Glory's from bone marrow."

I stare at the clone for another moment. He looks almost like Calix, but now that I've had a moment to take him in, I see there are subtle differences. His eyes are more pronounced than Calix's. His hair is wavier. "If he looks like Calix does that mean he's got Calix's marrow?"

"Yes, and . . . someone else's." Griffin's voice falters.

I know that intonation. He sounds guilty. I stop and turn to look Griffin in the eyes. "Whose exactly?"

Griffin looks at the ground, moving the dirt haphazardly with the front of his boot. "That's the thing . . . "

"Whose bone marrow?" I ask more vehemently. I'm starting to draw a few connections myself.

"Yours was the only other specimen I had to work with after I took Cole out of the lab." Griffin looks anywhere but into my eyes.

I remember the numerous times I offered my bone marrow up willingly to Griffin, thinking it was all going to our baby. I turn toward the wall and punch my fist into the dirt. The idea that this clone is the embodiment of me and Calix intertwined together is too much for me. I want nothing to do with Calix, and now his DNA and mine are mixed together in this monster?

"Griffin, how could you?" My voice rises with the accusation. I stare at the clone for a few more seconds. "Get back to work," I order the clone. My tone is gruff and offers no friendliness, even though the thing tries to win me over with another slight smile. At my words, Cole walks forward into the tunnel, completely willing to do my bidding.

"Really," Griffin says, "you can be nice to him. He's not the real Calix."

"He was made from Calix's bone marrow, wasn't he?"

"Yes, but . . ."

"Then to me, he's the same thing. Same evil inside."

"Maybe you'll learn to like him," Griffin says, moving a few stray hairs off his eyes, "after you've seen what he's constructed."

I grumble, "I don't think that is possible."

"You'll be surprised." Griffin grins, teasing me as he rubs his thumb over my elbow. He never seems to comprehend I'm angry at him. Or maybe he does and this is Griffin's way of soaking my anger out like a sponge. "He certainly has some of your good nature," he teases again. "Come on. Let's start walking."

I purse my lips together, watching Griffin move forward into the narrow tunnel. With a sigh, I bend down to finish tying my sneaker and then follow him. Margareath and I watch as Griffin boards up the entrance with wood again. Cole stands farther into the tunnel, a small shovel in his hand. Even though the tunnel is already expertly carved, Cole follows my instructions, continuing to work with his tool. He pats at the dirt and stone walls, smoothing them. As I wait for Griffin to finish nailing in the passageway and covering our tracks, I keep one eye poised on Cole, ready to strike if he turns on us. If he's one part me, he is at least three parts Calix. And I know all too well what a snake Calix is.

But Griffin's right about one thing. The four of us start walking into the dimly lit enclosure, and I look around at the clone's handiwork. He's done fine work with this tunnel. Even working round the clock, Cole must have used special machinery to dig something this good in less than two months. As if on cue, Cole touches the handle of his shovel, and it springs to life, vibrating and pulsing. It's an exact replica of the moving shovel I saw in the Mind Multiplier.

The four of us walk in silence for what feels like a long time, but none of us has a timepiece, so maybe it's only minutes.

"Why is Calix creating clones of himself?" I ask when we stop to pick up a set of canteens Griffin stashed in a crevice.

"Because Mid's Elected is worried optogenetics will wear off eventually, and then cancer will be widespread again," says Margareath.

"But Calix is safe. He's got the purple pills," I say.

"If optogenetics ever stops working, you can bet people will stage a coup and raid his supplies," says Griffin. He leans in to whisper in my ear. "Calix planned to harvest organs from the clones if he ever fell ill."

Even though I detest the machine-like human being walking in front of us, I can't help feeling disgust at the idea. No one deserves that kind of fate, even this look-a-like Calix. Then again, if Calix is cruel enough to grow himself a backup body and Cole has the same genetic wiring in his head, it's just one more reason to distrust the clone who shares Calix's genetics. I grimace at the back of Cole's head.

We keep walking through the night, not stopping to sleep, even though I'm sure we would all relish the rest. Finally, I see Margareath's feet dragging ahead of me. She's slowing down.

Griffin sees it too. "We should stop to eat and grab a few hours shut eye."

"I'll take first watch," I offer, knowing at least I had some sleep before Griffin woke me in the hospital. Who knows the last time he got any rest.

"No one need take a watch," says the clone. He turns around and smiles widely, the perfect white color of his teeth a sharp contrast to the semi-blackness of our underground passage. "We can all sleep. The tunnel's completely hidden from Mid's view."

I blink at him, still wondering how and when he'll try to turn on us. "Hidden from Mid," I say. "But not from you."

"I would never hurt you, Elected," he says. "I cannot wait to see my glorious East Country and return you to its helm."

I almost laugh out loud at the clone's childish optimism. I sincerely doubt the remainder of my three hundred countrymen will take me as their Elected now that they know I've broken so many of the Accords *and* failed to ward off Mid's attacks. *Glorious* East Country? In my mind, yes, it will always be glorious. But wait until he sees the damage done by Mid's bombs. I'll be happy if there's even one structure left intact. I'm about to say something to Griffin about his supremely rosy programming of Cole, when I realize maybe he and Margareath don't actually know what's been done to East.

"Did you finish the tunnel?" I blurt out in Cole's direction.

"No, Elected. My orders were to dig until I hit Mid's side of the Nirogene mines, then stop."

"So you never went above ground."

"No, Elected."

I nod absently. He hasn't seen it. Cole couldn't have reported back on East's state of welfare to Griffin or Margareath.

Margareath interrupts my thoughts with a loud, drawn-out yawn. She leans against the side of our tunnel with her hands clasped behind her head. "I can't wait to see my children and Albine again. Now that I remember them." She laughs lightly.

I turn around so she won't see the look of horror quickly spreading across my features. Her family. Who knows if they even survived the repeated bombings? Maybe they are part of the three hundred people held by Mid's guards, but the odds are against that. I shudder, and it's enough of a twinge that Griffin notices. He grasps my arm and leads me away from Margareath and Cole who are nestling close against the wall to sleep.

"What's wrong?" he whispers.

I don't look him in the eyes. "Umm . . . nothing."

"I can tell. Something's the matter."

I think again of all the times Griffin's left me out of his plans "for my own good." Part of me wants to keep him in the dark now, if for no other reason than a desire to stave off his grief. His stepmother, Brinn, in her fragile state, was surely one of the people who didn't make it. But I'm tired of keeping secrets, especially from Griffin.

"Let's sit down for this, okay?" I lead Griffin toward the floor. If I'm going to pour out all of my recent knowledge about East, we might as well rest at the same time. Heaven knows Griffin will need to sit when he hears the news.

I spend a good part of Cole and Margareath's slumber telling Griffin everything Calix said about the damage to East. How anyone who is left is now held under watch by Mid guards. I tell him about Tomlin's sickness. I give Griffin all the details of the bombings. There is no more White House. No more remnants of the national monuments. I tell him last I heard, Vienne was still alive, but who knows what's happened in the last weeks. And his and Vienne's baby . . . surely the infant died, but I can't bear to say the words out loud. My voice trails off in the middle of the sentence.

For my entire description, Griffin sits silently next to me in the dirt. He doesn't move a muscle, and when I finally finish, I turn my body so our knees touch. I reach out and hold his hands inside mine. They are two times the size and don't fit within my palms, but I latch my fingers through his anyway, waiting for the onslaught of his reaction. I'm no longer mad at him for using my marrow to construct Cole. Now I just feel the pain etched across his brow. His grief is yet another outcome of my failure at being his Elected.

When he doesn't utter a word, I say, "What are you thinking?"

"You don't want to know."

"Yes, I do." My eyebrows scrunch together, bracing myself for fury or despair. Or both.

He shifts on the ground and looks away from me. I wait a few moments longer, allowing the silence to fill the tunnel in both directions. It feels like the quiet has a shape of its own, growing from a filmy haze to something thick and suffocating. Finally Griffin opens his mouth and the words tumble out fast. "I'm thinking that nothing will ever be the same and that we should have followed the Technology Faction instead of the Accords. Our forefathers were wrong to think the Accords would hold the world in any kind of order." Then he pauses.

I swallow, allowing myself to digest all of the rage Griffin is obviously trying to repress. I can see it just bubbling under the surface. I know he's trying to hold it in for my benefit, but I deserve to hear how he blames me and my family for East's demise. I wouldn't let him tell me the extent of his fury before, but now I deserve it. "What else?" I ask.

Griffin looks toward the wall. I think this is it. He'll finally burst, yell at me, and tell me I wasn't the leader they needed after all. I wait for him to remind me that I killed his father, the one man who could have protected us from Mid. I take a deep breath, steeling myself to hear the words from someone who's believed in me for so long.

"I'm glad you weren't there in East when it happened."

I don't say anything. I suck in air, recovering the oxygen I didn't know I'd been depriving my lungs for the past few seconds.

"Don't get me wrong," continues Griffin. "I wish everyone in East was gone when Mid attacked." His voice grows lower, almost into a growl. "Brinn, Vienne, and the baby. All of them. We don't know what we're walking into tomorrow. It could be a complete bloodbath."

He's right. I have to steel myself for anything. Mid could be deciding right this minute to kill everyone left in East Country as retribution for my escape. The thought is sickening, and I don't know why I didn't consider it earlier. Should I have stayed behind in Mid to ensure my people's safety? I don't give myself much time to contemplate my answer. I stand up, walking directly to where Cole and Margareath sleep. "It's time to get walking," I say.

They do as I instruct, groggily standing and equipping themselves once again with flasks of juice and water. I said walk, but in actuality I know we need to move faster than that. I start out at a run, the other three wordlessly matching my pace. Hours later when my legs feel too heavy to go forward, I switch to jogging, still resisting the pain and the cramps.

"Hey," says Griffin. "We can stop again. You didn't get any sleep earlier. It's your turn."

"Yours too."

"I wouldn't mind a second of sleep, that's for sure." Griffin runs a hand through his sweaty hair. It's so grimy, covered in dirt from the low tunnel, whole bunches almost stand on end.

I sigh, knowing we have to rest again soon or we'll just die in the tunnel instead of in East or Mid. I agree reluctantly, and this time Margareath keeps watch. I won't leave Calix's clone alone while we sleep. For all I know it's just waiting to grab a knife and stab us when our eyes are closed.

We go on like this for the next eleven hours with Griffin and me sleeping for a few hours at a time while Margareath and Cole stay awake and vice versa. The catnaps rejuvenate us, so we stick to a solid running speed. Finally, up ahead I see a wall of compacted dirt. I practically bash into it in the dark, but Cole obviously knows where his tunnel stops and halts us a few paces out.

"You said to stop digging before I reached the mine's entrance. About fifty miles outside of Mid," he says to Griffin, almost like a defense for not finishing the entire route.

"We need to dig from here. I didn't want anyone from East's mines finding out about the tunnel ahead of time and thinking it was Mid trying to burrow in," says Griffin

"East would've plowed in the tunnel if they'd have found it," says Margareath.

I don't look at Griffin because I know he now realizes East's people couldn't have done anything of the sort. Instead, I concentrate on the task in front of us. We each work at the packed soil and rock with our automated shovels, and I am amazed how much earth we move in such little time. Before I know it, we burst into Mid's side of the Nirogene mine. Now it's just a matter of plowing onward to East's side. We walk through Mid's abandoned, open caverns and find a thick wall at the opposite end. Again, we start digging. Instead of climbing the border to get to East, this time, we're excavating our way through.

The whole process takes us half a day more, but with the automation shovels in-hand, my arms hardly ache. The tool slices and digs through the mountain rock like crumbling cheese. I can now see how Cole dug the tunnel with just this one gadget. I hold the shovel lightly in my hand, often glancing at it with appreciation and awe. My parents would be ashamed of how much I relish using the technology.

We start to see specks of dim moonlight shining through our tunnel, and I know we'll soon hit East's caverns. When we do, it'll just be a matter of running through into my country.

A few minutes later the job is done. There's a small hole now connecting East and Mid's mines. The four of us shimmy through and then run at top speed through East's long mine shafts. We can't wait to get into our country.

But when we're close enough to the gaping hole leading into East, we see our way is blocked by a ground-to-ceiling fence. Metal bars keep us from exiting the mines. Or from anyone entering them. Margareath slams into the fence with her whole body, shaking the frame. "For Heaven's sake!" she curses.

"Get back!" Griffin says. He pulls at Margareath's shirt. A flood of blinding light passes over the entrance right as he shoves her out of its path. The beam illuminates our tunnel for a split second, and then it's gone again.

"What was that?" Margareath asks as we all follow the beam of light with our eyes. It bobs along the sky and then circles back down again. We shimmy against the cave walls to avoid the beam as it flashes across the entrance again. This time right as it glides off, we take our opportunity to peer through the fence for a first glimpse into my country. I hold my breath, not knowing what to expect. Will we see destruction right here along the border or smoke rising from the ruins of East in the distance? I press my face against the metal, holding onto the rungs with both hands like Margareath did moments earlier.

Outside the entrance to the mine are makeshift tents and stone rimmed fire pits. Encircling all of that in the distance is another tall metal fence with nasty barbs poking from its top. Along the fence are three watchtowers, one of which is the origin of the long ray of light that keeps scanning the whole area. I know exactly what the dusty campsite houses.

"Internment," I whisper, remembering the walls built around the Japanese in the United States during the Second World War. It's amazing how much insight my history books provide about our current state of affairs. It seems civilization hasn't matured as much as we think it has.

"This is where Mid keeps its prisoners," says Griffin in a mumble under his breath.

"The what?" asks Margareath.

My mouth turns down, knowing it is time I gave Margareath the same information Griffin heard yesterday. I sit her down and Griffin stands nearby, still peering out into the quiet city of tents. Cole listens close by, moving his mouth as if to speak a couple of times.

"I don't understand . . . ," he starts to say.

I hold up one hand in his direction, refusing even to acknowledge him with my gaze. He doesn't have a right to talk about East's demise. The very same fibers in Cole's body exist in the man who did this to our country.

Even before I finish the explanation, Margareath stands. She runs at the fence and then falls to her knees. She rattles the bars, calling out her husband's name. Griffin lurches forward, catching her arm. "What do you think you're doing?"

Margareath's eyes are wild. "Getting out of here and looking for my family!"

"You can't just waltz into the country," says Griffin. "You'll alert Mid's guards, and I'm sure if the fence was easy to wrench down, our people would already have escaped into the mines."

Margareath stares at her feet, but I can see her legs shaking. It's taking all her willpower not to propel out of Griffin's grasp and keep calling for her husband. I understand how she feels. I want to do the same thing for Vienne and Tomlin.

"Let's think this through," I breathe out, giving my own nervous energy an outlet. "We can hide here until morning and then show ourselves to the first person from East who walks by."

"If there's anyone even left in the tents." Margareath's aggravated hiss holds a note of misery.

"There are people inside," says Cole, finally able to get a word in edgewise. "Otherwise Mid wouldn't waste the energy keeping their floodlight on all night."

I purse my lips. His logic is infallible, but I don't give him the satisfaction of agreeing. Instead, I stare ahead of us, listening for even one voice emanating from a nearby tent. All is deathly quiet, though, and after a while I sit down on the dirt floor, mentally exhausted.

"It's a good idea to rest," says Griffin. "There's nothing else we can do right now."

He sits next to me and holds my hand as we wait for the sun to rise. A few hours will show us exactly what devastation Calix brought to my people and who exactly is left, but for now, I sink into Griffin's side. An eerie thought hits me just as I'm about to fall asleep. This is technically the first time Griffin and I've been able to hold hands in East without fear of my people seeing. It's funny how that doesn't even matter anymore.

Now we only have to make sure Mid's people don't see us.

No one has to wake me when morning arrives. My eyes flutter open on their own at first light. It's the smell of smoke that truly rouses me, and I'm on my feet in an instant.

Griffin jumps up almost as quickly, his hand still clutching mine. "What's going on?"

Margareath is already awake, against the fence on her knees, hands clamped to the metal lattice. We run to her side, still careful to remain close to the mine's walls.

"Is something burning?" I ask her. She turns and sees the panic in my eyes.

"It's just campfires starting." She knows I was picturing worse, and the lines across her forehead crease deeper.

I keep waiting for Mid to retaliate for my escape. In fact, my dreams all included ghastly bombings and firing squads. I try to shake the images out of my head, realizing they were just twisted figments of my imagination. But they still feel real, and at any moment I know Mid could do exactly what I envisioned.

"Just make sure Mid's guards don't get a glimpse of you before any of our people do," Griffin says to Margareath. "You might want to step back a little." He rubs a weary hand across his brow.

"We could just dig our way out through the rock around the fence. We don't have to wait," says Cole. I squint over at him across the tunnel. His face is bright with a ridiculous grin. He's excited, like this is some big adventure for him. I wonder for the millionth time when exactly he's planning to turn on us. Once I get all of my people out of Mid's prison, my countrymen and I will run for the wilds, scouting a place to live that's not too hot or otherwise uninhabitable. Somewhere Mid won't think to look for us. One thing's for sure; Cole isn't coming with us. I'm sending him right back through the tunnel to Mid, where his heart can be harvested in place of Calix's blackening one, for all I care.

"They'd hear the shovels whirring," I say, rubbing my eyes. I feel the weariness from last night's restless sleep on the inside of my dry eyelids, like there are grains of sand scraping against each pupil. I look down at my shoes, scuffed with a hole starting to form by my big toe. I kick the dirt, throwing up a cloud into the air. I'm hungry and thirsty, and even though I won't admit it to Cole, I'm tired of waiting, too. I don't have a plan for how we can get into my country without Mid's guards seeing us. What's more, I keep hearing my mother's voice in my head. My parents wouldn't like who I'm starting to become: an advocate for technology with a growing bloodlust thumping through my veins at all times. I remember my father saying we didn't relish executing people who broke the Accords. It was a necessary evil. But I do relish the thought of killing now. I picture Calix's face marred by my old fencing sword and smile inwardly. I'm no longer the righteous Elected my father raised. I've been hardened by assassination attempts from so-called friends, the fear of execution in Mid, seeing my parents killed before my eyes, and the feel of my baby being ripped out of my womb. Now, I want vengeance, and killing my enemies doesn't just seem necessary. It sounds alarmingly satisfying.

Griffin's voice breaks through my thoughts, the deep resonation of his tone pulling me out of my private, internal war. "It'll just be a little longer 'till someone comes close enough to hear us whisper. Then we'll devise a plan to distract the guards while we dig out, as Cole's suggested."

The clone rocks back on his heels for a moment, proud that Griffin has given his idea credence. I just grimace and start cleaning my shovel to get it ready for its next task. It's not more than a half hour until a man walks near enough to the cave's mouth that Margareath takes the risk of calling to him.

"Allister!" she whistles through her teeth.

The man turns toward the sound emanating from within the tunnel's shadows, peers further, and then opens his eyes wide when Margareath steps forward. His mouth forms into a round O, like he's seen a ghost.

Which, of course, is probably exactly what he thinks. Margareath was supposed to have been executed, and it doesn't look like Vienne told East's masses that Margareath is still alive.

The man stops and looks backward to see if anyone else is hearing voices or sees the apparition. When he realizes he has no backup nearby, he leans the top half of his body toward us.

"Yes?"

"Get over here this minute!" Margareath says. "You're supposed to be one of East's guards. Not some lily-livered youngster still afraid of his own shadow!"

Now I recognize the man. He has grown taller since I saw him as a new guard, holding my horse's reigns on the steps of the Old Executive Building. Allister was the guard who almost foiled our plan to save Griffin. That night an unlucky gust of wind revealed Griffin's ankle underneath Vienne's robes, and we were sure Allister saw it. I can't help feeling a surge of pride for the young man as he follows Margareath's order. However timid he seems now, he made it through Mid's onslaught of carnage. He didn't run. He stayed behind to defend the city, and for that I'm grateful.

I step forward so he can see my face alongside Margareath's. I pull my hair up tight so he can focus on my likeness without the more womanly features clouding his vision. "Do you know who I am?" I ask.

He doesn't say anything for a moment but then creeps closer to the fence, placing a full pail of water on the ground so lightly it doesn't spill a drop. "You're our Elected." His voice carries awe, and for a second I'm surprised he still calls me by my official title. I was sure the people of East would now only refer to me as Aloy.

"Yes. And we need your help." Griffin steps into the light, keeping a watchful eye out for any Mid guards dressed in their customary gray and black uniforms. "We need to break out of here and talk to all of you without Mid seeing."

Allister's eyes widen yet further. Griffin's is another face I'm sure he never expected to see. His nose crinkles, and he looks like he wants to ask us more questions. However, after a second Allister merely says, "How can I help?"

"Find Tomlin and Vienne," I say. "Bring them here when it gets dark." I hold my breath to see what answer he'll give me when I say their names. What if they're both dead?

Allister scrunches his brow but then just nods and picks up his pail. He walks away, turning his head left and right to check if he's been seen speaking into the mine's entrance. If he has, I hope Mid's guards will just think he's crazy, talking to himself.

"I didn't get to ask him about my children," Margareath groans, sliding down the rock wall.

Cole immediately comforts her, crouching with his arm around her shoulders. "All in good time. We'll hear soon how they're doing."

It's exactly what I would have said if I weren't so jittery. Even this half-man, half-robot can dig up more empathy and hope than I can.

I pace back and forth across the tunnel, head down for the rest of the day, slightly aware that Griffin's watching me intently. In the evening, Griffin finally stops me in the middle of one rotation.

"You're going to wear a line in the ground. We'll trip into it, it's getting so deep." When I don't say anything he sighs. "You did what was necessary leaving Glory behind in Mid." I don't answer him, just bite my pinky nail and keep pacing. "He'll be okay, and I'll return for him as soon as possible."

I stop, turning on my heels. "Maybe that's the thing." My words come out achingly slow like molasses oozing from a tree's knotted trunk. "I don't want to send you back into the lion's den just because I failed my original mission. I don't want other people to have to protect me. If anyone goes back, it should be me."

"That's ludicrous." Griffin balls up a fist, rubbing it across his forehead.

"Is it? I wasn't able to convince Calix that East was innocent. I couldn't find my parents soon enough. I couldn't even keep Glory out of his hands. And I couldn't save our countrymen. I can't risk anyone else's life because of my failure."

I stumble toward the wall, my arm outstretched to catch myself as I lean forward. I think I may throw up, even though there is hardly anything in my stomach to regurgitate. The weight of all my failures feels like it's pushing my shoulders down.

My back is turned away from the entrance, so I don't initially see the face of the person who speaks next.

"You did save us, Aloy. Three thousand, three hundred of us."

My head cocks for a moment, the lull of that one voice enough to stop my heart from thumping so hard. It's like drinking a cup of hot chocolate on a chilly winter's morning. I rush at the gate, forgetting for a moment that we should be careful lest Mid's guards see us. "Vienne!"

She smiles and pushes her hands through the fence to clasp mine on the other side. I stare at her like I'm alleviating thirst by drinking in her image. Her blonde hair sweeps across the sides of her face in parallel waterfalls, almost hiding the myriad of scars dotting her skin. The marks travel down her neck to the top of her dress, and I see the lines again on her hands. The rest of her body is covered with long sleeves and a full flowing skirt. Even with her features marred, she still glows. She looks better than the last time I saw her. I'm afraid to blink for fear she will be gone again.

"What did you say?" I ask, incredulous not only at seeing her again but also by the number she's just uttered.

"Because of your warning, we were able to get almost three thousand people out of East's city center into the surrounding marsh land before the bombings started. Including all of the children." She points to her flat belly and smiles wider at me. "Eve is there too."

I throw a hand to my mouth, trying to grasp the breathtaking news. She said so much in those few sentences; it's hard to grasp everything at once. Griffin walks closer to me, wrapping an arm around my waist. I look up at him and feel the warmth of his smile widening as he too understands that Calix's estimation of our people was wrong. Just because only three hundred remain confined in Mid's makeshift prison, it doesn't mean the rest of our people were obliterated. From the corner of my eye, I see Margareath clutch her heart, look up to the heavens, and mouth a tumultuous set of thankful prayers.

"Hello, Vienne," Griffin says. "So we had a girl?"

Vienne nods and grasps one of his hands through the fence as well. "A beautiful one. Strong and fierce just like her three parents."

With our hands in a triangle, we look almost the same as we did before Griffin drank the hemlock, almost a year ago. Two of us on one side of a partition, the third within a prison. I start to say something about us being the most resilient family I've ever seen, when I realize someone's missing. A man stands back-to-back behind Vienne, but it's not my tutor. "Where's Tomlin?" I ask suddenly. "Did he make it through Mid's attack?" I cringe, waiting for bad news, knowing he was sick even before the bombs came. In his weakened state, I wonder if Tomlin found shelter fast enough.

"He's with us here. But he doesn't leave his tent often anymore."

Cole moves forward out of the recesses of the cave, a look of utter curiosity across his face. "What are the rest of your people doing out in the marshes?" I turn and give him a hard look, but he doesn't seem to notice. Cole just doesn't know when to leave us be.

Vienne stares at the stranger but gives an answer before I can stop her. "Waiting for my signal to revolt." She gazes deep into the tunnel past us, waiting for yet more people to walk forward just like Cole. When no one else emerges, she looks toward me and Griffin again, questions deepening a small line above her brows. "Did you bring defectors from Mid?"

"I'm not a defector. I'm a . . ."

I stop Cole mid-statement. "There's no one else with us."

Vienne shifts on her feet, an anxious expression clouding her usually light demeanor. I know her next question before she asks, so I give the answer fast with finality to my voice. "I had a boy."

I can't bear to tell her we left our baby behind. How can I explain about Glory's lungs, and how it's safer for him in Mid than East? I know Vienne's waiting for me to give further details of the baby's whereabouts, but I can't bring myself to tell her what a wretched mother I am. I avoid her gaze, letting her reach her own conclusions.

Upon hearing my words, the man behind Vienne tilts his head, flinching with an awkward shrug of one shoulder. I can think of only one person who would be slightly disappointed to hear I have a legitimate heir. Grobe shields Vienne's smaller body with his lumbering frame so no one can see that she's talking to us. He finally turns his head to nod our way.

"Nice to see you," Griffin says, a rough edge in his voice. Here is the man who accused Griffin of breaking the Technology Accord just so he could steal away the Technology Faction's lead role. The two adversaries eye each other over Vienne's shoulder. Grobe holds onto a large stick, and I see him slightly raise the makeshift weapon. But Vienne reaches around, placing a hand on Grobe's upper arm. He immediately calms, shuffling his feet and pulling the rod back against his body.

"Nice to have you back." Grobe's voice is gruff, but his tone is deferential.

I stop staring at our former nemesis. We have bigger enemies now. Instead, I look back at Vienne, trying to ascertain what she's thinking about me and my baby. She looks at me with pity. Perhaps she thinks my son died in birth or maybe at the hands of Mid's Elected. I feel guilty letting this idea settle in her mind, but I don't want to explain what really happened. She is so obviously proud of her baby. There is no way she'd understand that I'm just as proud of Glory, even though I chose to leave him behind.

Griffin looks back and forth between the two of us, waiting for me to give a more satisfactory explanation of Glory's location. Instead I say, "I don't know how much time we have, so we should get down to the most crucial information."

Griffin raises an eyebrow in my direction but doesn't press the subject. The truth can wait until later, and he knows it.

"How many guards surround the camp?" I ask.

"Twenty," says Grobe over Vienne's shoulder.

"And weapons?" asks Griffin. His eyes, normally a rich brown, are steely gray in this light, already readying for an impending battle.

"Guns mostly," says Vienne, breathing out. When I chance a glance her way, I see she's still staring at me. I turn around and pace the tunnel's floor, one hand on my brow and the other linked within the folds of my robes.

So twenty armed men to surround three hundred of my people. That's one gun for every fifteen unarmed East countryman. I turn back around, part of the group once again. "Can anyone hear us right now?" I ask, pointing somewhat ashamedly at Vienne's arms and legs.

She grimaces but knows exactly to what I'm referring. "No. I found the chip and destroyed it."

"Where was it?" asks Griffin stepping forward to look at her more closely. I see the concern flash across his features, and for the first time I'm not jealous of it. I realize this is the first time he's seen Vienne with all her scars.

"The pad of my heel."

"The very last place she looked," says Grobe, spitting, like it's our fault Vienne suffered.

I swallow my words instead of arguing with him. He's the one who put her in isolation so she had to extract the chip without the help of East's herbs and chemists. I wonder what changed his mind and when exactly he got so protective of her.

"How were you planning to revolt?" I ask instead, thinking it's lucky they waited until now. My people can't possibly imagine what Mid's capable of. But I've witnessed their cruelty first-hand. Mid thinks it's killed most of my countrymen already, and they won't be averse to slaughtering them all again.

"Our people are gathering resources from the marshland. Anything they can find. Stones. Logs," Vienne says.

"We figure thousands of people against twenty guards, even if they're armed and we're not, is enough to win hand-to-hand combat," says Grobe.

I nod, but casually glance at Griffin. He seems to understand my unspoken words. Now that we've gone from thinking almost everyone was killed to realizing that three thousand three hundred of our people remain alive, I can't stand to take even one casualty. A single guard from Mid could mow down a hundred of our people, letting bullets loose like deadly rain.

"We'll still need to be strategic about our attack plan," Griffin says.

"A full-on offense. No holds barred. That's what I think," says Grobe, grimacing with resolve.

"Help us distract the guards, so we can get through the fence to you. Let's start the battle now," says Margareath. She jumps up, pulling on the metal lattice with both hands. Her face is pleading. She isn't thinking straight. Who knows how long it will take to signal our people outside the encampment? She wants to be with her family and out from under Mid's thumb just as much as I do, but I have to stop her zealous approach. I go to put a hand on her shoulder before she climbs higher, but someone reaches her first.

"Slow down, Margareath," Cole says. He tugs on the bottom of Margareath's pant leg as she clings to the top of the fencing. She can't climb over because there's no space between the fence and the rock overhead, but Margareath rattles the metal above us anyway. "Come down. You're not being prudent."

When Cole's face is illuminated in the moonlight, Grobe inhales sharply. "You brought people with you from Mid? He could be a spy! We can't let any of those fiends into our midst!"

For the first time ever, Grobe and I might agree on something, but for some reason when he talks about Cole like an intruder, I come to the clone's defense. "He's not exactly one of them."

Grobe starts to protest again. "If he's from Mid, then he's an enemy. Kill him already and let's start this war!"

My warning months ago saved thousands of my countrymen, but I only think of the seven hundred lost when I say my next words. Grobe and Margareath may be eager to launch an offensive, but they haven't read the history books that are now burned to ashes inside the destroyed White House. Tomlin's relentless quizzing on the five World Wars taught me a thing or two about battle tactics and the element of surprise. Cole's foray into our discussion has offered me another idea too.

"Wait," I say. "I've got a different idea."

27

IT TAKES SOME CONVINCING, especially with Griffin, but finally everyone agrees my plan is the best option we have. We stay concealed within the mine for three more days—the amount of time it takes one of Griffin's old hawks to fly to the marshlands and back with a signal in its claws. Vienne lays food and water in tiny hollowed stones near the fence for us. We don't even try to dig our way out through the surrounding rock. It won't be necessary for what we have planned.

We also don't risk any more unnecessary visits to the mine's entrance for fear we'll be noticed by Mid's guards prematurely. Instead, we catch up on sleep and spend our waking hours far enough inside the caves so we can't be seen. We can still hear voices, though. Grobe disseminated information about our arrival among the three hundred captives, so a few people can't help themselves, casually walking by the cavern's entrance to give their hellos. All are quickly shooed away by Grobe who relocated his tent to be closest to us. When someone gets near enough, he pops out from under the tarp, waving them away like a mother hen. I'd actually laugh out loud if I didn't think my mirth would attract attention.

Vienne's assurance about the number of people my warning saved does wonders to uplift my spirit. I hold hands with Griffin practically all day long, and we sleep next to each other at night, bodies closely intertwined on the earth floor. I can't remember the last time I felt so refreshed.

But each day, as soon as my eyes flutter open, I remember that three hundred East people are still in captivity and my boy is still held in Mid's dangerous hands, so I review our plans for battle again. A piece of chalky, white rock in my hands serves as a writing implement against the stone walls, and I copy and recopy the blueprints of our plan.

On the third evening, one whispering voice beckons me away from my scribbling and into the shadows close to the entrance.

"Aloy, may I speak with you?"

I inch forward against the wall, close enough I can see Tomlin's face aimed away from the mine's entrance. He doesn't dare gaze into the cave for fear of being caught, so I have the luxury of slowly perusing my old mentor's frame without him seeing my facial expressions. I don't even know if I could have hidden my surprise in a polite way. Tomlin was never physically fit, but now he's hunched over, using a cane. His hair is matted around his skull, and he looks to be in considerable pain. I instantly want to reach for him, but I keep my arms rooted across my stomach.

"I'm here," I whisper.

"Ahhh. I have yearned to hear your voice again, and it is like a salve." His smile is shaky, but I can see it grow wider from my angle.

"You're ill," I say, my voice breaking on the second word.

"Nothing the rest of our people haven't all contracted at one point or another. Now is just my turn."

He says it like he's getting a chance to play a privileged game. Only, I can see the yellow of his skin and know it's no game tinkering with his body.

"I've heard your battle plan from Vienne. Are you sure you want to do this?"

If there's anybody who might talk me out of it, Tomlin's the one. No one else has offered a better plan so far, but Tomlin is wise enough to think of an alternative. I wonder if Vienne sent Tomlin just for this purpose. Either way, I'm glad he's here. I let out a loud breath. "I don't want to be protected any longer. I'm not the same leader I was when I left East, timid and afraid of change. I know exactly what I want now. And how to get it."

Tomlin chuckles but coughs on the last intake. "I can see that. But still, what you're planning is a risk to yourself."

"My father would do the same in my situation." For once I know what I say is absolutely true. He and my mother faced Mid's firing squad instead of revealing me as the true spy. To the bitter end, they were loyal to me and the country.

Tomlin shades his eyes with one hand, looking out at the horizon. "Yes. I heard from Vienne that you found them at long last."

"That's not exactly how I'd put it." My voice is hard. Battle worn.

He doesn't elaborate more on the way they died. We both know, and that particular memory doesn't have to be exhumed. "Your parents were always proud of you. You know that, right, Aloy? You don't have to prove anything by sacrificing yourself."

"I'm not trying to do it to prove something. I'm just carrying out the scheme that'll work the best."

Tomlin is quiet for a moment. I wait for him to offer a better solution, a more surefire offense against Mid's guards. But when he furrows his brow and instead just keeps staring into the sun, I can tell he doesn't have anything guaranteed to work better. I lick my lips, tasting the saltiness from the dank cave. I didn't expect that Tomlin would sway my mind, but now there's no one else to object. A few beads of perspiration appear on my forehead out of nowhere, but I forcefully rub them away with the inside of my arm. I will not be anxious about this. I will be brave and act as an Elected leader should. For years it was truly a performance, but now I don't have to fake a low, resolute voice or a hard demeanor. Those attributes are as much a part of me now as my newly long hair.

It's funny how just as I'm allowed to be myself, I become the leader my parents always wanted.

"Fine. It's settled then," I say. "Has the hawk returned yet?" I know only the bird can fly over Mid's fence to give the signal for battle and return again without suspicion. It clutches two phrases on a piece of parchment within its talons. "A new day is ours. Strike at the next dawn." Once it returns, we know to ready for a battle.

"Yes. It flew in a few hours ago. I was just coming to tell you."

"So tomorrow morning then. I'll let the others know." I point in back of me to where Margareath, Griffin, and Cole reside deep within the tunnel. "We'll be ready."

"Heavens be on your side tomorrow," Tomlin says.

I nod. "A new day to you. Always a new day." I try to smile but it comes out half-crooked.

Neither of us wants to say goodbye, so he just murmurs, "Yes. We look to the future." Tomlin spares one fast look at me and then shuffles away, as if he's just been idly standing by the rock to collect his breath before moving onward.

Later that night, as planned, we wait until everyone is asleep and the sky is darkest. Then we let the automatic shovel dig out a small enough section of rock next to the fence so an arm can fit through the hole. The whirring noise it makes is faint enough to blend with all the nocturnal insects trilling nearby. Griffin lays the instrument on the ground outside the wall within a shadow. It's not even one minute later when we see one of East's people, darkly cloaked, grab the shovel and whisk it away for further use. Tomorrow when the guards' attention is elsewhere, the shovel will be used to cut precise lines through the outer fence around the encampment. I can almost picture the guards' surprised faces when their precious enclosure comes crashing down and my people from the marshes descend on them.

"You doing okay?" asks Griffin, when I lie my head down across his arm on the floor of the cave late that night.

"I'll kind of miss this place," I say, referring to the tunnels. With all of the twists and turns, it's given me and Griffin a small degree of privacy that we never had within either Mid or East Country. We've purposefully bedded down in a completely different area than Cole and Margareath. We're far enough away that their voices are mere whispers echoing against the cave's walls. I don't let myself say it, but I can't help thinking this could be our last night together. I don't want to let it pass without some kind of meaningful exchange.

I raise my head and kiss Griffin lightly on his mouth. He returns my gesture, pulling my body closer against his and deepening the embrace. In the cold of the cave, I like the warmth of his arms around mine. I can feel where his touch is going, and my whole body aches with anticipation.

"You're not too anxious about tomorrow morning to . . . ?" he asks. I can hear the hopefulness in his voice, even through his restrained words.

I look up into his eyes, which sparkle in the moonlight bending its way into our enclosure. "Distract me."

"My pleasure." He grasps the back of my hair, running a hand through the locks until they're all shaken free. Then he kisses me hard along my bare shoulder. It's a fast and urgent intimacy, and I'm drawn into the immediacy of our mutual need. I can't get enough of his proximity, pulling him closer and closer until there is not a centimeter of space between our bodies.

I'm reminded of the Satisfaction Room in Mid as Griffin expertly traces his lips across the bottom of my earlobe, sending electricity and chills down my spine. Griffin holds himself over me, and I drink in the image of his arm muscles so strong and defined above me. I pull him closer so he's directly on top of me. It has been a year since we've had the pleasure of creating Glory. At almost every moment our chances for intimacy were thwarted in Mid. Finally, we can be free to touch each other without fear. There are no people to judge me for my gender. There are no cameras from Mid watching our every move.

We glide together like our bodies were made to fit, sweaty and urgent. His arms intertwine with mine, and I revel in the feeling that we aren't two distinct people, but two pieces of an interlocking puzzle. We so easily fall into place against each other, I can't help smiling as I kiss Griffin's neck and then his mouth. This is so much better than the simulation. So much better than the pretend robot. I let myself lose myself in the moment, pushing out all other thoughts of yesterday and tomorrow. For now, the present is bliss.

The next morning, it's Margareath who wakes me and Griffin as the sunlight doesn't quite reach the depth of where we ended up finally falling asleep. She turns her back as the two of us unhinge our bodies from each other. Griffin stands up quickly, rotating a shoulder and cracking his back. "How long now?" he asks.

"Less than a half hour," says Margareath. "Allister let us know the shovel finished its work on the outer fence. Just enough cuts to render the metal easily broken by the onslaught of our people. The thousands are close enough now that they'll hear the call once you've set things in motion."

"Good," I say. "And is Cole ready?"

"Just waiting your word," she says.

"And our people inside the camp?"

"The three hundred are going about their normal morning routines so as not to tip off Mid's guards. They know the specifics for when the battle starts—fall in line among the three thousand who storm the fence."

An eerie thought clouds my mind as I remember the group of children we left behind in Mid, the ones who the doctors and Calix forced to help with their dirty work. "Our East children aren't part of that mob, are they?"

"Course not," says Margareath, shaking her head. "Anyone under fourteen's stayed behind in the marshes."

I nod my approval. "So everyone's just waiting on me?" I look toward Griffin, "You're absolutely sure Cole will go along with the plan?" I ask Griffin for the millionth time.

"Positive. He's on our side. Not Mid's."

"We're putting a lot of faith in him, you know."

"Sometimes you just have to believe in people." Griffin gives me a pointed look, and I recall the time at the shack, deep in East's marshes, where he told me he believed in me. I hope I can finally be the leader Griffin said he was waiting for.

I'm prepared for Cole's reversal of sides, though. I don't have the luxury of relying on anyone except my closest friends. I pick up a sharp, long rock from the tunnel's floor. The moment Cole reneges on his promise to help us, I will plunge the tip into his kidney.

"Come on, then," I say, sighing deeply. "Let's get this started."

28

Cole and I stand at the entrance to the mine, in plain view. He clutches my wrist and uses his other hand to hold my arm behind my back.

"Grip it harder," I grunt at him from within closed teeth.

He maneuvers his hold on me so his fingers dig into my arm. I glare at him until he increases the pressure so my skin turns white under his fingertips.

I give him one final look and then call out as loud as I can. "Help! Let go of me!"

Cole shouts, his voice reverberating around the cave, hitting me with its strength. I haven't heard this tone from him before. "You escaped us once, and we're putting an end to this!"

I watch from a distance as three Mid guards run toward us from across the encampment. They're yelling to each other and waving wildly to their comrades. I suck in air one last time, knowing this is it.

The fastest guard arrives at the fence within seconds, his fists clutching the metal wiring like rib eye steaks around a skewer. In his hand is a mean weapon, black and long. It's cocked right in our faces. "What's the meaning of this?" he growls.

Then, as if struck in the face, the guard's whole demeanor changes. He stops in his tracks and looks back at the other guards as they arrive just one tick after him.

"Elected!" one of the other guards says. His mouth is open wide, staring at Cole.

"A patrol from Mid caught East's leader on her way here. I've apprehended her myself and will see her executed in East in front of all her people," Cole says. He is a dead ringer for Calix in both speech and demeanor. I know he's playing a role—the exact one I told him to—but that doesn't stop my stomach from roiling at the sound.

Ten other Mid guards join in, all of them staring at the two of us with a mixture of both fear and glee.

"Of course, Elected," says one guard who I presume is their chief. "Anything you wish."

"Where is the rest of your patrol, Elected?" asks a guard from the back. The chief gives the younger man a shameful look but then peers into the cave expecting to see a large squad, as suggested.

"They're following behind," says Cole. "For now, I need every single one of you to help rip down this fence so we can proceed with the execution."

Cole doesn't even have to ask for all of Mid's guards to assemble. A total of twenty men have already run over, one at a time, or in groups. I count and recount, ensuring that all twenty are there. Their weapons are either drawn, pointed at me, or they're tucked into seams of the guards' suits. I see the thick butts of each gun, long and lethal up against their legs. I swallow as one guard in particular keeps his gun trained on my head. He leers at me, and I hope he's the first one taken down in the ensuing fight. He cocks his weapon, enjoying the challenge of our eye contact.

I stop looking at Mid's guards and instead stare past them. I see the influx of a crowd stealthily gathering in the distance. It is an immense mob of my people, but they're as quiet as the sun rising.

Cole does a remarkable job of keeping the guards' attention on us, uttering command after command. He gets them busy removing the cave's fence by telling them to slam the butts of their guns against the metal.

At the same time, I can almost feel the collective pulse of my people ready to launch. As if we are all one mind, I brace myself for the loud crash even before it comes. I see the crowd rushing against the outer encampment fence, and I know the barrier is falling even before I hear it hit the ground. The battle has begun.

The earth at our feet shakes for only a mere moment, but that coupled with the war cries from thousands of my people, draws Mid's guards away from their reverie of Cole. They turn at the last second just as my people devour them, throwing their bodies on top of the unsuspecting

Mid squadron whose backs were turned away from my rushing people. The Mid guards are crushed in the onslaught, but they fight back.

"Let go of me!" I yell at Cole, and he drops his hands from my body instantly. His eyes are wide, watching the spectacle play out before our eyes. He's never seen war before, and he's like a child witnessing death for the first time. At first it seems like he doesn't understand, but I see him put a hand to cover his mouth as a rock bombards the head of one guard. I can hear the crack of a skull bone breaking. The sound makes me wince, but Cole falls to his knees in the dirt at our feet, his reaction more horrified.

I feel badly for him and am surprised at his show of solidarity with East, but I can't spare him any more time. I run toward the mine's entrance and push it away easily since Mid's guards did most of the work. Shots ring out through the crowds, and I know some of my people are hit. I have to help. I have to get the guns away from the guards that are left. My people don't know where the guns are hidden on the guards' bodies, but I do.

I know Griffin is standing next to me before I even hear his voice. It's hard to hear for all the screaming around us. "Aloy, run!" he bellows.

"My people!" I yell back to him over the combat. "They're killing our people!" I feel a crazy willfulness tingle through the layers of my skin.

"No! Aloy, no! They're not just aiming for our people!" Griffin grabs my hand, but I'm already stepping out of the cave's entrance into the light to join the fight. That's when I see the Mid guard off to the side, his back up against the cave's outer wall, a small, evil smile still creeping across his lips. The one who seemed to be enjoying my demise still has me within his crosshairs. He's staring right at me, and his gun is up.

Before I can even move, I hear the bullet leave the chamber. I know it will hit me somewhere, and I know I can't outmaneuver it. As if in slow motion, I see Griffin jumping across me, pushing me down onto the ground with the whole of his body.

"No!" I scream, and my voice carries the word in a gust of air as the wind is knocked out of me. I land on my back with Griffin on top. I see red liquid bubbling smooth and frothy on my hands, but I know it's not mine. "No!" I scream again. "Griffin, no!"

A group from the crowd descends on the guard. His gun is pulled out of his hands, and they hit him over the head with it until he collapses, knees buckling.

Griffin looks up at me, pulling himself off my chest with one arm. "You've been shot!" I say. "You shouldn't have leapt in front of me!"

"What did you think . . . I was going to do?" he asks through grunts. His voice pulls at my heart. It's choked and raw with pain. But where is the pain originating from? I pull on his shirt sleeves, ripping them away. They are soaked with blood. "When you concocted this plan," he coughs out, "to offer yourself as the distraction, with all of Mid's guards pointing their guns at your head, what did you expect me to do? Just sit idly by?"

"Yes!" I shout. For once, that's what I thought he would do. I told him I didn't need anyone risking their lives to protect me anymore—that I was ready and willing to take the consequences of my actions. I should have known he agreed to the plan too easily.

Griffin just smiles at me, and I cradle his back against my legs. His eyelids are drooping. I turn again to the task of finding the bullet hole. I move his arm around my waist, and he lets out a bellow. The shot is in his back, and another hole ripped through his shoulder. He's losing a lot of blood.

While I bunch the material around Griffin's wounds, I hear the battle around me receding. There's a considerable amount of my people lying still on the ground around us, but a large number of Mid's twenty guards are also down. Four Mid guards who remain alive are fast being rounded up and bound at the arms and legs.

We've won. We've done it. I close my eyes and am about to say this to Griffin, when I see a dead guard sprawled against the ground just meters away from us. In his limp hand is an idle radio. Its static is barely audible over the roars of shouting.

My heart plummets in my chest. Before I can even say anything about the communication device, I hear the rumble of airrides overhead. My people duck their heads instinctively, stooping under the high winds created by engines so close.

Five black airrides burst into the airspace above East Country. Thousands of my people gather together in one large cluster. If they bomb us, East will be completely decimated. All of my people will be killed at once. I brace myself for a bomb's impact, saying an internal goodbye to everyone still alive that I love. I hold Griffin's hand hard, and he squeezes back. We didn't expect this turn of events, and there's nowhere to run now.

But instead of striking us in a fatal onslaught, one of Mid's airrides lands inside the encampment. The other jets hover overhead, the whirs of their engines quieting to mere snarls. A door of the grounded airride opens, and a group of monstrous Mid fighters run at us, guns raised above their heads, ready to fire.

"Where is your Elected?" one of them shouts. "Show yourself!"

They're looking for *me*? After all this fighting, Mid is still just looking for me? I look up to the heavens one final time, steeling my nerves. I begin to move Griffin's body off my own, ready to stand and announce myself, when I hear a voice from the crowd in front of us.

"Me. I'm East's Elected."

Grobe stands tall among my people, and the crowd parts to let him through. He thumps his chest and stares unflinching at the Mid guard.

The man looks confused for a moment. He opens his mouth to speak and closes it again, like a fresh trout captured from the Chesapeake Bay. I stare at Grobe, confused why he's just offered himself up. It's me they want, not East's current Elected.

The guard shakes his head. "No. We're looking for East's Elected who resided in Mid for the past year. A woman."

I start to stand again, but Grobe's insistence halts me. "Yup, that's me." He doesn't seem to blink as he stares them down.

The guard pushes past Grobe, almost knocking him to the ground. "No, I'm looking for Aloy. A *woman*. Show yourself, or I'll start shooting your people at random!" He growls in frustration.

"I'm the Elected," says another voice, soft and fluid.

No. Not Vienne! She walks right up to the Mid Guard, offering him her hands outstretched, ready for confinement. The guard stares at her, trying to make up his mind if this woman is the correct one. I can't let this happen. They will *not* take Vienne in my place. I'm about to yell out, when someone else's voice breaks in.

"No, I'm the Elected," says Margareath, coming to stand next to Vienne.

Now Mid's guards look completely confounded. They glance back and forth at each other, not knowing what to do.

"I'm the Elected," says another voice. Then another. Women and men rush forward to protect me. All of them offer themselves in my place. There are so many shouts into the air, so many people proclaiming themselves as East's Elected, Mid's guards can't come to any resolution.

All the guards can do is look around the throngs of my people in bewilderment. I smile, feeling weightless, lifted up on the fealty of my people. Nothing could have prepared me for their bravery.

"Enough of this!" booms a voice from the back of the crowd.

A thick blanket of despair pushes me back down to reality. I'd know the voice anywhere. It's the one Cole used less than an hour earlier to fool Mid's guards. The real Calix steps out of the grounded airride, wrapped in thick black velvet robes.

"Step aside! I know what she looks like!" He wanders through the crowd, surveying my people, one by one. When he finally comes near to me, I'm already standing, matching his look, eye-to-eye.

"Hello, Calix," I say.

"Why, Aloy. How nice to see you again." He grins, the whites of his eyes shiny like fish.

"What do you want with me? Can't you just leave me and my people alone already?"

"Alone?" He laughs a brittle. "Why ever would we leave East alone when Mid was bombed again immediately after you escaped?" He looks out across my people. "You act insignificant, hiding among the swamps with your sticks and stones. And yet somewhere you also have a store of airrides and bombs. We will *not* be fooled so easily!" His voice booms on the last sentence.

"It wasn't . . . ," I start to protest, but Calix raises a hand in front of my mouth.

"Don't you want to see what I have here in my arms, Aloy?" I hate the way he says my name, taunting me with a high voice on the second syllable.

I look down, noticing him pull something bulky from within the large folds of his robe. I was so busy looking at his eyes; I failed to see he was holding a bundle. The package squirms, and I know what it is before Calix even pulls back the fabric.

"Your son." Calix starts to present me with my boy but then pulls back at the last moment.

My breath catches in my throat and a sharp moan escapes. Glory cries out, his head lolling toward me, following my voice. His big, blue eyes find mine, blinking. He reaches toward me with both arms. I lunge to grab Glory out of Calix's hands, but he steps out of my way.

"Ah, ah, ah. Not so fast."

"Give me my son," I snarl. "You are not keeping him. Do what you will with me, but you are not taking Glory off this ground." I point my finger down at the earth of East Country.

"You'd risk yourself and your entire country for one mere baby?" Calix laughs out loud.

"Not my people. Just me."

"Well, that isn't a choice you get the luxury of making," Calix says. "I have another proposition for you."

I stand with my hands on my hips. "I don't want your treaties. They're no good. I see how well you follow the Accords."

Calix laughs again, the hollow sound hitting the still air around all of us like nails. "I assure you, this is one treaty you won't want to refuse."

I stand silently, my feet planted to the ground. If this is the last thing I do, Glory will not be ripped away from me again.

"Come back with me," Calix says. My mouth hangs open, ready to protest, but he keeps talking. "It's either your baby or your country. You can come back to Mid as my Madame Elected and save your baby and spare your countrymen. Or you can decide to stay here. I'll take your baby back to Mid with me either way, but in the second scenario, East gets bombed to smithereens. Your choice."

"You want our surrender?"

"What a fun word that is, isn't it?" Calix says.

I look down at Griffin for a moment. His head rests against Vienne's shoulder. I spy Tomlin staring at me across the crowd. I try to discern the right decision from him, but he doesn't give me any sign. That's because there is no good choice. Either I leave, never seeing my country, Vienne or Griffin again, and Glory gets raised in the awful, emotionless Mid Country; or I stay in East, lose Glory, and the fighting continues.

If I don't leave East, Mid will bomb us as they threaten. If I do leave, I abandon my people into Mid's hands, giving them life, but with a prison sentence attached. East will always be under Mid's clutches, a slave country with a cruel master next door.

I'll be the mistress to the main master—to the man who killed my parents and who holds my baby as ransom. I can barely manage to look at him, let alone be his wife.

Calix grows impatient, grinding his foot into the dirt. "What'll it be, Aloy? Your country or your baby? If you stay, you can try to fight us, but those four birds above carry bombs enough to leave your state a crater.

How fast can you all really run?" He looks this time out at my people, frightening them with his words.

I look out at my people too, expecting them to be crying or on their knees begging for mercy. But everyone stands tall like me. We are a proud group.

I look one more time down at Vienne holding Griffin's head in her lap. Vienne gives me a small smile. She understands just how much this decision will cost all of us. Yet, she still manages to provide me this one hope-filled smile. I remember everything she has ever said and done for me in this one millisecond. The sacrifice she made looking for Mid's microchip. How she managed to control Grobe enough in my absence to keep our country from dividing internally. How she told me long ago that sometimes you just have to take the plunge.

When we were kids, Vienne dared me to sneak out of my house and defy my parents to see the annual dance. The situation now is far from similar, but as Vienne closes her eyes and takes a deep breath, I feel her strength transfer to me like it's a sinewy, invisible mass snaking through the air between us. I feel her telling me it's okay to make a decision I feel is best. She'll support whatever I choose.

I look further down at Griffin. I see him wince in pain, but when he knows my eyes are on him, he winks at me. Even with everything happening, nothing can take the roguishness from the twinkle in Griffin's eyes. I know no matter what I choose today, he won't stop fighting. He will fight the bullet wounds now and then he'll battle Mid. If I'm taken away, Griffin will come to find me and keep his promise to Mid's children. I don't doubt it for a second.

Whichever option I choose, it won't be a perfect solution, and it won't stay static. I will keep fighting too. I will *never* give up.

Because what Tomlin said to me yesterday is true: Each day is a new day. And each day holds a different future. I just have to choose one for today.

Tomorrow, however, all choices can change.

To Be Concluded

Stay tuned for the thrilling finale to the Elected trilogy.

PERFECTED

Nothing is finished until it's perfected.

With two futures in front of her: leave East Country behind as Calix's wife or stay and prepare for battle with Mid Country, which will Aloy choose?

Reader Group
Discussion Questions:

1. What decision do you think Aloy will choose? What consequences do each of the choices hold? When faced with duty versus desire in your own life, what have you chosen to do?

2. The Elected Series covers the topic of technology usage and how much is beneficial versus unhealthy, either for the individual or for the environment. What are your views on technology use in your daily life? In what ways does technology help you versus harm you or your family?

3. If you could, would you prefer society reverted to the simplistic style of East Country? Or do you prefer the technological advancement in Mid? How does the style of healthcare in each of the countries compare to different cultures across the world now?

4. There are many instances in Mid Country where science has advanced into questionable territory: using clones for body parts, knowing ahead of time what diseases people will contract in their lifetime, etc. Is there a line crossed when experimentation and advancement becomes immoral? Who should decide where the line is drawn?

5. Vienne usually uses psychology and her persuasive words to achieve what she wants. Sometimes Aloy and Griffin use diplomacy as well, but there are times they advocate for the use of force to gain the upper hand. Where in Suspected did Aloy try to use persuasion without it working? On the other hand, where in the story could Aloy have used her words instead of force to achieve better results? In current world events, which methods do you think would gain the best results?

6. Suspected delves into the topic of parenting. Children are raised in a group with specialized nannies taking care of them while the parents

focus on advancing society and completing their work. While the style of Mid Country isn't one to be revered, is there a time and place in our current society where you think trained professionals would serve children better than their parents? Or are parents always the best resource for their child's development? How does this translate into schooling and education?

7. Mid's people are forced to only care about work. How does this relate to our current society's views of work/life balance?

8. And last, but not least . . . what did you think of the Satisfaction Room? If we had the technology to create such life-like fantasies now, do you think it could be a viable option for replacing or supplementing other types of physical contact? When is it detrimental versus a safer option? Could it relieve any societal problems we have now?

Acknowledgements

Thank you to the many people who helped launch SUSPECTED, both the first printing through Silence in the Library Publishing and the second printing in 2020.

To my parents who continued to read every bit as I wrote it. My dad who thought Aaron should be Mid's Elected and who is always giving me his intellectual musings about the future of the world. And especially my mom who did a stellar job editing so that I could give my publisher a grammatically tight first draft in 2015. My husband Jason and children, Marlena and Ellie, who encouraged me to keep writing and gave me the precious gift of time to get it done. I write your personality traits into the most brave and compassionate of all my characters.

To Silence in the Library Publishing, who saw ELECTED's potential and brought me onto the team for the first publication of this book. Janine Spendlove, Ron Garner, Tanya Spackman, Kelli Neier, Bryan Young, and Maggie Allen. My talented cover artist Suzannah Safi.

To my writing critique group members: Clifton Tibbetts and Jon Sourbeer for your unfailing enthusiasm and the detailed analysis you gave the Elected Series. Beta readers who peeked at ELECTED when it was a very...very rough draft: Erin, Kat, Kim, Luke, Amy, Jon, Pina, Matt, Colleen, and Leif. You told me ELECTED seemed like a real book and that made me feel like a real writer. To Jonathan Neumann, my future co-writer. My writer friends: Diana Peterfreund, Marissa Meyer, Jillian Anderson Coats, Mark Henry, Kendare Blake, Lish McBride, Martha Brockenbrough, Jeanne Ryan, and Sajni Patel for many coffee dates and writing retreats.

To all of my long-time friends as well as the new ones from social media, for tweeting, blogging, facebooking, emailing, talking and, in general, sharing info about ELECTED. To all the Kickstarter backers who helped the first publication of ELECTED launch through Silence in the Library. There is an army of "East Countrymen" who helped place this book into the hands of readers.

To Nicole and Denise Entertainment for creating original music to go along with the series. I listened to songs "Away" and "The Journey" over and over again throughout the writing of SUSPECTED, and it helped keep me in the mood of various scenes.

Last, thank you to The Elected Series' readers. I am constantly overcome by the passion you have for Aloy and am grateful for your interest in her story. I hope we can all hold Aloy's unfailing hope within our own hearts and strive for a better, cleaner, and more tolerant world. A new day to you!"

About the Author

Rori Shay is a learning and development consultant living with her family, dogs, and enormous cat in Washington D.C. and Seattle, WA. She enjoys running 5Ks, acting in Halloween haunted forests, helping animal welfare organizations, and picking the perfect pumpkins for her doorstep every fall! She also reads voraciously, like books are her very nourishment.

Feel free to contact Rori at rorishay@gmail.com, on Twitter @RoriShay, on her website www.rorishay.com, or via her Facebook page www.facebook.com/RoriShayWrites.